Pet Peeves
An Oral History

Diane Michaels

MiddleRun Press
New York

MiddleRun Press
New York, NY
info@middlerunpress.com

First paperback edition: January 2019

ISBN 978-0-9977107-9-3

To Kevin

CONTENTS

Foreword

With twelve Emmy awards, an astonishing two hundred forty-four episodes, and eternal life in syndication, *Pet Peeves* reigns as America's favorite sitcom. Millions of viewers tuned in every Tuesday night for eleven seasons and followed the off-camera antics and romances of the cast with equal ardor.

A casual conversation between two members of the cast while they shot the final episode grew into a yearlong project of one-on-one interviews conducted with over three-dozen cast members, network executives, writers, crew members, and other people connected to the series. Their responses, stitched together into a collective oral history, tell the story of *Pet Peeves* from its creation through the series finale.

Chapter 1
The Beginning: Another Day to Live

Elvin Shatsky, co-creator, *Pet Peeves*

People forget that my sitcom, *Pet Peeves,* started out as soap opera.

Thelonious Trout, chairman of ABS Television Network

The daytime drama, *Another Day to Live,* began airing on weekdays at two o'clock beginning in September 2004. I hated to kill the show after only five weeks, but if I had let it continue to run, it could have cost me my job. I was paying off the mortgage on a vacation home in Oahu I had bought a few months earlier. The show's ratings were in the toilet. It was an easy call.

Stephen Burrows, producer (control room) and scriptwriter

It's possible the viewer comments made the network brass more nervous than the ratings did. Viewers had told us the storylines hooked them in and the actors were perfect in their roles. That's not where the problem lay. What kept coming up was people didn't believe the show fulfilled their expectations of what a daytime drama should be. I read somewhere we had viewers who found the show to be too funny.

Wayne Quimby, head writer, *Another Day to Live*

How can a daytime drama be funny? We were serious daytime drama writers with long, illustrious careers in the industry. No one has ever accused me of being funny.

I had worked my way up to head writer at *Things Just Keep Getting Worse* a couple of years earlier. I loved the show and didn't want to leave it, but I couldn't say no when ABS tapped me to create a new show. After getting the go-ahead to produce *Another Day*, we immediately hired Kendra to be our breakdown writer. She had spent about a dozen years in the writers' rooms of a couple of Emmy award-winning shows. We brought her in especially because she was the amnesia queen.

Kendra Lewis-Frost, breakdown writer, *Another Day to Live*

I had forgotten that they used to call me the queen of amnesia. I must have come up with fifty different amnesia storylines before I signed on to write for *Another Day to Live*. Let's see... On one show, a character forgot everything when he knocked his head against a rock whilst rock climbing. Mere days after he regained his memory, his wife fell out of a boat as it sailed through shallow waters. She hit her head on a rock, wiping her memory clean. These examples should provide you with an idea of the types of plotlines I had earned a reputation for developing.

Wayne Quimby

The basic premise of *Another Day* was two dueling families in one city. Archibald Edward Quinn II, a.k.a. Duke, was the CEO of a mega-corporation. He owned half the town and all the politicians. Harold Copeland was the district attorney. He had a real hard-on for Quinn. The story arc we had envisioned had the DA finding the evidence to put Quinn away at the end of season 3. Seasons 4 and 5 would then follow Quinn's quest for revenge from his prison cell. We'd have additional storylines about forbidden love, amnesia. You know, the usual fare.

David Solomon, director, *Another Day to Live*

I jumped at the chance to direct *Another Day* when they offered it to me. And not just because I needed the gig. I'm not saying my gambling debts had gotten out of hand or anything.

Kym Gifford, ABS Entertainment chairman

I had been the vice president of Daytime Programming when we first considered developing *Another Day*. I was sure we had a winning show on our hands. We cast Moishe Bronfman and Blaine Carson to play the patriarchs. They were both familiar to daytime drama audiences, Moishe from *All Our Scandals* and Blaine from *Whispers*. Bronwyn Davies, who we cast as Felicity Copeland on *Another Day*, was clearly a rising star. I first noticed her when she played the role of Patrick Blake's mistress on *From Boardroom to Bedroom*.

Bronwyn Davies, actor (Felicity Copeland)

I loved the plot twist on *Boardroom* when they revealed my character was actually Patrick's sister. I couldn't wait to see where they were going to take things next. But the actress playing his wife complained to the head writer that I was getting more lines than her. He must have had a thing for women who complained a lot because they started dating. Next thing I knew, they wrote me off the show by having the wife lace my lipstick with poison. My exit from the show also marked the end of my relationship with Frank, the actor who played Patrick.

Kym Gifford
Wade Hanson [the actor who portrayed Archibald Edward Quinn III, a.k.a. Trip] had a few small acting credits to his name when we cast him to appear in the role of Moishe's son. It was worth the risk of casting a near unknown in the role of Trip. His face alone sold me. He was born to play the scion of a billionaire on a daytime drama. Dark hair, broodingly handsome with a whiff of frat boy. Stiff as a board, but in a good way.

Kendra Lewis-Frost
Of course, Felicity and Trip would meet in the first episode and fall madly in love, unaware of the strife between their families. Who can resist a good retelling of the Romeo and Juliet story?

Julius Whelk, assistant director, *Another Day to Live*
I think where we went wrong was casting Austen Hughes as what we call an "under-five"—an actor with five or fewer lines—in the first episode.

Austen Hughes, actor (Peter Gluck)
My background was comedy. Mostly standup, but I had a couple of bit parts in movies under my belt when I appeared on *Another Day*.

Violet Vye, casting director

We needed a foil for Trip, someone who would, oh, say, prime the pump for when Felicity finally meets Trip. Wade had the smoldering good looks of a romantic lead in a daytime drama. Austen, well...

Austen Hughes

I fit a certain stereotype: chunky comedian. The guy whose body is perfect for physical comedy, in the mold of Chris Farley. I go for it when I'm on stage at a comedy club. If I happen to get hurt in the process, so be it. Well, provided the joint has insurance.

Wayne Quimby

So, the way we wrote it was in the first episode, Felicity lies in a hospital bed in the ICU. She's in a coma; she's been unconscious for three weeks. Trip is the handsome doctor treating her. They are fated to fall in love. Obviously, the romance would have to wait until she woke up. Before the action starts, Peter had found her on the beach. She was bleeding and unconscious. She had no ID on her. The scene begins with Peter hovering over her hospital bed. She awakens and asks him if he's her doctor. He tells her the story of when he found her and what has happened since. She doesn't remember a thing.

Kendra Lewis-Frost

They wasted no time in asking me to plot my fifty-first amnesia scene.

Julius Whelk

What should have happened was when Trip enters to check on his patient, Peter slips out of the room, never to be heard from again. Everything went according to plan in the rehearsals earlier in the day.

Austen Hughes

I was desperate for a gig. I told my agent to get me auditions for anything: dog food commercials, Off-Off-Broadway, cat food commercials. I wasn't ambitious, just broke. He sent me to read for *Another Day to Live*. I was thinking, *Are you sure you meant to send me to audition for a soap opera?* After landing the gig, I promised myself I would do everything in my power to keep them from writing me off the show after only one scene.

Sonia Santiago, production assistant, *Another Day to Live*

When we shot the scene, Austen backed away from the bed on cue and tripped over Wade's feet. They both went down, and the bed—someone had forgotten to put the brakes on—began to move. Bronwyn is a real pro. She had been sitting up in bed once her character had awakened from her coma. Here's her doctor on the floor and her bed in motion. What would the character do? Bronwyn pretended to faint. She had a reputation as a world-class fainter, a real asset for a daytime drama ingénue.

Bronwyn Davies, actor (Felicity Copeland)

I committed myself to staying in character, trying every trick I knew to keep from laughing when the bed started to roll. And not to end up with raccoon eyes because of the tears forming from the suppressed laughter. Nothing worked. I ended up choosing to collapse onto the bed to hide my face from the camera in case they were still shooting. I couldn't stop from convulsing, though. Maybe viewers would think I was having a seizure.

Al White, stage manager, *Another Day to Live*

Of course, we had to reshoot the scene. Four takes later, Austen had fallen four more times. I turned toward the booth, waiting for the director to shout in my ear to remove this doofus from the set.

David Solomon, director, *Another Day to Live*

Austen followed up each fall with panache. The camera loved him, and he was a very skilled improviser. When he stumbled during the sixth take, I gave the order to keep the cameras rolling. Wade finally managed to stay on his feet. Austen pulls himself up by the bed rails and says...

Austen Hughes

"Missed me, you fucking sniper!"

David Solomon

No one got the joke at first.

Kendra Lewis-Frost

Wade's lines right before the fall were, "We're aiming to start cognitive therapy right away. We can't promise she'll regain her memory, but we have to give it a shot." Even before I had made the connection between the words "aim" and "shot" and Austen's improv, I thought he had delivered a brilliant line.

Leslie "Tank" Watson, camera operator

I lost it. I love my job, but the set of a daytime drama isn't exactly the funniest place in the world. I crossed my fingers Austen would stick around for a few episodes to keep the mood fun.

Julius Whelk, assistant director

We couldn't shoot the scene again, what with the bruise forming on Austen's cheek and the bloody nose. I was able to splice the dialogue between him and Bronwyn from an earlier take onto the fall in the last one, minus the f-bomb, when I edited the scene. It was worth the effort. I thought the line he delivered after the final fall was pure gold.

Stephen Burrows, producer (control room) and scriptwriter

While everyone else was laughing, Julius had a fake smile on his face like he wanted to laugh, too, but didn't know why. He kept spinning his head around in hopes someone would let him in on the joke.

David Solomon

I made the decision to have Trip tend to Peter's wounds in order to give Austen, whom we had hired for this single scene, some bonus seconds of screen time. He had earned it. Julius and Sonia could worry about cutting the show down later.

Sonia Santiago, production assistant

Wade must have caught the improv bug. While tending to Austen's wounds, he diagnosed him with amnesia and admitted him to the hospital. Somehow the writers and director lost control of the scene. Next thing you know, we stopped filming so the stagehands could bring a second bed onto the set. And now we had a third-wheel subplot to develop for future episodes.

The original shooting schedule for day one included three additional hospital scenes, none of which had anything to do with

Hughes. With the curtains drawn around his bed, the actors proceeded to follow the original script, making no reference to the patient lying in the bed just out of the shot. The writers assembled in haste to write Hughes into the story. He next appeared in episode 4 with two lines of dialogue.

Kendra Lewis-Frost, breakdown writer

I knew the second they wheeled a bed onto the set for Austen the first day of shooting, I wasn't going to sleep that night. I'd be counting ways to add his character into future scripts instead of counting sheep.

On a daytime drama, the head writers develop the big story ideas. I was the breakdown writer at *Another Day to Live*, charged with outlining each episode and introducing the details the scriptwriter would incorporate into the script. When we finished shooting day one's scenes, Wayne [Quimby, head writer] furrowed his forehead in thought, snapped his fingers, and said, "Make the doofus one of Quinn's henchmen."

Stephen Burrows, producer (control room) and scriptwriter

We didn't have to make major tweaks to the scripts we used during the first week of shooting. I rewrote one scene to remind viewers of the second amnesia patient from the first episode. I was under strict orders to write his part as an under-five again. The producers were adamant about not bumping up his pay. I played it safe and gave him only two lines to leave room in the event he added in a line or two of his own improv.

Wayne Quimby

We didn't give Austen much to do, but who could blame us? We didn't know if someone had made a mistake bringing him back. I figured if he screwed up again, we'd cut the scene, have him die from his injuries off-camera, and tell Hughes not to let the door hit him on his ass on the way out of the studio.

David Solomon

I knew we hadn't made a mistake bringing back his character. Austen was the first actor to sign in the morning we shot his second scene. He knew his lines before the start of the rehearsal. With him stuck in a hospital bed, it would have been impossible for him not to keep up during the blocking rehearsal. No, he was obviously a consummate pro. It's a good thing he was. I had a thousand dollars riding on a bet with Wayne that Austen would work out.

Sonia Santiago, production assistant

David had me on Austen like a tick. No way he trusted him. Because they had committed to paying him for a second day, it was on them if things hadn't gone well.

Austen Hughes

The suits had to worry about whether I was a total moron, but I had the right motivation to show up early and do a good job. It was late July when we filmed the first week's episodes. Rent was due in a couple of days. Plus, unlike the studio, my apartment didn't have AC.

Managing Hughes was but one problem the producers faced. Hanson and Davies, while visually attractive as a couple, fell short of conveying a believable spark between their characters, Trip and Felicity.

Al White, stage manager

Even a viewer normally impervious to romantic tension between characters would have picked up on the lack of chemistry between Wade and Bronwyn. They had none. Nada. Zilch. It was akin to watching the mating ritual between two annelid worms. Bad example. I'm not saying either actor could only love him or herself. I meant organisms that rely on asexual reproductions don't get aroused when they encounter another member of their species. Crap. I'm digging myself in a hole here. You know what I'm trying to say, right?

Bronwyn Davies, actor (Felicity Copeland)

During the casting process, Wade and I read together. The second I saw him, I was panting because he is off-the-charts hot. I mean, damn! While we read, I snuggled up against his chest. His voice buzzed everywhere in my body when he read his lines. Mmm. Of course, we nailed the scene.

Wade Hanson, actor (Archibald Edward Quinn III, a.k.a Trip)

Bronwyn's a cutie, don't get me wrong. A tiny bundle of curls and curves. She has a cartoon character's bounce about her. But I wasn't thinking about her in any way except as my work partner when we were on camera. And off.

Bronwyn Davies

His voice should have been the clue. A guy who looks great on camera and has a voice like hot fudge but can't emote his way out of a paper bag probably should have pursued a career in broadcast journalism.

Wade Hanson

Everyone always assumes the romantic leads won't be able to keep their hands off each other when the cameras stop rolling. So, yeah, a few people made cracks about me needing to keep it in my pants when I was hanging out with Bronwyn off set. I knew resisting her charms wouldn't be a problem for me. In retrospect, I can understand how I might have been overly committed to remaining professional, even on camera, but I wasn't getting notes to play it steamier, either.

Al White

So, Wade played a character called Dr. Quinn. Someone came up with a nickname for him—Dr. Quinn, Medicine Woman—after his first couple of scenes. He could easily have been a straight female frontier doctor treating a female patient, considering his unsexy bedside manner in his scenes with Bronwyn.

Julius Whelk, assistant director

Off-camera, Bronwyn flirted with everyone except for Wade. Early bets were on her hooking up with Blaine Carson, the actor who played her father, the DA. Thankfully, the heat between them cooled before we shot their first scene together. The network would have killed the show much earlier if Davies and Carson hadn't toned down their flirtations when the cameras were rolling.

Blaine Carson, actor (Harold Copeland)

I have a weakness for blondes. What can I say? Ask my ex-wives. On second thought, don't.

Bronwyn Davies

I will tell you right now I had no interest in Blaine. Ew! He's old enough to be my father.

I can't understand why everyone calls me a big flirt. I'm friendly, that's all. I swear I've promised myself each time I've walked onto a new set, I would not hook up with another actor.

Al White

She said what? Ha! I had worked with her before. She treats the acting world like her own dating app. Trust me. She had done a lot of right swiping before joining the cast of *Another Day to Live*.

Austen Hughes

I'm not saying anything that anyone hadn't already figured out, but yes, it wasn't just the paycheck enticing me to return to shoot my next scene. But women in Bronwyn's league don't notice guys like me.

Hughes hovered around Davies like a puppy waiting to be adopted. His ability to make her laugh only encouraged him to try harder.

Bronwyn Davies

When Austen came back to the set a couple of days after we began shooting, I hadn't made friends with anyone in the cast yet. I figured he'd be fun to hang around with during my downtime. They were shooting all the hospital scenes for two different episodes later in the day. I was in all but one of them—his scene. At that point in the shooting schedule, my character still had the memory capacity of a cup of Jell-O.

Austen Hughes

I couldn't believe it when Bronwyn Davies sidled up to me in the commissary on the lunch break. Why would the star hang out with a fat extra who probably didn't belong anywhere near the set of a soap opera? I was nervous as heck, but I'm a comedian. Saying funny things when life got tense was pretty much all I did from seventh grade until I graduated from high school. Hearing her laugh reminded me of taking the first swig of beer on a hot day. It left me craving the next sip.

Bronwyn Davies

Man, what were we talking about at our first lunch together? I can't remember. Ha! That's funny! I was playing an amnesia patient. Get it? But seriously, he was a hoot. He became an instant best friend. I don't tend to notice guys who aren't hot enough to play the leading man. Shoot me. I'm awful. But I did find myself staring into his eyes. Even today, his sense of humor and the calm, clear green of his eyes can stop me in my tracks.

Austen Hughes

You know the weird mix of confidence and debilitating self-awareness you feel when you spend a lot of time with someone you have a crush on but whom you never get to kiss? That's pretty much everything I remember from shooting *Another Day to Live*.

Felicity Copeland regained her memory at the end of episode 5. According to the script, sparks were already flying between her and Dr. Quinn. DA Harold Copeland appeared at his daughter's bedside at the start of the second week. When he discovered her doctor was the son of his nemesis, he tried to quash the budding "romance." Peter overheard Copeland talking about Duke Quinn behind the curtain separating his bed from Felicity's. Recognizing his boss's name, he recovered from his bout of amnesia. In episode 10, Hughes graduated from being an under-five to a day player. His promotion guaranteed an increase in his lines and scenes in each episode as well as a raise.

Kendra Lewis-Frost, breakdown writer

After maintaining a wide berth around Bronwyn during the first week, Wade showed a bit of interest in hanging out with her whenever she and Austen were together. I found the trio's off-camera dynamic to be a good source of inspiration for future plots.

Letitia Higgins, head hairdresser

Heaven help me if Bronwyn, Wade, and Austen came to hair and makeup together. I couldn't hear myself think. Bronwyn has this laugh. You probably could play a recording of it for a random person on the street, and they would recognize whose laugh it was.

Austen Hughes

Picture Bronwyn choking on a highly vocal mouse. Her laugh starts with a wheeze component followed by a tattoo of squeaks. When you hear the donkey bray, you know she has run out of air. I've never had to put my CPR training to use, but I always remain on high alert when she laughs.

Wade Hanson

Austen changed the dynamic backstage, that's for sure. He reminded me of my roommate from summer stock the year after college. Erik Bautista. Erik drew everyone to him. You'd come alive in his presence. I… Sorry, what was I saying? Oh, yes. Austen. Love the guy.

David Solomon, director

Wade related well to Austen on camera. The couple of hospital scenes they had together brought out the best in his acting. Dr. Quinn, Medicine Woman became good old Trip Quinn when he was treating Peter's injuries. It was clear they should become friends when Peter went back to work for Duke. And the dual loyalties set up a great conflict between Duke and Trip. Duke endeavored to keep the unsavory side of his business dealings hidden from his son, but now Trip was acquainted with the guy who not only knew where the proverbial bodies were buried, he might have played a role in burying them, so to speak.

Wade Hanson

I haven't thought about Erik in years. I wonder what he's up to.

Wayne Quimby, head writer

They didn't hire Hughes as a contract actor, of course. But when we expanded his role beyond enabler of Duke's nefarious schemes to Trip's sidekick, it doubled his onscreen time. One thing we couldn't do, though, was give him his own plot. Maybe we should have. Then again, I don't know if it would have changed anything.

Stephen Burrows, producer (control room) and scriptwriter

I'll admit I bear some of the responsibility for the direction the show took when Austen was in a scene. I loved what he did with the lines I wrote, and his acting in each scene inspired what I would write into the next script. He and I entered into a symbiotic dance. I was one of several writers on the show. But I kept getting assigned the outlines with his scenes.

Wayne Quimby

We called on Hughes to be a character actor in the role of Peter. Not that there is anything wrong with having someone in a small role on a daytime drama adding a little color or comic relief. But a little goes a long way. With Hughes's performances, we were heading for Mars.

Moishe Bronfman, actor (Duke Quinn)

No one in the cast complained about the increase in the number of lines they wrote for Austen. Well, maybe Blaine did. But you know Blaine. If he doesn't have anything nice to say, he speaks up.

Blaine Carson, actor (Harold Copeland)

I was wondering, *Who is this guy? Why does he have nearly as many lines in each script as me?* Had I known then that he'd be responsible for us getting canceled, I would have brought it to the producer's attention. I did check to make sure he was a SAG-AFTRA [Screen Actors Guild - American Federation of Television and Radio Artists] member. Unfortunately for me, I mean, fortunately, he was legit.

Kym Gifford, ABS Entertainment chairman

By *Another Day to Live*'s debut in September 2004, we had six weeks' worth of episodes in the can. It was clear the show had its strong points. The cast and crew should have been proud of their efforts. But I had a nagging suspicion early on that when the episodes from weeks four and five aired, it would appear as if a star from a sitcom had gotten lost on his way to his set, winding up at *Another Day*'s studio instead.

Austen Hughes

All right. I'll finally fess up. I got a little lost on the studio lot back at the beginning. I was by myself, walking through the sets during my downtime. I thought it was cool how you could move from, say, the ICU set directly into Duke's office and then into the Copelands' living room. I was by myself, doing a bit, giving a make-believe group of people a tour of a weird house where none of the rooms made any sense next to each other. "And we're walking…" I ran out of rooms at the back of the set, went through a door, and it locked on me. I was stuck in an alley in Queens with nothing but a bunch of dumpsters to keep me company. Someone in the group had warned me not to go through the door, but did I listen? No. It pissed me off when my tour group refused to let me back in.

David Solomon

Things took an odd turn right around the premiere. We were, admittedly, having a ball on set. The actors were giving it their all, production was moving like clockwork. And we had become one big, happy family. But when I considered the show we were offering viewers, I had serious doubts. I was caught between wanting to share our show with the public and panicking whenever I thought about reviews and ratings. Oh, and I may have had a wager going with Wayne about whether the show would be renewed for a second thirteen-week period.

Blaine Carson

It was obvious to me well before the show first aired we weren't going to make it. The role of Peter served no purpose in driving the plot. He entertained but to what end? But who listens to an actor complaining about another actor?

Bronwyn Davies

I gave Blaine a nickname: Henny Penny. *The sky is falling! The sky is falling!* Shut up already. And stop looking at my boobs.

Sonia Santiago, production assistant

We were in the studio filming week seven's episodes during premiere week. The reviews were okay. We hit our target ratings numbers. Network brass came to the set to congratulate us the day after the premiere. The cast and crew members breathed a collective sigh of relief.

Kym Gifford

I, along with other executives from the ABS Network, had been on the set once or twice each week before the show aired. I can't say I didn't have a clue about the Austen situation. But if you were there, watching him act, he'd put you under a spell. You saw him hamming it up a bit, sure, but he was otherwise flawless. He memorized his lines and cues immediately. He was always on set before they called him. And when I reviewed an episode during editing, his performance drew me in. I couldn't separate the quality of his work from the appropriateness of his presence on this particular show.

Leslie "Tank" Watson, camera operator

I saw the fatal moment first. In a scene we shot the day after the premiere, Trip and Peter are having bro time at a bar. Peter gets a little talkative after his third martini and mentions that Duke has him digging up dirt on one of the bigwigs at the hospital. Wade was supposed to step in front of Austen and stay still for a tag at the end of the scene. I zoom in, but Wade isn't in the shot.

Austen Hughes

I love tags. They're the funniest things about soap operas. The scene ends, but instead of a fadeout, the characters freeze with these over-the-top expressions on their faces. I could go take a leak and come back, and they'd still be mugging for the camera. I never was supposed to be the one on camera at the end of a scene while I was at *Another Day*. No matter how Peter was feeling about whatever had gone down during the scene, the writers didn't care. It was always another actor who was on camera for the tag.

But Wade missed his mark. I noticed the camera on me was hot and decided I should do the tag. I made a *whoopsies* face and held it for all I was worth.

Kym Gifford

The bubble burst. I finally saw Austen clearly. He wasn't a daytime drama actor. None of the footage we had of him showed him to be anything except for a comedian. I knew *Another Day* would not survive with him in the cast. They had to write him off the show. But my brain was in overdrive. I dearly wanted to hold on to this actor and keep another network from turning him into a star.

Peter took a bullet meant for Duke in the episode they shot the next day. They hired a stand-in to play him. The attempted assassination scene is in one of the twenty episodes that never made it to air. After the fourth week that Another Day to Live *was on the air, the cast and crew were given a one-week vacation. The network canceled the show five days later.*

Blaine Carson

Fucking Austen Hughes.

Chapter 2
The Art of Grand Gestures and Verbal Acrobatics

The start of the fall TV season comes at the end of pitch season. Before the networks know which of their fall series will succeed or fail, they hear pitches for potential shows they could plug into the next fall's lineup.

Amongst those pitching shows to the ABS Network in the late summer of 2004 was Elvin Shatsky, a producer whose shows IBS, a rival network, could count on to print them money season after season. While Shatsky has many storied sitcoms to his credit, one show on his résumé continues to haunt him.

Elvin Shatsky, co-creator, *Pet Peeves*

It's clear to me now. I should have offered [Fred] Grandy more money to star in *Gopher!*

Stephen Burrows, producer

Even if Grandy had starred in *Gopher!* I doubt the show would have survived beyond the three episodes they aired. But the guy they cast in his place? He wasn't fooling anyone by pretending to be the original Gopher from *The Love Boat*.

Austen Hughes, actor (Peter Gluck)

I watched the show. I was maybe in high school when it came out? The Gopher I remembered from seeing the reruns of *The Love Boat* wasn't built like a defensive end, and he had brown hair. The replacement's lisp kind of threw me, too.

Kym Gifford, ABS Entertainment chairman

The morning of the premiere of *Another Day to Live*, Elvin had pitched an idea for a sitcom to the network. It was about a shady commercial real estate agent and the IRS agent intent on bringing him down. Sounds familiar, right? It's uncanny how similar it was to the premise of *Another Day*. We didn't love Elvin's pitch, but we loved the thought of having him produce a series for our network. We hoped teaming him up with another writer would result in a better idea.

Kendra Lewis-Frost, breakdown writer

My agent called me the afternoon after the premiere to ask me to come up with a short pitch for a sitcom based on the premise of *Another Day to Live*, only to make it different. The key element was for me to write a character in the vein of Peter. In the vein of how Austen played Peter. And I was to pitch my idea at the ABS offices in Midtown Manhattan the next afternoon.

Elvin Shatsky

My first thought when they invited me to attend someone else's pitch meeting the next day was, *You're bringing in a writer from a soap opera to tweak my pitch? I don't need this shit.* But my last hit had gone off the air in the spring. The timing was perfect for developing relationships with another network. Also, I may or may not have slept with Braithwaite's [Rex Braithwaite, chairman of IBS Television Network] wife.

Rex Braithwaite, chairman of IBS Television Network

Elvin pitching to networks other than IBS was a real punch in the gut during an unsettled period for me on the home front. Things came out okay in the end, though.

Kym Gifford

I had this burst of inspiration about Kendra and Elvin making a great team. Two days later, it dawned on me what a ridiculous idea it had been, but by then I knew Kendra was likely to be unemployed soon. I wouldn't have wanted to rob her of an opportunity. Besides, the meeting had already taken place.

Kendra Lewis-Frost

I'm the last person anyone would have asked to write a sitcom. Coming up with a pitch was probably the most agonizing writing experience of my life. And that includes the assignment I was given at university where I had to write a love scene between my mother and the man to whom she was about to lose her virginity.

While creating a pitch was tough for Lewis-Frost, one could argue that her afternoon and evening were a walk in the park compared to the day Hughes had to endure.

Austen Hughes

At the same time I was getting out of makeup, the producer, who was in the same building as me, called my agent to tell him I was fired instead of telling me to my face. My agent then left the news in the general mailbox on my home voicemail. My roommate was a real douche when he told me I had been canned.

Kendra Lewis-Frost

News about Austen buzzed through the set the minute he signed out. The burden of creating a vehicle for a now-unemployed Austen added to my worries.

Bronwyn Davies, actor (Felicity Copeland)

Poor thing! The excitement we had experienced after the premiere left the building with Austen. Part of me felt sad for him. And part of me was anxious for all of us. Cast changes early in a run rarely mean things are okay. It was best for me to distance myself from him.

Austen Hughes

Everyone I knew from the show forgot about me almost right away. Wade and Bronwyn each texted me the day I was sent packing to offer their condolences, but that was the last I heard from them. Their radio silence informed me they missed me the way I miss the case of toenail fungus I battled back in high school.

David Solomon, director

Boy, were the actors on their best behavior the day they let Austen go! We finished shooting early, which is good because I had to get to a meeting. My bookie would've killed me if I had shown up late.

Kendra Lewis-Frost

On my way back home, my cab driver must have thought me to be a raving lunatic. I'm surprised he didn't deliver the nutter mumbling to herself in the back seat about a man named Peter to the good folks at Bellevue Hospital.

The one element for the new show I had in place was Peter needed to be a fish out of water. Perhaps he was an idiot savant employed by a high-profile firm? A country bumpkin in the big city? A standup comic on a daytime drama?

Lewis-Frost wavered on whether to keep her meeting. Professionalism, rather than a sense of commitment to the project, led her to the ABS Headquarters the next day.

Kym Gifford

Kendra came into the meeting room like a terrified baby giraffe, all gangly legs never finding their footing. Most in attendance were strangers to her. She knew me, of course, and her agent. Two of the executives from the network sat like stern lumps of oatmeal in a pair of armchairs off to the side of my office. And Elvin, squished next to his agent on the love seat, had his arms crossed against his gargantuan chest, challenging her to fail.

Kendra Lewis-Frost

I swallowed my cappuccino in three gulps, singeing my tongue and the roof of my mouth in the process. That everyone in the room understood even a single word of my pitch was a miracle.

Elvin Shatsky

As far as pitches go, it wasn't the worst. Maybe I liked the pitch because I liked the looks of the broad delivering it. Her fancy British accent didn't hurt, either.

Kendra Lewis-Frost

I recently found my original pitch on my laptop. Would you care to hear it?

"This is a show about families, love, and loyalty. A daughter and her parents are partners at one law firm. A son, his parents, and a clueless new hire better suited to animal husbandry than the law are partners at another. A long-standing rivalry between the firms means they can't leave their battles behind in the courtroom. While the younger generation may have donned wingtips of their own to follow in their parents' footsteps, it's the friendships and romances they form while tiptoeing behind their parents' backs that may spell doom for the rivals."

Dick Babcock, senior vice president of ABS and Entertainment

I found it to be on the basic end of pitches, but it did dovetail nicely with Shatsky's idea. I preferred the idea of a show about lawyers to one about an IRS agent with a bee in his bonnet. And Lewis-Frost did make me want to meet a character who should have gone into animal husbandry instead of the law.

Kym Gifford

The ideas started flying around the room after Kendra finished speaking. She, meanwhile, devoted herself to draining the contents of a pitcher of water rather than taking part in the brainstorming session.

Elvin Shatsky

Someone, maybe me, thought about making the show about doctors who share a floor in a medical building in New York City.

Kym Gifford

There were plenty of doctors on TV that season: *ER, Grey's Anatomy, Out of Practice...* We were still debating lawyers vs. doctors when Kendra returned from her bathroom visit.

Kendra Lewis-Frost

Who leaves a pitch meeting to head to the loo? This idiot, the writer who had shown a greater talent for drinking beverages than for coming up with a viable idea for a show.

Kym Gifford

Kendra took her seat, and with no fanfare, said, "Veterinary surgeons."

Elvin Shatsky

I didn't know what the hell she was talking about.

Kendra Lewis-Frost

I hadn't had the time to consider occupations for my characters the night before the pitch. *Lawyer* popped into my head exactly because it's such a clichéd career on TV. But who needs another show about lawyers? Posters from the ABS hit shows line the hallway outside the executive suite. A family pet on one of the posters had caught my eye on my way to the restroom. The idea came to me while I was washing away the cappuccino mustache I had apparently been flaunting throughout my pitch. Vets. I could name only two shows about vets— *All Creatures Great and Small* and *Vets in Practice*—and both were off the air.

Kym Gifford

It was brilliant. A show about vets would stand out from the pack. I imagined vets could be much funnier than lawyers or doctors, too. I put my foot down, however, on the writers relying on poop jokes.

Elvin Shatsky

When I figured out Kendra was talking about vets, I pitched three new storylines about incidents involving dog shit. Comedic gold.

The Network asked Shatsky and Lewis-Frost to co-write a script for the pilot of a sitcom about rival veterinary clinics. The team tentatively dubbed the project Pet Peeves. *Shatsky agreed, reluctantly, to work with Lewis-Frost on the script.*

Kendra Lewis-Frost, co-creator, *Pet Peeves*

I was gobsmacked. The pilot project could translate into a massive promotion for me. If we received the green light to make a pilot, I would be listed as both co-creator and executive producer. For a sitcom. There wasn't enough Valium in New York to calm my nerves. What did I know about comedy?

Elvin Shatsky

I had pitched to ABS with the intent of creating my own show. I wasn't in the market for a writing partner, especially one whom I guessed couldn't tell the difference between a joke and a banana. Kendra is easy on the eyes, certainly. I didn't mind the prospect of sharing an office with those legs. I sure hoped this redhead who had usurped my pitch meeting wouldn't give me a case of agita, though.

Kendra Lewis-Frost

I figured it best to acquire a basic understanding of veterinary practices and medicine. Elvin could put in the jokes later. Of course, the first thing I researched was whether pets suffer from amnesia. I stumbled upon information regarding feline cognitive dysfunction, which I used in a little writing exercise.

ACT [I]

SCENE [2]

OPEN ON:

INT. VETERINARY CLINIC EXAM ROOM - DAY

MRS. GLADYS PEMBERTON is standing
worriedly next to a cat carrier on an
exam table.

TABITHA, a tabby cat, yowls and hisses
from within the carrier.

DR. HAROLD COPELAND enters the room with
NORA, a vet tech.

DR. COPELAND

I see the reason you've
brought in Tabitha is because
you believe she is suffering
from amnesia. What behavior
led you to make the
appointment?

MRS. PEMBERTON

She doesn't recognize me. Not
even when I call her in our
special way.

DR. COPELAND

Let me take a look.

Misunderstanding, MRS. PEMBERTON bends
over, and with her head between her
calves, she calls to the cat. The cat

yowls, reaching its paw through the cage to bat at Mrs. Pemberton's derrière.

> MRS. PEMBERTON
>
> It was all I could do to lure her into the carrier.

MRS. PEMBERTON's cell phone rings. She puts it on speakerphone.

> MR. PEMBERTON
>
> Where are you?

> MRS. PEMBERTON
>
> I'm at the vet.

> MR. PEMBERTON
>
> Why didn't you bring the cat?

DR. COPELAND and NORA remove the cat from carrier to examine it. It struggles and fights back.

> MRS. PEMBERTON
>
> What do you mean? Tabitha is here with me. [To cat:] Who's a good girl? Mommy loves her little princess! [Purring come through the phone.]

> MR. PEMBERTON
>
> Are you sure you brought the cat?

DR. COPELAND and NORA share a knowing look when they check the cat's genitalia. MRS. PEMBERTON investigates the hindquarters of the cat, perplexed.

MRS. PEMBERTON

Honey, I need to call you back. [Hangs up.] I don't remember Tabitha having a pair of those.

Elvin Shatsky

Until they killed her daytime drama, Kendra and I connected primarily through email. I was fine with not having to work with her directly. She forwarded me ideas nearly every day. I wasn't sure if her storylines were meant for our show or for her soap. Cats with amnesia? What's next? Reunited twin goats scheming against their mother from whom they had been separated at birth?

Kym Gifford

My assistant became well acquainted with Elvin in the early days of script development. Listening to him whine about Kendra was below my pay grade. Who cared if he didn't like her ideas? He's the man with half a dozen hit comedies to his name. What had he contributed to the new show thus far? I stopped taking his calls faster than you can say over-the-hill hack.

Kendra Lewis-Frost

I had to outline another twenty-two episodes of *Another Day* between the day I pitched *Pet Peeves* and the day they canceled our show. It was tough coming up with plots for each show, especially when Elvin kept shooting down every proposal I had for ours. Mind you, he wasn't sending me any ideas of his own. I decided my time would be better spent learning the inner workings of sitcoms. I read *Clues for the Clueless Sitcom Writer* so many times, my dog-ears had dog-ears.

Kym Gifford

I wished I could have given Kendra additional support or let her know she could commit herself a bit more to developing *Pet Peeves* than to writing outlines for *Another Day*. Every day I was fighting with the network to keep the show on another day. Listen to me! I had never thought about how *Another Day to Live* ended up living up to its name until now. Sorry. As I was saying, I also couldn't share the news with her about my conversation with Austen's agent.

Austen Hughes, actor (Peter Gluck)

My agent had promised me he'd hustle to find me a commercial or something. I heard from him about a month after I had gotten the boot from *Another Day*. He spoke in industry code, in the manner of a handler giving me the details of my next spy mission. He didn't have a job for me, but he did. But not really. I was supposed to hang tight next year, maybe from February through May. I shouldn't head out of town for any gigs late winter into spring. No promises, though. His coded message went on for so long, I'm pretty sure Jack Bauer figured out my location through a phone trace and triangulation.

A naturally curious and studious person, Lewis-Frost continued to study the sitcom genre to help her to find her comedic voice.

Kendra Lewis-Frost

I graduated from books about sitcoms to watching the shows themselves. TV writers tend to be avid TV viewers. My housemate shared my television viewing habits. Together, we feasted on comedies during the early days of developing the *Pet Peeves'* pilot script.

I took what I knew from writing daytime dramas and mixed it with what I had learned about comedy in my research. I needed to find my voice. I prefer a little drama mixed with intelligent comedy to the in-your-face, dumbed-down, laugh track-dependent drivel plaguing so many TV shows. *Gilmore Girls* was in its sixth season that fall. I decided Amy Sherman Palladino should be my comic muse. My mantra became WWASPW: What would Amy Sherman-Palladino write? Her characters were all about the grand gestures and verbal acrobatics. Her tone was what I aimed to emulate.

Elvin Shatsky

When Kendra and I began sketching scenes, I sent her highlight reels from my hit shows for her to learn from. My previous shows had a certain tone. We used laugh tracks, of course. Gotta help the viewers get the jokes to keep them watching. Not that I wanted our jokes to aim too high in the first place.

Kendra Lewis-Frost

Yes, I watched everything he sent to me. They were instructional. I knew after viewing the reels exactly what I wished to avoid in *Pet Peeves*.

Kym Gifford

Elvin and Kendra sent a detailed outline to us a couple of weeks after the pitch. It resembled a pair of conjoined twins who loathed each other and, unable to run in opposite directions, refused to participate in outside conversations involving their twin.

In mid-October of 2004, following the cancellation of Another Day to Live, *Lewis-Frost and Shatsky began to write together on a daily basis at his office in Midtown Manhattan. The cast and crew of* Another Day, *meanwhile, scattered like dandelion seeds in a spring breeze.*

Wade Hanson, actor (Trip Quinn)

I was sorry to see the show end, but life on the set hadn't been the same once Austen left. On rare occasions, a bit of casting magic happens. After having experienced the enchantment firsthand, I now make a point of chasing after magical moments rather than seeking out the perfect role.

Bronwyn Davies, actor (Felicity Copeland)

I thought the show had legs. I was killing it. Someone at the top at ABS noticed me and offered me a holding deal. I took it, agreeing to work exclusively for the network for the rest of the season. They did manage to come through with the occasional guest spot for me on other ABS shows.

None of us from *Another Day* stayed in touch. It's not as if any of them could have helped my career.

Wade Hanson

A week after the show ended, I auditioned for the Off-Off-Broadway production of *Qaddafi's Christmas Tree*. I landed the role of Qaddafi.

Stephen Burrows, producer

I put out a call to Kendra, asking if she had any leads for writing jobs. She didn't. For an out-of-work writer, she didn't sound worried about her own prospects, though.

Kendra Lewis-Frost

The cancellation was, honestly, the best news I could have received. Not only could I devote myself fully to *Pet Peeves*, but the network hinted about inviting some of the actors from *Another Day* to audition for roles in the new show. I found it much easier to write characters with specific actors in mind.

Elvin Shatsky

Kendra was such a busy little beaver. It had been a few years since I had developed a new show. During the later years of my last two shows, which were long-running series, if you remember, I spent less time writing. I had brought in great writers, and the shows kind of ran themselves. It freed me up to pursue other pleasures.

Kym Gifford

Elvin had earned tremendous respect in the industry and for good reason. But he also had another reputation. When he couldn't delegate a task to another writer or producer, he usually put off completing it until the last minute. I had heard credible rumors as to how he spent his time instead.

Elvin Shatsky

I was talking about golf. What did you think I meant by other pleasures?

Kym Gifford

I prayed for a snowy November in order to keep him off the links. The first draft of the script was due by Thanksgiving.

Kendra Lewis-Frost

We were still tinkering with the outline by the beginning of November. I was unaccustomed to writing at such a slow pace. I wrote up to six or seven outlines per week in my days as a breakdown writer.

Elvin Shatsky

Kendra and I couldn't even agree on the character types we were writing for. Ya gotta have your basic sitcom characters: the logical one, the guy or girl who lives in their own universe, the buffoon. But Kendra wasn't familiar with sitcom tropes. She came from the world of heroes, villains, and amnesia victims.

Kendra Lewis-Frost

We had retained the same character names and relationships from *Another Day*. Their personalities, well, that was another matter. Elvin based the characters in his version of *Pet Peeves* off of those in *Friends,* which had its finale the previous spring. To him, Peter was Joey, Trip was Ross, Felicity was Rachel, and so forth. Partly because I didn't want to write a derivative script and partly because I couldn't imagine Austen playing the role of Joey, Wade as Ross, or Bronwyn as Rachel, I fought him on this particular point every day for a month.

Elvin Shatsky

Advertisers are a bunch of scaredy-cats. They only want to place ads on hit shows. Pitch them a new concept, and they run away like cockroaches when the lights come on.

Kym Gifford

ABS sought an original show in the vein of *Arrested Development,* one that would stand out in the schedule. But we weren't interested in developing our own version of *Arrested Development* any more than we wanted to air a revamped *Friends.*

My reasoning behind picking Kendra to develop the show with Elvin was I hoped the pairing of their lines of professional expertise would yield an original show. I wasn't entirely off-base. She brought the drama to their relationship, and he behaved like one of his beloved clichéd sitcom characters. And no, I'm not referring to the logical one.

Kendra Lewis-Frost

The first bone I threw to Elvin was regarding having our characters be roommates. I consented to Felicity living with her parents and having Trip and Peter live with Trip's parents.

Elvin Shatsky

We fought over the location. I wanted to set our show in New York City, but Kendra insisted there weren't any vets in New York. She rattled off alternative state names like a proud Brit who had finally gotten to know her new home country.

Kendra Lewis-Frost

I couldn't guess where Elvin had come up with the notion of me believing New York was devoid of vets. What I had meant was I associate vets with the country. And if we're searching for a rural location, why not look beyond New York?

To me, if you're talking about pets in the City, I'm conjuring images of posh salons and dog walkers holding a dozen leashes attached to dogs of varying sizes. Of course, at least three of the dogs are poodles and one a Bernese Mountain Dog or some other mammoth breed you can't imagine living in a tiny flat in Manhattan. Oh, where was I? We toyed with the idea of setting up rival pet hotels on opposite sides of a street at one point.

Elvin Shatsky

The network wanted a show about vets. If Kendra was going to get her way by casting some unknown in the fish-out-of-water role of Peter, wouldn't it be best if he were a country bumpkin in Manhattan?

Kendra Lewis-Frost

I kept waiting for the moment when the supposed genius of Elvin would radiate in all its glory, but I began to lose hope.

Kym Gifford

The ABS executives tried to stay out of the way. We left the two of them alone to work with the notes we had supplied, but we weren't out of the loop. By the middle of November, when we learned they were still tweaking the outline, the network chairman suggested we pull Kendra from the project. With Elvin's track record, [Thelonious] Trout knew he would eventually receive a script from him. I reminded him the ideas we had agreed to develop had been hers, and it was worth giving her another chance.

Kendra Lewis-Frost

I became a stranger to sleep the week before Thanksgiving. We—and by we, I mean me—compromised on enough points to finish the outline late Sunday night. Two twelve-hour days of frantic writing and two restless nights of editing later, we had something bearing a resemblance to a draft of a pilot to hand to the network.

Elvin Shatsky

I've never missed a deadline. I wasn't worried we wouldn't have a script to turn in. At four o'clock the day before Thanksgiving, I was on a plane to Nassau for a quickie. With the guys. A golf trip, you pervert. Quit it with the insinuations. I wasn't aware of the fact that Braithwaite's [Rex Braithwaite, chairman of IBS Television Network] wife would be in Nassau.

The Network returned the script to the writers in early December. They had three weeks to revise it based on suggestions provided by the network executives

Kendra Lewis-Frost
I slept through most of Thanksgiving weekend. I figured it might be the last scrap of free time I had until Christmas. The script came back on the first of December along with plenty of notes regarding changes the network wanted us to make. What was missing was Elvin.

Elvin Shatsky
What's the big deal? Everyone lands in jail at some point in their life, right? It meant I got to spend an extra week in Nassau. Who could complain about that?

Rex Braithwaite, chairman of IBS Television Network
For the record, I'm not the one who called the police.

Kym Gifford
It was a tense week at the network. Not only was our most famous potential showrunner in jail, but also the trades broke the news he was developing a script for us. The IBS Network was decidedly not happy with us for having poached their cash cow.

Bronwyn Davies, actor (Felicity Copeland)
I didn't know Shatsky personally, but the headline in Backstage was so juicy, I had to read the story. I learned he was developing a comedy for the ABS Network. I called my agent and asked her to put out feelers in case Shatsky's little legal problem didn't impact him getting the green light on his series. I had the feeling he'd be a hoot to work for.

Kendra Lewis-Frost

Kym called me the moment she heard about Elvin's arrest. It turned out he and Rex's wife had been impersonating ghosts one night in a graveyard in Nassau. How is it he had yet to have come up with anything half as creative as his real-life escapades when it came to writing the script?

Elvin Shatsky

When all was said and done, we only had to pay a fine. I missed my Sunday tee time while I was in jail. I had hoped to stay an extra day to get in one last round, but the Bahamian government was intent on seeing the back end of me.

Kendra Lewis-Frost

While the extra days without Elvin weren't enough for me to finish the script, in his absence, I was able to incorporate the smartest of the network notes into my favorite elements from the script to create a new outline.

Elvin Shatsky

Because I didn't have access to email while staying in the government-run hotel down in the Bahamas, I wasn't caught up to speed with what the network wanted us to change until I was on the plane back home. None of the emails waiting in my inbox were from Kendra, surprisingly. I figured she must've gone into hiding, assuming the network would drop us like a hot potato because of my adventure. She could keep hiding for all I cared. Thinking back on something I had learned from the constables on night patrol at the graveyard in the Bahamas, nothing good comes from people who scare easily.

Kendra Lewis-Frost

Elvin walked into his office a week later than originally scheduled and ordered me to bring him a coffee before he had even sat at his desk. With not a hint of emotion, while asking him if he wanted one sugar or two, I slipped my outline in front of him.

Elvin Shatsky

Cheeky. Very cheeky. The little mouse had been busy while the cat was away. I'm joking, of course. Her outline proved she had what it takes to write a sitcom script. She earned my respect through her initiative. Not that I agreed with most of what she wrote, but at least it was something.

Kendra Lewis-Frost

Writers refer to revising a script as developmental hell. It can be an epic battle trying to give the network what they want without having to edit out everything you want, everything you believe in from the script. I agreed with much of what the network suggested, and my week without Elvin had been heaven. Upon his return, the descent into hell began.

Elvin Shatsky

Here's the reason I had produced each of my previous shows without a partner. I know the ins and outs of striking a compromise with network brass after they give me notes. But Kendra? She actually expected me to compromise with her. One set of balls to tickle was plenty, thank you very much.

Kendra Lewis-Frost

I counted on Elvin's preference for procrastination to work in my favor. I developed a script from my revised outline, expecting him to stall out before completing his own. He did quite a bit of cursing and not a lot of typing during his first three days back in the office.

Elvin Shatsky

I drew a blank. I had to come up with a better outline than Kendra's, but nothing came to me. I decided to write something, anything—you can't edit a blank page, as they say. The outline I handed her Friday afternoon wasn't much different from the outline we had used for our first draft. Let her be under the impression I had committed fully to our early ideas, and she would just have to get on board.

Kym Gifford

I had heard they were at an impasse. We requested copies of the competing outlines. Elvin was a producer with a track record; Kendra simply didn't have that kind of clout. My colleagues had assumed she was the weak link and would have to go, but her outline proved them wrong.

Kendra Lewis-Frost

We were running out of time. We submitted our competing outlines one week before the deadline to hand in our final draft. I spent the last weekend finishing a script based on my outline. I hoped Elvin would find at least scraps of what I had written to be salvageable.

Kym Gifford

Sunday night, I sent each of them a request for a script based on Kendra's outline.

Elvin Shatsky

The network's recommendation came a day after I had resigned myself to going along with Kendra's outline.

Before I had heard the news, I ordered a flower bouquet to be delivered to her at the office first thing Monday morning. I didn't include a personalized note. In the event the network wanted us to continue with my outline, I figured she could conclude the flowers were an offering of consolation.

Kendra Lewis-Frost

My relationship with Elvin changed over the course of the last week of script writing. Instead of shooting down my ideas, he revised them to make the jokes land. By the third week of December, he could go for up to four hours at a stretch without saying, "Not bad for a soap opera writer."

Kym Gifford

Their script arrived on my desk an hour before I left the office for my Christmas vacation. I couldn't wait to read it.

Elvin Shatsky

I had to get the damned thing off my desk and move on to more pressing matters. Like figuring out where the hell they'd let me play my next round of golf.

The script of the pilot episode of Pet Peeves *was one of many each of the executives at the network took with them to their beach houses in Barbados and ski chalets in the Swiss Alps. Shatsky and Lewis-Frost would spend the next few weeks chewing their fingernails down to the quick while they waited to hear if their show would be green-lighted.*

Chapter 3
The Birth of the Pilot

Following the mad scramble they faced to submit the final script, Shatsky and Lewis-Frost settled in for a restless holiday season while they waited for news from the network.

Kendra Lewis-Frost, co-creator, *Pet Peeves*

Silent Night? More like Silent Fortnight. My family was glad to be rid of me at the end of my five-day visit with them back home in Stoke Poges for Christmas, what with my propensity for anxious blabbering as I waited in vain to hear anything about the status of our script. I flew from England straight to St. Lucia for a week of pacing back and forth on the beach. Pitiful way to spend one's holiday.

Elvin Shatsky, co-creator, *Pet Peeves*

Do you have any idea what it took to book my timeshare in the Bahamas for both Thanksgiving and Christmas in 2004? I don't know why the hell I agreed to buy a timeshare in the first place. It took me nearly two years to unburden myself of that albatross. Damn you, Bahamian magistrate!

Kendra Lewis-Frost

Dare I say I missed Elvin the teensiest bit? He had started to grow on me. I feared if I reached out to him to commiserate on the challenge of waiting for a response from the network, he'd return to viewing me as a babe in the woods unsuited to the realm of sitcoms.

Elvin Shatsky

I had considered inviting Kendra to spend a few days with me down in Palm Beach. My partner in crime from Thanksgiving had begun to look like an old hag compared to a babe like Kendra. Florida had a bit of the old hag appearance to her, too, when compared to the Bahamas.

Kym Gifford, ABS Entertainment chairman

I haven't enjoyed a proper vacation over the holidays since before my promotion to Entertainment chairman at ABS. My view of the blue-green waters of the Caribbean each winter is obscured by whatever script I have in my hands. I know, poor little rich girl. But you should read the dreck some writers turn in each year. I guarantee it would put you right off your vacation, too.

The winter holidays were equally festive for the former cast of Another Day to Live.

Wade Hanson, actor (Trip Quinn)

I was in New York for Christmas, starring in *Qaddafi's Christmas Tree*, an Off-Off-Broadway show. The New York Times called the play, "Not the most awful, perhaps not even the second most awful way to escape the tourist-clogged, gray slush-covered streets around Times Square." The run was a success. One night, we filled nearly three-quarters of the seats in the theater.

Bronwyn Davies, actor (Felicity Copeland)

I was dating Jackson Everly, the guy who had the lead in, oh, what was that movie? I can never remember the names of movies and shows if I'm not in them. JK! We snuck away to Aspen for two weeks. I'm still picturing how cute his butt looked in his tight ski pants. Good vacation!

Wade Hanson

My parents flew up from South Carolina to spend Christmas with me. The theater would have hit the three-quarters-full mark had my mother gone to see the show. But Mother refused to watch her son play a terrorist. She didn't have the stomach for it.

Moishe Bronfman, actor (Duke Quinn)

I remember December 2004 particularly well. Hanukkah started on Christmas Day and ran into the New Year. My family always rented out rooms at Harris's Happy Hunter Hideaway each year for our Hanukkah celebration. The Catskills are in our blood. Skiing? Not so much. But the hotel was kosher, which made Mama happy.

An out-of-work actor was a greater insult to my family than being married to a shiksa. I was already one of those things and on the verge of being both. Let's just say there was no room at the inn for me that year.

Austen Hughes, actor (Peter Gluck)

I went back home to Lee's Summit, Missouri in the middle of December and stayed for nearly a month. I took the opportunity while I was in Missouri to do a couple of sets at comedy clubs out in the Midwest.

My mother worried about the state of my career back in New York. During my stay, she had taken to combing through the want ads for me, hoping a steady income would lure me back home for good. One too many newspapers full of listings for part-time gigs unloading stock at big box stores in the Kansas City metropolitan area left open on my placemat was incentive enough for me to head back to Manhattan. I was ready to fulfill my dream of landing a gig Off-Broadway, you know, maybe at the Home Depot half a block west of Broadway on Twenty-third Street.

A team of tanned and rested ABS network brass returned to their executive suites in early January. Once they had finished reading the scripts, they would send the best of the bunch to the president of the network for his decision as to which should receive pilot orders.

Kym Gifford

I was ready to stab my eyes out before I reached the end of my stack of scripts.

Kendra Lewis-Frost

Did I complain earlier about spending five days in a quaint English village and a week in a beachfront hotel room in St. Lucia? Try waiting it out in New York during the month of January. I was as interesting to my friends as a slushy puddle at a crosswalk.

Kym Gifford

I brought the stress home with me each evening. I'd crawl through the front door to my apartment an hour later than planned and spy a beautifully set table. It broke my heart, shattering the promise of a romantic dinner. Between my exhaustion and the fact that the only thing on my mind was a topic I had been banned from discussing at home, I could not have been an easy person with whom to maintain a relationship.

Elvin Shatsky

By late January, I had nearly forgotten I had submitted a pilot script to ABS. I'm not going to lie to you: there are worse fates for a guy than being out of work, receiving a steady stream of residual checks from past shows, and spending time with a beautiful woman who owned a home out in Palm Springs.

On Wednesday, February 9, 2005, Thelonious Trout, the president of the ABS Network, ordered pilots for eight of the comedies he had reviewed. Pet Peeves *made the cut.*

Kym Gifford

I don't know which made me happier: *Pet Peeves* getting a pilot offer or regaining permission to talk about my job at home.

Kendra Lewis-Frost

I had a single moment of blissful celebration with a friend followed by the chest-crushing realization Elvin and I had barely two months in which to hire a director, cast the roles, find studio space and locations, shoot, and edit the bloody thing.

Dirk Romano, director, *Pet Peeves* pilot

Shatsky and I have collaborated on several shows over the years. He found me in between projects when he handed me the script to *Pet Peeves*. I was kind of on the fence about it at first, to be honest.

Elvin Shatsky

Romano had been hesitant about accepting a gig on every pilot we've ever shot together. It's a thing with him. Until he can attach an actor to each role, the words on the page don't speak to him. He didn't have to love it. So long as he showed up and didn't screw it up, I'd be happy.

Dirk Romano

I'm not saying I thought the script wasn't fit even for lining a litter box. No more than a typical Shatsky pilot script, anyway.

Kendra Lewis-Frost

Things started to move in the right direction once they gave us the green light. We received a massive piece of good fortune. The studio in Queens where we had shot *Another Day* was unoccupied and ready for us to move back in.

Elvin Shatsky

One huge advantage of shooting in New York was most of the pilots the networks had ordered would be shot and produced in California. True, New York hemorrhaged a great deal of talent out west each year during pilot season. But the competition for everything from studios to actors was less intense in New York. I always have better luck when the actors who aren't smart enough or hungry enough to head to LA during pilot season figure out they are stuck either auditioning for me or not working at all.

Kendra Lewis-Frost

We still needed to scout locations for exterior shots. The script we had turned into the network at the end of the previous year placed the veterinary clinics in a town in Westchester, New York. Thelonious Trout challenged us to find a new town that was, in his words, "Somewhere out in the sticks."

Elvin Shatsky

When Kendra talked me out of setting the show in the City, I chose Westchester. No way in hell I was traipsing around in some backwater burg for a few exterior shots.

Fred Long, location scout

I limited my search for the ideal town to northern and central New Jersey. The location needed to be somewhat isolated, and its population couldn't sustain more than one veterinary clinic. I stumbled upon the town of Califon out in western New Jersey. I couldn't imagine a better setting for our comedy.

Elvin Shatsky

Where the fuck is Califon?

With Gifford's support, Lewis-Frost made several casting recommendations, basing her choices on actors from Another Day. *Shatsky, of course, had suggestions of his own.*

Austen Hughes

My agent sent me to an audition to read for the part of Peter Gluck for a sitcom pilot. I thought it was weird my character in the pilot had the same name as my character from *Another Day*. It never dawned on me someone would have written the part with me in mind.

Bronwyn Davies

My agent wouldn't reveal anything about the show beyond the fact that I would be reading for the role of Felicity Copeland. Hmm, sounds familiar, doesn't it? Assuming this was a reboot of *Another Day*, I hoped Wade and Austen were being considered to reprise their roles. It would be fun to work with everyone again. Well, everyone except for Blaine.

Blaine Carson, actor (Harold Copeland)

A sitcom? Are you kidding me? Unfortunately, because I needed the work, I agreed to take the audition. I heard Bronwyn was up for a role in it. A sitcom started to sound real nice to me.

Spencer Little, actor

I felt great after reading the part of Trip. They called me back to do a chemistry screen test with Bronwyn Davies. The woman could not have been a bigger flirt when we were introduced, but during our scene, she might as well have been playing a nun, given her prudish interpretation of the role. It totally threw my performance.

Bronwyn Davies

At my request, my manager hunted down my chemistry test with Wade from when they cast *Another Day*. Knowing how Wade and I weren't the sexiest of couples in daytime drama, I didn't want to leave anything to chance.

Elvin Shatsky

During his audition, Wade struck me as too handsome for a sitcom. And a little stiff when he introduced himself. Romano whispered to me about the potential he saw in Wade, so I signed off on him. I came around to Kendra's side when I met Bronwyn, who was one part Doris Day, one part Mae West. She could come up and see me anytime she wanted.

Moishe Bronfman, actor (Duke Quinn)

I was tickled they invited me to audition for a sitcom. I hadn't chosen to build my career in daytime drama; the career chose me. As it happens, I have borscht running through my veins, and by that I mean my people come from the Borscht Belt. By way of Schenectady.

Violet Vye, casting director

At his audition, Austen wasn't the actor I had envisioned casting in the role of Peter Gluck. At least physically. But when he read the part, well, I couldn't imagine anyone else playing Peter.

Kendra Lewis-Frost

Violet called back two or three actors for each role to read for Elvin, Dirk, and me. I was at the tail end of a phone call when one actor up for the role of Peter introduced himself, and I missed his name. I turned around to face this gorgeous creature. Not my type, mind you, but you had to be blind not to find him handsome. He was tall with sandy blond hair flopping seductively over eyes so green, every shamrock in Ireland must envy them. I'm not one to notice these things typically, but the way his t-shirt failed to constrain his muscles, well, you could excuse me for staring. And that tan. Having been stuck in Manhattan since the beginning of the year, I was the color of a blank Word file.

Austen Hughes

A couple of weeks before my first day on the set of *Another Day*, one of my roommates began dating a fitness instructor from Brazil. She had been an officer in the Brazilian Army. Maybe not, but she sure knew how to bark orders. A woman who considered each man she met to be her personal project, she set her sights on all two hundred eighty pounds of me. I can't believe people will shell out money to suffer the kind of abuse she dished out to me for free.

I had been on a first-name basis with the cashiers at every fast-food restaurant within a five-block radius of my apartment. When I stopped buying each of my meals and snacks from these fine dining establishments, I'm surprised they didn't have to apply for federal aid to survive the economic downturn.

By the time I went to my audition for *Pet Peeves*, I was ninety pounds lighter. The Girl from Ipanema—and I apologize to her for forgetting her actual name—recommended I get a spray tan and new headshots before the audition. As surprised as I was to see Kendra, I got a kick out of the fact that she didn't recognize me.

Kym Gifford

The last round of casting was in the hands of the network. I had encouraged Elvin and Kendra to write the character of Peter specifically for Austen, as in, the pasty, overweight Austen who had dazzled me the previous summer. His reading for us in the callback was pitch perfect. But physically, he didn't fit the character we were casting. We had to pass.

Kendra Lewis-Frost

I'm not going to lie; I took the casting decision regarding the role of Peter quite hard. When I had a moment alone with Kym, I let her have it. I prayed my outburst didn't torpedo the show or my part in it.

The table read occurred in early March. For the first time, Shatsky and Lewis-Frost would hear their words come to life. Gifford and Dick Babcock, senior vice president of ABS and Entertainment, were on hand to protect the over one million dollars they had invested in producing the pilot. Any actor who stumbled over lines, any joke that didn't land would be on the chopping block.

Wade Hanson

I was nervous as heck our first day at the studio. I had no experience with comedy. I figured if any of us from

Another Day had a shot at starring in a sitcom, it would have been Austen.

He used to loosen me up back when we were shooting *Another Day*. I imagined if he had been cast on *Pet Peeves*, he would have helped me to believe I could play the straight man in a sitcom. I wasn't feeling particularly confident when I sat down at the table, squished between Bronwyn and an actor I had never met. Elvin Shatsky sat across from me, studying the lot of us and tapping his pen aggressively on his legal pad.

Bronwyn Davies

It was like déjà vu all over again, sitting around a table with many of the leads I knew from *Another Day*. I kind of wished we had welcomed more new actors to the set. Another guy in Wade's league, perhaps. I was overdue for a break in my dating lull.

Rob Flowers, actor (Peter Gluck)

I had been a member of the Sunday Company at the Groundlings. My manager suggested I take auditions in both LA and New York during the 2005 pilot season. I crossed my fingers in hopes I'd receive an offer for a project in LA, but the role of Peter was too good a fit for me to turn down simply because the gig was in New York.

Wade Hanson

Rob was a nice guy. Funny, too. But the chemistry, the magic, wasn't there. I learned a lot by playing Qaddafi. Stepping into the role of a dictator with a hankering for terrorism eight times a week for six weeks taught me how to scrub away every trace of Wade while I was onstage.

I worked through some acting exercises before the table read of the pilot such as getting in the mindset of a man who had the hots for Bronwyn's character. Same for playing against Rob. Um, you know what I mean. I needed to make sure Trip and Peter's bromance was credible.

Elvin Shatsky

For a bunch of soap opera actors, the cast surprised me. Moishe especially. You talk to him before he gets into character, and he looks and sounds like a guy from Crown Heights. All he was missing was the big black hat and one of those scarf thingies. Who would imagine a guy called Moishe Bronfman could pull off the role of Archibald "Duke" Edward Quinn II?

Moishe Bronfman

I've been up against Peter Gallagher for a couple of roles. If you squint when you look at me, we could be brothers from different mothers. You could say I hired a WASP coach to help me to delve into Duke's character. On Valentine's Day 2005, I married the love of my life and Brahmin extraordinaire, Abigail Wentworth.

Blaine Carson, actor (Harold Copeland)

Just as I had expected. My part was far smaller than it had been on *Another Day*. I had two lines, to be exact. At least that imbecile Austen hadn't been cast. Small victories.

Bronwyn Davies

It was fun reading with Wade again. The low-key chemistry we had developed on the set of *Another Day* during the Austen era had returned.

I can't deny it; Rob was terrific on his first day. I resented him for not being Austen, but he brought many of the same qualities to the role.

Moira O'Shea, actor (Claudia Quinn)

In the pilot episode of *Pet Peeves*, Claudia was little more than a cameo role. Elvin promised me he had ideas for my character later in the season, should we be so lucky to be picked up. I was going to hold him to it.

Kendra Lewis-Frost

Wow! What an experience it is to hear actors take the words you've written on a two-dimensional sheet of paper and add a third dimension to them during a table read.

Dirk Romano, director

I saw potential in the script. What separated it from the last three or four pilots I had shot with Elvin was the change in tone, which I attributed to Kendra. But these actors weren't even a little bit funny. You'd think they were extras from a failed daytime drama or something.

Kym Gifford

In the win column, Rob and Moishe were terrific. The script needed some work, but they all do at this point. On the casting front, well, I began to worry I had made the wrong call by approving a few of the actors.

Elvin Shatsky

What was on my mind the day of the table read? I was coming up with ideas for new shows to pitch to the network in June.

The pilot called for three exterior shots and one scene between the actors playing Trip and Peter to be shot on location in the town of Califon, New Jersey. With the timeframe of the pilot set during mid-July, and with spring-like weather predicted early in the week that shooting began, Shatsky decided to take advantage of the weather and shoot in Califon on March 28.

Elvin Shatsky

I teased Kendra, asking her if I needed to update my vaccines before traveling to New Jersey, but honestly, they had picked a great location. It inspired a few of the jokes we wrote into the pilot.

Kendra Lewis-Frost

If hearing the actors read the script at the beginning of the month had banished the anxiety of waiting to hear if we would get the green light, seeing members of the cast on location, in costume, had me over the moon.

Wade Hanson

Rob and I rode together in a van with the crew. It was a good bonding experience. I wanted to run our scene with him on the way out, but he comes from an improv background. I tried to play it cool when he said he wanted to keep rehearsal to a minimum to maintain the freshness of the jokes.

Rob Flowers

It was a mystery to me how Wade could have landed the gig. He had far more TV experience than me, but he reminded me of this guy back in high school who had one line in the school production of *The Music Man*, which he insisted on reading with me before every rehearsal since I was the star of the show. Don't waste my time, man!

Filming picked up at the studio in Queens the next day, continuing into the following week.

Kendra Lewis-Frost

Elvin told me to buckle up for a bumpy ride. I'm thinking, "Six or seven days to shoot one half-hour episode? Try writing and filming a minimum of five one-hour-long shows in five days." He wouldn't last a week on a daytime drama.

Elvin Shatsky

This was when the burden of writing with someone who didn't have a clue about comedy became apparent. The jokes weren't landing. We could always add in a laugh track in postproduction, but putting a Band-Aid on the stump of an arm right after it's been blown off isn't going to improve the situation by much.

Kendra Lewis-Frost

Again with the laugh track. I found it stunning how he thought every line we had to edit had come from my hand, not his.

Dirk Romano

The ensemble as a whole was strong, but getting a few of them, Wade and Blaine especially, to loosen up was like getting my wife to go down on me any day except my birthday. You didn't need to know that. Can you erase it?

Wade Hanson

Shooting the pilot was a blast! Rob and I really clicked.

Rob Flowers

I carried all my scenes. I love playing against a straight man. A good straight man is often the best comedian on set. Think of Audrey Meadows on *The Honeymooners*, for instance. Believe me, Wade was no straight man.

Wade Hanson

On *Another Day*, I had never believed Trip and Felicity had anything in common besides their pretty faces. *Pet*

Peeves introduced a new perspective, having the characters both be vets. Now it made sense for us to fall in love.

Bronwyn Davies

My character, Felicity, first meets Wade's character, Trip, in a hotel bar. They're both attending a veterinary convention. They're supposed to have a super-sloppy make-out session at the bar. The first take was like a sixth-grade dance at a Catholic school. We had measurable space between us. Every actor I've ever kissed on set has been into me. I worried that if Wade didn't want to kiss me, maybe no one else would, either. I was certain I had lost my sex appeal, which got in my head for the next couple of takes.

Dirk Romano

Bronwyn was great in the first take. And then she stepped up her game, showing a hunger, a sense of desperation. But she wasn't the one with whom I had a problem.

Wade Hanson

Go deep, Wade. Be the guy who can't keep his hands off of a woman he picked up in a bar.

Dirk Romano

I'm off by myself watching the video monitors. Wade wasn't doing much with the suggestions I sent down to him via the assistant director. I decided to take it in a new direction. I told him to press Bronwyn up against the bar, lose his balance, and then flail around a bit to regain his balance without breaking contact. If we couldn't get passion out of him, we should aim for funny.

Floyd Martin, assistant director

He didn't break contact. At least he got that part right.

Wade Hanson

Who knew the bar they had constructed for the set was so hard?

Bronwyn Davies

The edge of the bar is digging into my shoulder blades. I'm in agony but I keep going with the kiss. Then Wade shouts, "Dammit to Hell!" I start laughing. I mean, he sounded like my grandfather.

Wade Hanson

I couldn't believe she laughed. I had just broken my hand on the bar, and all she could do was laugh?

Elvin Shatsky

Screwed up the shooting schedule, that's for sure. They carted Wade off to the emergency room. The only scenes we had left to shoot that didn't involve Trip were the scenes for Duke's storyline. The dog wasn't available to come in a day ahead of schedule. What obligations could possibly keep a dog from showing up to work? "Sorry, can't film today. There's this squirrel, you see."

Kendra Lewis-Frost

I was going bonkers trying to come up with viable ways to explain the cast on Wade's hand, should he come back with one, when we shot his remaining scenes.

Bronwyn Davies

I rode with Wade to the hospital. I felt bad for laughing at him. In retrospect, I should have gone home instead.

Wade Hanson

The X-rays came back negative. The swelling in my hand went down pretty quick, and I was back to work the next day.

Trips to the ER and dogs with busy schedules aside, filming wrapped up only one day late. Shatsky brought in a post-production crew to cut down hours of footage into a twenty-two-minute show and add in the visual and sound effects.

Bronwyn Davies

Filming the *Pet Peeves* pilot was the oddest experience of my professional life. While having five days to film a half-hour show felt ultra-luxurious to me, not having a clue if the pilot would be picked up kind of impacted the mood on set. I guess no one wanted to forge team-like relationships since we didn't know if we'd be working together on future episodes. I've had deeper bonding experiences with my castmates while shooting a laundry detergent commercial.

Wade Hanson

Everyone at *Qaddafi's Christmas Tree* was so committed to staying in character, it was hard for them to accept me into their family, what with me playing the bad guy. I somehow expected it would have been more fun shooting the pilot for *Pet Peeves* than it was in reality. Rob and I never quite hit it off, and Bronwyn wouldn't stop teasing me after the whole hand incident.

Moishe Bronfman

My favorite part of shooting the pilot? My scenes with Larry. He played the role of the pregnant dog.

Bronwyn Davies

On a daytime drama, we'd shoot way more pages each day than we did for the pilot. With fewer takes, the process was efficient, and we'd end up with a better sense of how the show would turn out. Honestly, with *Pet Peeves*, I had no idea whether we had created a viable pilot or a weeklong blooper reel.

Blaine Carson

I hoped they hired a good editor, that's what I thought when we finished shooting.

Lucy Hernandez, editor

The pilot of *Pet Peeves* wasn't your usual Shatsky project. It—he's going to murder me for saying this—had a soul and a brain. I didn't find most of it to be memorably funny, though, and the acting wasn't the best, either. I figured it was a long shot, at best, for it to get picked up.

Dirk Romano

Lucy does good work. I gave her notes after I saw the first cut, but there was only so much she could do with the footage we had foisted on her, especially the bar scene between Wade and Bronwyn. I've seen soap operas with more laughs.

Elvin Shatsky

Hernandez had worked on her edits for two weeks before she gave me a copy to view. She still had tweaks she could make with the sound editors.

Our budget didn't allow us to go with anyone big for the theme song. Hernandez's nephew has a decent voice, the guitar playing was fine. I wasn't sure about the lyrics, though. I guess he thought the phrase *pet peeves* meant it was a show about a psychiatric practice. I was in need of a session or three after I heard the theme.

Diego Hernandez, singer/songwriter

My aunt helped me land the gig. When I sat down with my guitar and a sheet of paper, I made the decision not to take the literal route and write lyrics about vets. My concept operated on a couple of levels. I'm proud of it. [He sings], *The way you ape me, hound me, I'm having a cow...*

Kendra Lewis-Frost

Ooh, boy. My baby was out of my hands for the next two weeks. Let me tell you, waiting to hear from the network hadn't gotten any easier.

The production team signed off on the pilot, submitting it to the network on April 25, three weeks before the upfronts. The ABS Network presented their fall lineup to advertisers on the morning of May 16. In addition to three new dramas, they introduced two new sitcoms: Love Me, Love My Sister, *a vehicle for Nicole West, the star of Shatsky's last hit comedy; and* Quad Wrangle, *a show about romantic entanglements between students attending MIT. Pet Peeves had been left behind like a toothless and flatulent mutt on pet adoption day.*

PRODUCTION DRAFT — 03/29/2005

PET PEEVES

Episode #100

Pilot

Written by
Elvin Shatsky and
Kendra Lewis-Frost

Directed by
Dirk Romano

<u>PET PEEVES</u>
Episode #100
Pilot

<u>CHARACTER LIST</u>

ARCHIBALD "DUKE" QUINN II

PETER GLUCK, DVM

CLAUDIA QUINN

ARCHIBALD "TRIP" QUINN III, DVM

FELICITY COPELAND, DVM

ANITA COPELAND, DVM

HAROLD COPELAND, DVM

WOMAN WITH DOG

RESTAURANT HOSTESS

LAB LECTURER

PET PEEVES
Episode #100
Pilot

SET/LOCATION LIST

INTERIORS:

VETERINARY CLINIC
— LOBBY
— EXAM ROOM

HOTEL
— BAR
— BALLROOM FOYER
— BALLROOM
— HOTEL ROOM
— RESTAURANT
— KITCHEN

EXTERIORS:

"WELCOME TO CALIFON" SIGN
VETERINARY CLINIC
HOTEL

COLD OPEN

OPEN ON:

EXT. "WELCOME TO CALIFON" SIGN - DAY

                                CUT TO:

EXT. VETERINARY CLINIC - SAME

                                CUT TO:

INT. VETERINARIAN CLINIC LOBBY - SAME

DUKE unpacks office supplies.

PETER puts supplies away.

CLAUDIA moves everything PETER puts away to a different location.

TRIP, a forlorn expression on his face, sits on a chair in the waiting room.

                    DUKE

     Son, in one week, all of this
     will be yours.

                    TRIP

     A veterinary clinic next door
     to a country store. Just what
     I've always wanted.

DUKE
Technically, it's next door to the general store. The country store is a mile up the road.

PETER
I would have given anything for my hometown back in Ohio to have had a country store. Or a general store.

TRIP
Aren't we just so lucky to have both? I'd gladly trade one of them for a Michelin-starred restaurant.

PETER
Or hills. I wished we lived somewhere hilly when I was a kid. Ours was the flattest town in America, my pa always said. It was as flat as a week-old opened can of pop.

DUKE
Trip, every student in your class at veterinary school would kill to have a brand-new clinic two years after graduating. Now, quit moping and give us a hand.

CLAUDIA
Should we have gone with a marble floor in the lobby?

TRIP

You realize half the dogs who come in here are going to pee when they figure out where they are. Vinyl makes more sense, Mother.

CLAUDIA

I don't want to live in a world where vinyl flooring makes sense.

DUKE

My deepest desire is for you to be happy and successful, Trip. But I still don't understand why you'd prefer to stick your hands inside an animal rather than join my investment firm. When you work with money, you can keep your hands clean.

TRIP

Then why do they call it filthy lucre?

PETER

All this talk of sticking hands inside of an animal has me itching to do a bowel retraction on a ferret. Too bad we still have another week until we finally open our clinic. I'll have to make do with participating in the wet lab at the veterinary conference this weekend.

DUKE

You say wet lab, I say wet bar. Speaking of which, the two of you should head down to New Brunswick. You don't want to miss the opening cocktail reception.

CLAUDIA

At least one skill I've taught you will come in handy. Go. Mingle. We'll have everything in its place before you come home on Sunday evening.

TRIP

Home? I'm not ready to call this outpost home.

PETER

Don't make it too pretty, Mrs. Quinn. If it can't be hosed down at the end of the day, it's no good to us.

CLAUDIA

Remind me not to bring you in to consult on the design when I next redo our penthouse.

END OF OPENING

ACT [I]
SCENE [2]

OPEN ON:

EXT. HOTEL — NIGHT

CUT TO:

INT. HOTEL BAR — SAME

TRIP and FELICITY sit on bar stools.
One empty stool stands between them.

                    TRIP

    [To FELICITY:] You here for
    the vet thing?

                    FELICITY

    Yeah. You?

                    TRIP

    Yup.

TRIP raises his beer glass in a toast.
FELICITY reciprocates with her
cocktail. He moves to the seat next to
hers.

                    FELICITY

    You are aware that you could
    be drinking for free at the
    meet and greet?

TRIP

That would mean I'd have to meet and greet a bunch of vets. Why aren't you meeting and greeting and drinking for free?

FELICITY

I've met enough vets for the day, thanks.

TRIP

Well, then I won't introduce myself to you.

FELICITY

[Surveying TRIP with a smile:] I suppose it wouldn't hurt to meet another vet. I'm Felicity.

TRIP

[Shakes her hand.] Nice to meet you. Trip.

FELICITY

You see, Trip, the other problem with going to the reception is it would be impossible to escape my parents. Tomorrow's keynote speaker canceled. They asked my mom to give a lecture in his place. She's probably strolling around like she has been elected queen.

TRIP

They don't elect queens.

FELICITY nods her head, agreeing. Reconsiders.

FELICITY

Prom queens. They elect prom queens. You're supposed to network at these things, but everyone I'd introduce myself to at the reception would say, "Oh, you're Anita's daughter." It's bad enough having to work in her shadow at my parents' clinic, but getting stuck in her shadow at a reception? No, thanks!

TRIP

How about your father?

FELICITY

He has worked in her shadow for so long, he uses it as his mailing address. [Takes a sip of her drink.] Where's your practice?

TRIP

I spent the last two years at a clinic on the Upper East Side in Manhattan. My father is helping me set up a clinic somewhere in western New Jersey. Market research indicates we'd do best if we built it in a forgettable small town. We — my best friend and I — open our practice next week.

FELICITY

What town's it in?

TRIP

Hell if I remember. And yours?

FELICITY

Not a chance you've heard of it, I'm sure.

Awkward pause. They shyly glance at each other and their drinks.

FELICITY (CONT'D)

Forgettable Small Town must be far away from your girlfriend.

TRIP laughs nervously. He catches himself and studies her expression while ruffling his hair.

TRIP

No one's gonna miss me while I'm stuck out in the boonies. In other words, I have an opening for a milkmaid or whatever it is they call country girls.

FELICITY

Some of us country girls are
called Doctor.

TRIP

My apologies. But you do have
the rosy cheeks and innocent
gaze of someone who grew up
on a farm.

FELICITY

You've obviously read the
wrong books about milkmaids.
Besides, there's nothing
innocent about my gaze.

FELICITY undresses TRIP with her eyes.
He slides off his stool and places his
right hand on edge of the bar behind
her. He angles her name tag up with his
left hand.

TRIP

Does the green dot on your
tag mean you're available?

FELICITY

I suppose it could. Either
that or it's to let them know
I registered to attend the
lab session on Sunday. I see
from your tag you're not
going to the lab. Or does not
having a green sticker on
your name tag means you're
not available, at least where
milkmaids are concerned?

> TRIP
>
> It means I may be very lonely
> on Sunday while you're honing
> your tooth extraction
> techniques.

> FELICITY
>
> Why don't we make up for lost
> time now?

FELICITY leans in for a kiss. TRIP's
hands move to her shoulders. The kiss
deepens.

END OF SCENE

ACT [I]
SCENE [3]

OPEN ON:

EXT. HOTEL — DAY

CUT TO:

INT. HOTEL ROOM — SAME

TRIP enters the room while PETER is getting dressed the next morning.

PETER

Good morning to you! This sure takes me back to veterinary school.

TRIP

At least I'm not stumbling into our apartment at the last second before I have to run off to my first class.

PETER

Um, perhaps you've forgotten why we're here? The first lecture begins in fifteen minutes.

TRIP

So maybe it's a little like school. Oh, by the way, my dad left me a message. He and

79

my mother are going to put
out flyers around town to
advertise our free rabies
clinic next weekend.

PETER

I had hoped to start my
career at our new clinic with
something a little more
heroic than vaccinating pets.

TRIP

You're thinking like a vet.
My father thinks like a
tycoon. We'll make a bigger
impression on the locals by
giving a service away for
free. And by doing it on a
Saturday, we're letting the
town know that our clinic,
unlike our competitor's, will
be open on Saturdays. My
father believes the town
doesn't have enough pet
owners to sustain two
clinics. If we play our cards
right, ours will be the last
one standing.

PETER

The clinic being open on
Saturdays: it won't translate
into "Peter sees patients at
the clinic on Saturdays while
Trip enjoys breakfast in bed
with his latest conquest,"
will it?

TRIP

You overestimate the eligible
population of whatever
godforsaken town we live in
now. I imagine I'll have to
grow accustomed to waking up
alone on Saturdays and every
other day of the week.

PETER

Welcome to my world, friend.
Welcome to my world. I'd love
to tell you about the joys of
celibacy, but I want to make
it to the first session.
They're talking about dental
radiographic interpretation.

TRIP

You make it sound sexy.

PETER

When you have better luck
getting a kiss from an animal
than from a single woman,
you've got to meet sexy where
it lives.

TRIP

Maybe if you eye every
woman's mouth as if it were
begging for an X-ray, you'll
up your game. Do I have time
to grab a bite of breakfast
before the lecture?

PETER

You have no concept of time, do you? The best I can offer you is whatever coffee's left in the pot.

TRIP

[Looks in the sink next to coffee maker.] Peter, why is there a cat head floating in the sink?

PETER

I'm thawing her out.

TRIP

Let me put it a different way. Why is there a cat head thawing out in the sink?

PETER

It's for tomorrow's wet lab on feline tooth extraction techniques.

TRIP

Since when do they require you to bring your own cat head to a lab session at a conference?

PETER

Since now because I didn't register for the lab. I can't

afford to pay the extra eight hundred dollars. I'm still paying off my student loans, you know.

TRIP

You should have mentioned it. I would have been glad to have asked my father to fund your extraction ambitions.

PETER

He's done enough for me already. Why aren't you going to the lab?

TRIP

Attending a conference was your idea. I'm not as excited about going back to school as you are.

PETER

Is running a clinic together going to be like it was back in school? I can see it now. You'll do the bare minimum, copying my homework when you fall behind.

TRIP

I learn better by doing than by reading. I can hold my own as a vet. You still haven't explained why you have a cat

head if you're not registered
for the lab.

PETER

I'm going to find a way to
slip into the lab.

TRIP

I guess there is more than
one way to skin a cat.

END OF SCENE

ACT [I]
SCENE [4]

OPEN ON:

EXT. VETERINARY CLINIC EXTERIOR — DAY

CUT TO:

INT. LOBBY OF VETERINARY CLINIC — SAME

DUKE and CLAUDIA are decorating the lobby. A woman carting a medium-sized dog in a red wagon enters the clinic.

WOMAN WITH DOG

Are you open?

DUKE

Not until next weekend. Have you tried the Copeland Animal Hospital?

WOMAN WITH DOG

I have. They're closed on weekends.

DUKE

Oh, right. I believe you'll find several independent vets locally who specialize in horses. I presume you're not seeking help for a horse?

WOMAN WITH DOG

Surely you can tell the difference between a horse and a dog.

DUKE

When it comes to helping animals, they are all the same to me: future patients for the clinic.

WOMAN WITH DOG

Well, the future is here now. I found this pregnant stray on my property.

CLAUDIA

Then what does she need us for? It appears she's done very well on her own.

WOMAN WITH DOG

I believe she's in the early stages of labor. She was fretting with the dirt under my hydrangea bush, digging a hole for a bed.

DUKE

She's panting. Perhaps she made the hole to lie in the cool dirt.

CLAUDIA

Perhaps she doesn't like hydrangeas.

WOMAN WITH DOG

Panting is another sign she may be in labor. I can't in good conscience leave her outside with her puppies. Not with foxes and coyotes out hunting for their next meal.

CLAUDIA

[Turns toward Duke.] You promised me this town was civilized.

DUKE

And it is. Didn't we find the most amusing Bordeaux in the liquor store last night? Besides, you see these wild animals as a threat. I see them as...

WOMAN WITH DOG

Future patients. So you've mentioned. But what about this dog? I'm on my way out of town for the weekend. You have to help her.

DUKE

What do I know about de-livering babies? Darling, you've gone through child-birth. What do you remember?

CLAUDIA

I remember being woken from a

lovely nap and handed our son wrapped up in a blanket. That's it! You can't give birth without blankets.

                    DUKE

I unpacked a box full of them. Is that what we're supposed to do? Leave the dog alone, handing her blankets if she gets cold?

              WOMAN WITH DOG

She'll need a whelping box. A large crate will do.

                    DUKE

Blankets, a crate. It sounds quite manageable.

              WOMAN WITH DOG

Then I'll leave her with you.

DUKE exits the room to move a crate from the back into an exam room. He returns and coaxes the dog out of the wagon. WOMAN exits the clinic, empty wagon in tow. DUKE exits the lobby, leading the dog into an exam room.

                  CLAUDIA

Oh, Duke? Tell our mother-to-be to remember to breathe. I believe breathing is the new epidural.

END OF SCENE

ACT [I]
SCENE [5]

OPEN ON:

EXT. HOTEL — DAY

                              CUT TO:

INT. HOTEL BALLROOM FOYER — SAME

TRIP and FELICITY loiter by a palm tree outside the entrance to the ballroom.

                    TRIP

Good afternoon.

                    FELICITY

Fancy meeting you here. You look like you're half asleep.

                    TRIP

I have you to thank for that.

                    FELICITY

You're welcome. Aren't you supposed to be in the lecture? It started a couple of minutes ago.

                    TRIP

I got a little behind.

                    FELICITY

But it's cute, nonetheless.

                    TRIP

        Thanks, but this derrière of
        mine should have settled into
        a chair in the lecture hall
        five minutes ago. Wait a
        second. Isn't your mom the
        one giving the lecture?

                    FELICITY

        That's why I'm out here.

                    TRIP

        My partner will kill me if I
        miss the lecture. You coming?

                    FELICITY

        I suppose.

                                    CUT TO:

INT. HOTEL BALLROOM

TRIP and FELICITY sneak down the side
aisle while the lecturer is giving her
introduction. Their commotion entering
the row where PETER is seated
interrupts DR. ANITA COPELAND.

                    ANITA
        Are you comfortable? Perhaps
        you'd prefer to be seated
        closer to the front?

                    FELICITY
        This seat is fine, Mom.
        Forget that I'm even here.

                    90

ANITA

I'd like to do just that if it's okay with you. I'm Dr. Anita Copeland of...

PETER

[Whispers to Trip:] Why didn't I get a cute vet in my conference bag?

TRIP

Considering how you helped yourself to three bags, I'm surprised you didn't wind up with at least a passable vet tech in one of them. Felicity, this is my partner, Peter. Peter, Felicity.

ANITA

Am I interrupting anything?

FELICITY

Sorry, Mom.

ANITA

For the final time, I, along with my husband and daughter — who has given herself quite the introduction today — run an animal hospital in Califon, New Jersey.

                    TRIP

     Califon? Why does that sound
     familiar?

                    PETER

     Maybe because that's where
     our clinic is? Oh, man! Does
     that mean your new girlfriend
     is one of the vets at the
     hospital we're trying to put
     out of business?

                  FELICITY

     Excuse me?

FELICITY tries to stand. Trip holds her
down with his hand. TRIP glares at
PETER and then turns toward FELICITY.

                    TRIP

     I had no idea.

FELICITY walks toward the exit.

                TRIP (CONT'D)

     Wait! I can explain!
     TRIP runs after her.

                   ANITA

     I'm going to assume our pair
     of disrupters has learned
     enough today to respond to a
     situation involving a cat
     with a gum infection.

END OF ACT I

ACT [II]
SCENE [6]

OPEN ON:

EXT. VETERINARY CLINIC — NIGHT

CUT TO:

INT. VETERINARY CLINIC — SAME

DUKE is fussing over the dog lying on a mound of blankets in a crate in the middle of a large examination room. CLAUDIA, seated on a couch, is growing bored.

                    CLAUDIA

    Are we sure we weren't scammed? How do we know the dog is pregnant? Maybe she's just fat.

                    DUKE

    Here. Feel her belly.

                    CLAUDIA

    All I feel are hard lumps. Oh! Something moved!

                    DUKE

    That, my darling, was one of the puppies.

CLAUDIA

Listen to you! You are quite
the magician when it comes to
investing money. By virtue of
having paid for your son's
education and his new place
of employment, you, too, are
now a qualified veterinarian.

DUKE

One doesn't need a degree in
veterinary medicine to know
the difference between an
overweight dog and a pregnant
one. [To dog:] You're
shivering, you sweet girl.
Here. Have another blanket.

CLAUDIA

She has plenty of blankets.
Maybe she's shivering because
you're making her nervous,
hovering around her like a
vengeful wasp.

DUKE

I am not hovering, nor do I
mean her any harm. You're
being unsympathetic.

CLAUDIA

I'm being unsympathetic?
We've been watching a dog do
nothing except for pace and
pant for the last five hours.
I, meanwhile, am famished.

Leave the dog alone and take me somewhere with decent food if decent food is at all a possibility in this burg.

DUKE

I don't want to leave her alone in her time of need. Why don't we order dinner to be delivered?

CLAUDIA

I shudder to think of what they would deliver. Do they even know what a Béarnaise sauce is so far west of Manhattan?

DUKE

Don't be a snob, dear. I've seen you eat pizza before.

CLAUDIA

I can't eat a red sauce. Not while I'm wearing a white Chanel suit.

DUKE

Then what do you suggest?

CLAUDIA

I suggest you call Trip for recommendations.

DUKE

For dinner?

CLAUDIA

No, Duke. For the dog.

DUKE

I wonder if the dog should eat in her condition.

CLAUDIA

I'm quickly losing patience with you.

DUKE

You lose patience with me every day, my love. And yet we survive. Why don't I call Trip and ask him when we should expect the first puppy?

CLAUDIA

I thought you'd never ask!

DUKE paces while talking with Trip, squats to examine the dog, and ends the call.

DUKE

He says it sounds like she's in the early stages of labor. It could be a few hours longer until the first puppy arrives.

CLAUDIA

We have time to go out to
eat, then. She won't miss us.

DUKE

I've told you I don't want to
leave her alone. You go. Take
the car. She and I will be
fine here on our own.

CLAUDIA

This is what it has come to?
You've chosen a dog over me?

DUKE

You know that will never be
true, darling.

CLAUDIA

I hope the two of you have a
very lovely evening together.

CLAUDIA kisses DUKE, eyes the dog
suspiciously, and leaves. DUKE, on his
hands and knees, examines the dog's
hindquarters.

DUKE

There's clear fluid coming
out of her. Trip mentioned we
should be on the lookout for
the fluid. Claudia, I think
it has started! Claudia?
[Peers out of exam room
window. To dog:] Well, my

lady. It's just the two of us. I hope you have some idea of what you're doing because I am quite out of my element.

DUKE arranges throw pillows and blanket into a makeshift bed for himself next to the crate. He sits down and strokes the dog's head.

END OF SCENE

ACT [II]
SCENE [7]

OPEN ON:

EXT. HOTEL — NIGHT

CUT TO:

INT. HOTEL RESTAURANT — SAME

TRIP and PETER enter the restaurant. FELICITY, ANITA, and HAROLD COPELAND are eating at a table in the back.

                    PETER

    So, no dinner plans with your new friend?

                    TRIP

    That ship has sailed. Maybe it would be best for all of us if you and I found someplace else to eat. Maybe find a new place to open our clinic while we're at it.

                    PETER

    I'm hungry. We're eating here. [To hostess:] Hi. Do you have a table in the "I'm sorry I screwed you before screwing you over" section?

                    HOSTESS

    Will that be a table for two?

TRIP

Yes. [Spies the COPELANDS at their table.] But perhaps you have a table open against the far wall?

HOSTESS

We don't have anything available in that section at the moment. Will this do, sir?

TRIP sits in a chair with his back to FELICITY and her parents.

PETER

It's a shame we're trying to put the other clinic out of business. Your vet friend is quite the looker.

TRIP

Quit looking at her. I'm hoping to eat my dinner in peace.

PETER hides behind a large menu, taking surreptitious glances at the COPELANDS.

PETER

Too late. She's seen us. She's — no, strike that — they're coming over here.

TRIP

Do I have time to run away?

FELICITY

You can't run away, Trip. Now I have to add conniving bastard AND a coward to my list of your flaws. I'd like to introduce my parents, two kind, generous, talented veterinarians who have slaved and sacrificed for years to build their humble practice.

PETER

Nice to meet you. I'm Peter Gluck and this is…

ANITA

I don't need to learn your names. What is this my daughter tells me about your plans to ruin our business?

FELICITY

Yeah, Trip. What was your friend saying earlier about you trying to put our hospital out of business?

PETER

[Extends his hand to FELICITY.] We met earlier. I'm Peter.

Felicity turns toward him, disgusted, and returns her attention to TRIP.

                    TRIP

The Califon Small Animal
Clinic hasn't even opened its
doors. We're two young vets
just starting out. Our clinic
can't possibly pose a threat
to an established hospital
like yours.

                    ANITA

So why did you pick Califon?

                    TRIP

It's such a charming town. We
immediately felt at home.

                    PETER

I thought you said you hated
living out in the boonies.

TRIP mashes PETER's foot with his under
the table, suitably distracting him.

                  FELICITY

You used me to get inside
information!

                    TRIP

I did nothing of the sort. I
didn't know who you were when
we met last night. I thought
we were having fun.

                  FELICITY

Well, we're not anymore. I
assure you, fun will be the

furthest thing from my mind when we're back home.

ANITA

I've heard you're holding a rabies clinic next weekend. Is that correct?

TRIP nods.

ANITA (CONT'D)

Good luck with your little scheme. Harold, tell them any attempt to lure our patients away from us with a carnival-like event will not go unnoticed.

HAROLD COPELAND

Er, yes. Please don't, um, do…

ANITA

As my husband has so eloquently put it, we will not tolerate your incursion.

ANITA and FELICITY storm away.

HAROLD

The flourless chocolate cake is quite good, by the way.

ANITA

Harold!

END OF SCENE

ACT [II]
SCENE [8]

OPEN ON:

EXT. HOTEL — DAY

CUT TO:

INT. HOTEL KITCHEN NEXT TO BALLROOM —
SAME

PETER peers through a partially opened
door leading from the kitchen into the
ballroom. Vets straggle into the
ballroom via the appropriate door,
taking seats at long tables laid out
with identical setups of medical
equipment. PETER occasionally hops out
of the way of passing hotel staff.

CUT TO:

INT. WET LAB IN HOTEL BALLROOM — SAME

PETER slinks through the kitchen doors
to claim a spot on the end of a table
in the ballroom. He seeks to avoid
attracting attention while he unpacks
the contents of his bag: dental
instruments, magnifying goggles with a
light attachment, a metal tray, and a
gray plastic bag. He pulls the cat head
out of the plastic bag and places it
into the metal tray, finishing the prep
of his workspace when the lecturer
steps to the front of the room.

LECTURER

Good morning! It's great to see such a large group for this morning's lab session on feline tooth extraction techniques. I'm excited to put into practice the techniques I introduced you to in yesterday morning's lecture.

LECTURER drones on. PETER shuffles his tools around, dropping one under the table by the feet of another vet. He awkwardly retrieves it. After sitting still for a minute or two, PETER leans back to inventory the rest of the participants. He spots FELICITY and quickly snaps forward. He follows the instructions the LECTURER gives for beginning the procedure. While taking another glance at FELICITY, PETER knocks the tray with the cat head off the table and scrambles to rescue it. The attendees, including FELICITY, focus their attention on PETER.

PETER

No worries. I have everything under control.

FELICITY

Hey. Wait a minute. You're Trip's friend, right?

PETER

That's right! I'm Peter. Peter Gluck.

FELICITY

Well, Peter. Peter Gluck.
Would you mind holding up
your name badge for a second?

PETER

Um, sure.

PETER pulls the badge from beneath his
lab coat and brandishes it in
FELICITY's direction.

FELICITY

Just what I thought. He
doesn't have a green dot on
his badge.

LECTURER

You're right. Excuse me, Dr.
Gluck. Have you registered
for my lab?

PETER

I, um, when I saw you were
giving a lecture and running
a lab at the conference, I
had to sign up. I've read
your articles in the Journal
of Veterinary Dentistry.
You're, like, my hero!

LECTURER

Am I now? It's always a
pleasure to meet my fans.

FELICITY

But he didn't sign up. He's crashing the lab without paying for it. Besides, you can't try out the techniques if you don't have one of the cadavers provided for each paying registrant.

PETER

Oh, don't worry. I came prepared.

PETER holds up his metal tray. The head flies out of the tray onto his neighbor's workspace.

LECTURER

If you haven't paid for the lab, I'm sorry, but I'm going to have to insist you leave.

PETER

Can I ask one question about the angle of the…

LECTURER

Go!

PETER stuffs cat, tray, goggles, and tools into his bag and exits the ballroom into the —

CUT TO:

INT. HOTEL BALLROOM FOYER — SAME

PETER pulls a cell phone out of his lab coat pocket.

> PETER
>
> Trip, it's me. Lab ain't happening. Pack our bags and meet me by the car. Looks like I'm the one who is going to require an extraction.

END OF SCENE

ACT [II]
SCENE [9]

OPEN ON:

EXT. VETERINARY CLINIC — DAY

CUT TO:

INT. LARGE EXAMINATION ROOM AT CLINIC —
SAME

DUKE is holding a puppy on his lap. The
dog, lying in the crate, nurses five
puppies. CLAUDIA enters the exam room,
holding a bag of donuts.

DUKE

[To puppy in his lap:] Don't
tell the others, but you're
my favorite.

CLAUDIA

While I'm flattered you
prefer me to your other
wives, I do wish you'd end
things with them once and for
all. Oh, my! Look at the lot
of them!

DUKE

Amazing, isn't it? Mama and
her babies are doing great.

CLAUDIA

Which begs an explanation for
why you chose to sleep here
instead of with me in a nice,
comfy bed. She clearly has no
need for you.

DUKE

There wasn't much sleep
happening. The last pup
wasn't born until at least
two in the morning. And then
I had to make sure the mother
passed the placenta.

CLAUDIA

Duke, I don't need the
medical details.

DUKE

Perhaps it's for the best you
left me to fend on my own.
The important thing is
everyone is healthy, and
she's such a good mama. She's
so proud of her pups!

CLAUDIA

She does seem quite pleased
with herself. Treating our
clinic like a free bed and
breakfast. Look at her,
eyeing your donut. No! Bad
dog! Not for you!

DUKE

Would you care to hold one of
the puppies?

CLAUDIA

No, thank you. Did you fail
to hear my thoughts on
matters regarding animals
each time your son begged for
a dog when he was little?

DUKE

The mystery of his choice of
career has been solved. He
turned down the opportunity
to join my firm simply to
seek revenge on you.

CLAUDIA

I dare say he genuinely
enjoys cutting animals open
and sticking things up their
rear ends. He must have
inherited that from your side
of the family.

DUKE

I never should have told you
what my cousin Fitz did to
the poor bird he found on
Martha's Vineyard when we
were children. While we're on
the subject of our son, isn't
that his car in the parking
lot?

CLAUDIA

Why, yes. He and Peter have
returned. We weren't
expecting them until this
evening.

TRIP

[From the lobby:] Mother?
Dad? Are you here?

CLAUDIA

We're in the executive suite,
dear. Your father is playing
with the puppies.

TRIP and PETER enter the exam room.

TRIP

She had her puppies! I wish
we hadn't missed it!

TRIP and PETER kneel down to cuddle
with the litter.

CLAUDIA

How was the conference? What
were the two of you up to
while your father played
veterinarian?

TRIP

The conference was fine.

DUKE

Aren't you home a bit early?

PETER

We ran into a little trouble
at the lab this morning.

DUKE

What kind of trouble?

TRIP

The short version is the
cat's out of the bag. Our
local competition is onto us.

DUKE

I've prepared for this. It's
all part of my strategy.
Don't you worry about a
thing.

PETER

Speaking of cats, if I don't
rescue mine from the trunk of
Trip's car, the only strategy
we'll be interested in is
finding the right car
freshener to mask the smell
of decomposing kitty.

THE END

TAG

OPEN ON:

EXT. "WELCOME TO CALIFON" SIGN — TWILIGHT

CUT TO:

TRIP and PETER regard the sign from the shoulder of the road.

TRIP

What the hell does Calphalon mean?

PETER

Isn't it a brand of cookware? Oh, did you mean Califon?

TRIP

Calphalon, Califon, Calgon. It doesn't matter what they call this godforsaken place. Just take me away. Hit me over the head with a frying pan and put me out of my misery.

PETER

I think I will be happy here.

TRIP

Suit yourself.

PETER

They named the town after California.

TRIP

That still doesn't explain why it's called Califon.

PETER

They ran out of room for the *I* and the *A*.

TRIP

[Examines the sign.] So where's the *R*?

PETER

[Spells California to himself using his fingers.] Oh, right. I'm guessing the drunk dude they hired to paint the sign was no better at spelling than he was at spacing the letters.

TRIP

So when a guy messes up the sign, they think it would be easier to change the name of the town than to paint a new sign?

PETER

Could have been the mayor.

                    TRIP

What?

                    PETER

The mayor could have painted
it. And everyone was too
intimidated to point out his
error to him.

                    TRIP

Or too drunk to have noticed.
Speaking of which, does this
town have a bar?

                    PETER

Two, I believe.

                    TRIP

I believe I need both of
them. So long as neither of
them is in the country store.
[Beat] Or in the general
store.

FADE OUT:

END TAG

Chapter 4
The Second Beginning

The cast and production crew had kept Monday, May 16 open in their calendars. They would have given a press conference during the day and attended the exclusive network soirée in the evening had their show been picked up. Not all of them had prepared for bad news.

Kym Gifford

2005 was the first year I had participated in the upfronts in the role of chairman of Entertainment. I was proud of the lineup we had offered to the advertisers. It had been a challenge to pick the best of the best, but I believed we ended up with the right shows. Of course, I had a soft spot for *Pet Peeves*, but in the end, it was one of eleven pilots we rejected.

Bronwyn Davies

My stylist had hooked me up with an up-and-coming designer for my upfronts wardrobe. I can't remember what I was going to wear during the day, but the formal dress! I think my disappointment over not getting to wear the dress may have been greater than my disappointment over our show not getting picked up.

Elvin Shatsky

You know what would have made our pilot better? A couple of poop jokes.

Kendra Lewis-Frost

I was heartbroken. I had received an invitation to attend the evening affair as someone's plus-one. Rather than stay home to nurse my wounds, I accepted the invitation because I didn't want to appear ungrateful for the opportunity the network had given me to create the pilot. It was all I could do to keep from sobbing into my caviar-topped blini at the reception.

Blaine Carson

One more show in the crapper. Too bad I couldn't blame Austen for this one.

Bronwyn Davies

So. My agent called me late Monday afternoon. I had been summoned to appear at the ABS offices the next morning at eight a.m. She had no additional information to tell me about the meeting. I figured they were going to blow smoke up my skirt, thank me for acting in the pilot, promise they'd consider me for something else, blah, blah, blah. How rude to make me come in at eight in the friggin' morning, though!

Wade Hanson

You could have pushed me over with a feather when my agent told me about the meeting the network had scheduled for eight fifteen the morning after they announced their lineup. My agent warned me not to get my hopes up that I'd walk away with a gig, but what else could it mean?

Kym Gifford

The day we announced the fall lineup was unusually chaotic. I had a few fires to put out. Our jobs didn't go into low gear the second we made the announcement about our lineup, that's for certain.

Bronwyn Davies

I showed up at ABS headquarters on the early side, but they didn't send me up to the executive suite until eight o'clock on the dot. I fully expected the network honchos to stagger in late, hiding their bloodshot eyes behind Ray-Bans. You can't blame me for wishing they had been crippled by hangovers from the night before.

Wade Hanson

I ran into Bronwyn in the lobby. She was pretty cynical about what was going on, but I refused to feel the same way. I was jittery as a June bug while we waited, though. They finally called us upstairs. She went into her meeting first.

Bronwyn Davies

I took inventory of the network brass in the room. I knew most of them. Except for one man. I'm telling you, I drank him in, thinking, *Hello, Mr. Hottie McHhhhhhhholy shit! Is that Austen?*

Austen Hughes

I figured the network was jerking me around again when they brought me in for the meeting. Everything changed when Bronwyn walked through the door. I lost control of my heart. It revved up and threatened to race right over to her.

Bronwyn Davies

I squealed like a low-level lieutenant in a drug cartel who had nothing to lose during a raid. Not particularly professional of me. I ran over to Austen and hugged that gorgeous, buff man for all he was worth.

Austen Hughes

They asked us to read a scene from the *Pet Peeves* pilot, the one where Felicity and Trip meet in the hotel bar. We got to the kiss and… I had been waiting two hundred ninety-six days for this moment. I knew it should be a sitcom kiss, but I couldn't keep it comical. If I ever managed to detach my mouth from her lips—oh, my god, those lips!—I would have to deliver a joke. Would I even remember what my next line was?

Bronwyn Davies

Humina humina. I played the scene differently than I had with Wade. How could I not? I pressed Austen up against Kym's desk, pinning him under me. My chest grazed against his. He was hot, temperature-wise. Not like waves radiating from him but rather this instant warmth that flowed into me the moment I touched him. It reminded me of wrapping my hands around a ceramic mug of tea on a cold morning. I have probably never acted less in my life. The teensiest part of my brain remembered I was in an audition. It took a great deal of self-discipline to pull myself away from him and take my hands off of the bulging biceps that had become their new home when it was time to read my next line.

Austen Hughes

I had studied comedy, not stage acting. There are

things they don't teach you in improv class. Things like how to, um, deal with the rush of, well, let's say, excitement during a scene. I used Bronwyn as a prop, turning her around to face our audience but keeping her planted directly in front of my groin.

Bronwyn Davies

Again, I didn't need to act. He delivered his line after our kiss. I giggled and snuggled up against him and said to myself, *I know what you're up to, Mr. Hughes!* Yeah, he clearly felt what I was feeling.

Austen Hughes

She didn't make it easy for me. What's the opposite of easy? Nah, that's too cheap a joke. Forget I said it.

Kym Gifford

I completely forgot about Wade when I saw those two act together. I mean that two ways. The scene I had just watched completely erased the memory of the tepid kiss between Bronwyn and Wade from the pilot. And of course, I had forgotten he was outside my office, waiting for his audition.

Wade Hanson

Bronwyn walked out of the meeting a little after eight fifteen. Her hair was definitely messier than it had been a few minutes earlier. And her cheeks were rather pink. I asked her what had happened in her meeting. She bit back a grin and shook her head. Kym's assistant sent me in before I had a chance to try to pry an answer out of Bronwyn.

Austen Hughes

I had barely recovered from kissing Bronwyn when Wade walked in. My heart had been pumping blood like a sump pump in a flooded-out basement. I pivoted from experiencing certain Bronwyn-related sensations to feeling a bit stressed. I began to perceive the importance of the meeting.

Wade Hanson

It took me a second to realize it was Austen who had wrapped me up in a hug. Now I knew why Bronwyn came out of the meeting with her cheeks flushed. I was blushing up a storm in his embrace, too.

They had us read the last scene from the pilot, the one where Trip and Peter are hanging out by the Califon sign. It felt so much better reading the scene with Austen than it had when I shot the scene with Rob.

Rob Flowers, actor

I came to New York in February primarily to audition for Saturday Night Live. You gotta take the audition when they invite you if you're an improv comic. It was my second try for the show, by the way. My manager added the *Pet Peeves* audition once I had booked the trip. It wasn't a disappointment to me when I heard about the show not getting picked up. I hadn't been feeling the whole *Pet Peeves* thing while we shot the pilot, after all. Around noon the first day of the upfronts, I got called over to Lorne Michaels's office. Walked out a few hours later with a gig worth moving to New York for.

Kendra Lewis-Frost

Kym called me around lunchtime on Tuesday. The first thing she said was, "You were right. Austen Hughes is the only actor who could have played Peter." I wasn't happy to hear her admission. Couldn't she have come to her realization during the original casting process?

Kym Gifford

I guess I buried the lede when I gave Kendra the news.

Austen Hughes

My agent didn't call me until a couple of hours after I had left the meeting. I had a good feeling about the audition, but I hadn't yet put two and two together for what it could mean for me.

Kendra Lewis-Frost

Not for the first time, I gave Kym a piece of my mind. She was uncharacteristically silent during my tirade. Usually, we have a bit of back and forth during these rows.

Kym Gifford

I let Kendra get it out of her system before telling her the news: ABS had picked up *Pet Peeves* to debut mid-season. We ordered six episodes.

Austen Hughes

They offered me a sitcom. A fucking sitcom.

Despite having an extra six months to produce six episodes, Shatsky went on a hiring spree in the early summer to ensure he could bring in his dream production, writing, and directing team. In addition to casting Hughes in place of Flowers, he replaced the actor who had originally played Dr. Anita Copeland. [1]

With notes from the network, Shatsky and Lewis-Frost rewrote the pilot to change the Felicity-Trip romantic arc to one

---

[1] **Helen Price, actor (Dr. Anita Copeland)**

I suppose I'll be remembered only as a footnote for my role in the pilot of *Pet Peeves*.

between Felicity and Peter. Davies and Hughes committed themselves fully to exploring their scripted relationship.

Bronwyn Davies

I was sort of seeing someone else at the time of the upfronts, but I didn't expect it to go anywhere. While I waited for Austen to come out of the meeting, I sent the other dude a text telling him it had been fun, whatever.

Austen Hughes

My knees were not even slightly functional by the time I left the meeting. My legs wobbled like the Scarecrow's in *The Wizard of Oz*. I hadn't heard the news about the show being picked up yet, but I knew I had killed it in there. Something good was about to go down.

But anyway, I'm walking like I've never owned a pair of legs before, and I spot Bronwyn. I galumphed over to the chair next to her, hoping she wasn't paying attention to my freaky gait.

Bronwyn Davies

You're familiar with how my mind works already, so I guess I won't shock you by admitting I thought Austen was walking oddly to hide what had come up during our reading. It had been about half an hour since the end of our scene. Impressive.

Austen Hughes

Bronwyn's eyes flicked between my face and my groinal region. A lot of parts on my body had changed since we had been on the set of *Another Day*, but not that one. I would have been plenty happy to have introduced her to it the previous summer had she asked.

Bronwyn Davies

I couldn't get over how friggin' sexy he was. I knew it would've sounded superficial if I had fawned over him for being thin. Searching for another topic, I wondered out loud if *Another Day* might have nine lives. I hadn't meant it as a pun on how *Pet Peeves* was about, well, pets including cats. But anyway, he picked up on the joke right away.

Austen Hughes

I pun when I'm nervous. So there I am, rattling off one-liners like how grrruff the network suits had appeared; no matter what happened today, we'd all land on our feet, especially if they were grooming us for a new project; how I wished they hadn't been so cagey. Bronwyn has her infamous laugh, the wheeze-squeak-bray thing. I'm checking her fingernails to make sure they aren't turning blue. Kym's assistant isn't having it. I guess it's unseemly for people to have fun in the executive suite. We definitely had to leave. But, of course, my legs are still wonky, and Bronwyn's careening around because of the laughter. We didn't make the smoothest of exits.

Bronwyn Davies

Man, it felt perfect having his arm around my shoulder, like being wrapped in a weighted blanket. Total security.

Austen Hughes

We waddled our way over to her apartment. I was still at her home a couple of hours later when my agent called to tell me *Pet Peeves* had been picked up. Hands down, one of the best days of my life.

The newly hired team of writers met at Shatsky's office until the show officially took up residence at the same studio space in Queens where they had shot the pilot. Nearly a year to the day after filming began on Another Day, *shooting began on season 1 of* Pet Peeves.

Kendra Lewis-Frost
Most people Elvin hired to produce the series came out of his ancient Rolodex. He allowed me one call.

Stephen Burrows, writer
I thought Kendra was pranking me when she called me out of the blue. The amnesia queen had created a sitcom? Actually, the image of her writing a sitcom itself was a good enough joke for me to believe her. I had picked up a couple of one-offs since they had canceled *Another Day*, but the chance to write for a series again, even if it were a comedy, was just what the doctor ordered.

Kendra Lewis-Frost
It wasn't simply to honor a promise I had made to Stephen the previous fall. If you recall, he played a huge part in turning the original Peter Gluck into the comic hero on *Another Day*.

Elvin Shatsky
Count 'em. I now had two soap opera writers.

D'Wayne Curtis, writer
You don't say *no* when Elvin Shatsky offers you a gig, but honestly, I wanted to work on a fresher project than the typical Shatsky series. When I read the pilot script, I noticed it had a subtle dryness to it; it read a little smarter in places. That provided enough motivation for me to sign the contract.

Dirk Romano, director

The first day of shooting, I knew we'd come out with a better show than we did with the pilot. Austen made all the difference. He's a director's wet dream. He even made the weaker actors better. Wade especially. Wade relaxed. He learned to land a joke. I guess not having to play opposite Bronwyn agreed with him, too.

Wade Hanson

It was great being on the set with Austen again! And Bronwyn. We started hanging out a bit, the three of us. Sometimes four of us—I'm totally blanking on the name of the woman I was seeing back then. She wasn't an actress. Maybe a dental hygienist?

Kendra Lewis-Frost

We fell into a good rhythm in the writers' room. Elvin prefers to write scripts independently, as did I in my daytime drama days. A sitcom is different. You need to bounce lines off of your fellow writers to identify what will make the joke funnier. Stephen and I paired off for a couple of scripts. It was natural for us to write together, having come from the same background. For me, the real excitement began when we'd bring a script into the writers' room, and the lot of us would go at it for hours.

Moishe Bronfman, actor (Duke Quinn)

The one disappointment I have from shooting the first season is I didn't get to work with Larry again. A few scenes from the pilot didn't require reshooting, including the scenes where I delivered his puppies. My character rarely appeared in scenes at the veterinary clinic in the later episodes because Duke wasn't a vet. It wasn't my show, anyhow. It was Austen's.

Elvin Shatsky

Austen could make any line funnier. He didn't need us to rewrite his lines. His vocal inflections alone were a thing of beauty. I wondered if his physical comedy, now that he was less-substantial—is substantial the PC word for fat?—would lose some of its punch, but then again, you've got a guy like Stan Laurel who was skinny as a bean pole and still could make you laugh without saying a word. Anyhow, Austen could deliver a line. We didn't have to teach him how to hold for a laugh, either. Bronwyn, on the other hand, moved at the speed of light. I thought I'd die of old age before she'd learn to get the pacing right, but she caught on, thank God.

Blaine Carson

I got a new wife on the show. She was prettier than the last one. But I also got stuck on a show with Austen again. The only things I didn't get were more lines.

I'm not being fair here. Austen bears the blame for the demise of *Another Day to Live*, certainly. I had been sure the show was the right vehicle for me to achieve Susan Lucci-like status in the world of daytime dramas. Austen belonged on a show like *Pet Peeves*. I would have preferred it if each of us could have landed our own shows without ever having to cross paths again.

Postproduction went smoothly. Once again, the cast and crew settled in for the long wait until the premiere in March 2006.

Bronwyn Davies

The first season of the show was in the can in time for the fall premieres, not that we needed it to be ready so early. We had over six months before the premiere. Austen and I made the most of our free time, traveling and being a part of the scene in New York. We could go anywhere and not be bugged by the paparazzi back then. What a drag!

Austen Hughes

I couldn't believe I finally had a girlfriend. I had had maybe two girlfriends in high school and college combined. I've always assumed they both had pity-dated me. In the years when I worked mainly in the clubs, I got laid exactly one time. Considering her interest level in me, maybe I should make that half a time.

Bronwyn Davies

So, Austen had roommates. A lot of roommates. I don't know how many, maybe three or four regular guys and then there was always another guy crashing on the couch. The apartment smelled like feet. And chili. I never wore nice clothes when I visited Austen. You could always count on a fair amount of beer spillage. But dude, these guys were funny. Professionally funny. They sat around and developed material for their sets. They were different from my friends. Way more committed to what they did rather than to how they looked.

I liked Austen. A lot. It made me feel bad that I hadn't been into him in the same way when we first met. A tiny part of me started to consider he may have been way too good for me.

Austen Hughes

Back when I was on *Another Day*, I caught a lot of flak when I did a set at a comedy club and word got around I was acting on a soap opera. I was the one laughing all the way to the bank. Plus I had access to the commissary each day I shot a scene. Suckers. They called me a sell-out when I landed the gig on *Pet Peeves*, but come on, what comedian doesn't want to star in a sitcom? Or bring home someone like Bronwyn

Flip Tuttle, one of Austen's housemates

Dude, Austen Hughes was funny as shit, but if you had asked me back then which guy coming up through the clubs was going to make it big and get to date Bronwyn Davies, I wouldn't in a million years have picked him. It would have been me, of course. The ratty couch I slept on for seven months never looked as good as it did when she sat on it. I always had the best dreams the nights she came to visit.

Kym Gifford

The fall was a rough one for me. We had introduced five new shows, and every one flopped. Do I wish we had picked up *Pet Peeves* for a whole season the previous May? I can't say. If the pilot had been as solid as the new first episode, things probably would have gone differently.

The beauty of TV is you'll always have next season. See? I have my optimistic moments. We began listening to pitches for the following year before the fall premieres. I already had my hopes pinned to a few of them before we had to pull the plug on four of our new shows.

Kendra Lewis-Frost

I watched the ABS sitcoms every night during the fall season. Is it awful of me to have wished both *Love Me, Love My Sister* and *Quad Wrangle* would fail? *Love Me* had an ideal time slot, Tuesday's at eight thirty, leading into *Dear Old Dad*. Kym wasn't amused when I expressed my hope we could land in their time slot in March. I can't blame her. The show hadn't been canceled yet.

Elvin Shatsky

I pitched a new idea to a couple of the networks that fall. Nothing panned out. Probably the longest stretch I was without a show on the air in years. On the plus side, my golf handicap had never been lower.

The network began to promote Pet Peeves *in February 2006. With no stars familiar to primetime audiences, it generated little buzz except for those involved with the show.*

Kendra Lewis-Frost

When I saw a promo for the show, you'd think I had never worked in television. Thank goodness for thick walls. I'm sure the people in the next apartment would have thought they lived next to a hyena in labor had they heard me shriek with glee.

Austen Hughes

My mom still has a promo poster from the first season hanging in my childhood bedroom back in Lee's Summit. You know the one with Bronwyn, Wade, and me in our white vet coats, standing behind a bulldog wearing an Elizabethan collar up on an exam table? Bulldogs are not the smallest of breeds. You can barely see us behind him. The dog took a piss during the shoot. You can imagine what happens when a forceful stream hits a stainless steel surface. The photographer caught it on film. I totally wanted them to use one of those shots. Our expressions were on point! Wardrobe hadn't brought along spare sets of scrubs and jackets, so that was the end of the photo shoot.

Kym Gifford

We lined up interviews for Elvin and the principal actors. Elvin was the only one we could get booked on a late night show, *Last Call with Carson Daly*. None of the ABS late night shows were interested. Daytime talk shows booked group interviews with cast members rather than one star at a time. About all we had going for us was the time slot, Tuesdays at eight thirty. I knew if *Pet Peeves* failed, I couldn't count on keeping my job.

Kendra Lewis-Frost

A few reviews came out before the premiere, and they weren't awful. Variety declared Austen to be an up-and-coming star. A few reviews were charitable toward Bronwyn and Moishe, too. My favorite quote is, "Buried under the usual sledgehammer-driven comedy we've come to expect from Shatsky, you'll notice a nuanced, drier, sometimes darker humor drawing the viewer to discover its hidden pleasures. If later episodes make better use of this voice, ABS may very well have a show on par with *The Office*."

Kym Gifford

We decided not to hold the premiere party at some big-name Midtown site to avoid any potential humiliation in the event we failed to draw a crowd. It may have been Kendra who came up with the idea of holding it at the Bronx Zoo.

Blaine Carson

This is what my career had come to: a premiere party at a zoo. In the Bronx.

Bronwyn Davies

I thought for a moment about wearing the dress I had planned to wear to the ABS Gala during the upfronts, a diaphanous pale blue gown with a train. Not exactly the right choice for traipsing around a zoo. I went with a short, tight green sequined dress. It was nearly the color of Austen's eyes.

Austen Hughes

It blew me away that Bronwyn and I were still dating. A victim of a life-long sexual drought, I had sort of envied friends of mine who hooked up with a different woman every night. In truth, what I had always dreamed of was a love-at-first-sight, celebrate-our-seventy-fifth-anniversary sort of romance. By the premiere, I wasn't sure if Bronwyn had the same dream. I had managed to drag her home to Missouri to meet my family at Thanksgiving. You'd think I had stuffed, trussed, and shoved her in the oven with a thermometer up her butt when I first invited her. She'll never admit it, but I was under the impression she ended up having a great time.

Ann Hughes, Austen Hughes's mother

I couldn't be prouder of my son. He's always been a good boy. Smart, polite. He had big dreams when he went to New York, but he's a softy. I worried a comedian's life would be too hard on him. While I believed in him, I had never imagined I'd attend a television premiere or witness him escorting a pretty little thing like Bronwyn down a red carpet. He wasn't the overtly ambitious sort. I still miss my chubby Austen and having to tuck his shirttails into his pants, but attending my son's first TV premiere was a special occasion for me.

Kendra Lewis-Frost

The weather was seasonable the night of the premiere. We were able to watch the first two episodes on a big outdoor screen without losing bits and pieces of ourselves to frostbite. Unfortunately, our reception site didn't have direct views into any of the animal enclosures. I almost forgot we were at a zoo. I hadn't thought about the food choices before the premiere, but after? Having just watched the scene where Moishe delivers a litter of pups, the idea of eating a pig-in-blanket was a bit off-putting.

Bronwyn Davies

I became a vegetarian the night of the premiere party. How could I work with those adorable creatures and then go and eat them? Not the puppies. Don't be gross. But my TV parents ran a rural animal hospital. We also treated cows and chickens.

Blaine Carson

We had a nice crowd at the premiere. Watching the show with a couple hundred folks laughing at all the right moments put me in the right spirit to hope the show did well. Gotta say I loved the grilled meat section of the buffet. It surprised me it didn't draw a bigger crowd.

Reviews came out the morning of the premiere. They were mostly neutral to good. Metacritic's aggregate score of the reviews from the first season was 61, allowing Pet Peeves *to squeak into the green zone. Austen received the most favorable press.*

Wade Hanson

Me, Austen, and Bronwyn hosted a viewing party in the lounge of her apartment building. I probably laughed the loudest. Well, Austen kept making Bronwyn crack up, but that doesn't count.

Elvin Shatsky

I didn't watch the show when it aired. Why would I want to see it with commercials?

Kendra Lewis-Frost

I watched it alone at home with my roommate. I knew when Kym watched it, she'd be focusing on the ratings, but for me, the wonder of seeing my show on the television set transformed it into something magical. I was speechless from the cold open through the tag.

Kym Gifford

We had sold out the advertising spots to a few prime companies for the first episode. And with it wedged between two high-performing shows, I hoped the ratings would be somewhere above the basement level. *Love Me, Love My Sister* had received great numbers for its first episode. The problem was no one tuned in for week two. Until I had six weeks' worth of strong ratings for *Pet Peeves*, I wouldn't be able to relax. Who am I kidding? I've spent so many years with my muscles tied up in knots, if I unclenched even a single one, my skeletal system would run to my therapist, complaining that I could no longer support it.

Over ten million viewers tuned in for the premiere of Pet Peeves. *The second and third episodes drew about five million each. The next two weeks saw additional drops in viewership. Nearly six million viewers tuned in to watch the finale, which aired a week before the upfronts. The cast and crew held their collective breath until the following Monday when the network announced it had picked up* Pet Peeves *for a second season with an order for twenty-two episodes.*

Chapter 5
The Comfort Room

Kendra Lewis-Frost

And the angels sang. We couldn't rest on our laurels, of course. We had a tremendous amount of work ahead of us. Before the first season aired, Elvin and I had discussed where we would go with the story should we be on the air for a second season. Beyond envisioning a narrative arc for a second season, we didn't put much thought into the future of the show. Elvin warned me not to get ahead of myself. With nothing better to do between completing production on season 1 and its premiere, I had ignored him, outlining several episodes for season 2 and sketching out a few of the scenes on my own.

Elvin Shatsky

Kendra shows up for the first writers' meeting after we were picked up for a second season with an overflowing binder of outlines. Who died and appointed her showrunner? I didn't bother reading any of her ideas for the simple reason I wanted to remind her I was in charge.

Kendra Lewis-Frost

Horrible person that I am, when I hadn't been rooting for the demise of comedies during the fall season, I prayed Elvin would receive the green light for another project. It wouldn't have been the worst thing to have seen less of him at *Pet Peeves*.

D'Wayne Curtis, writer

The writers behind the second season fell into two camps. There were the Shatsky devotees. And then there were those who were pushing for a less vaudevillian tone to the scripts. If you took anything away from the reviews from the first season, it was that the show succeeded in part because of Kendra's influence.

I saw her style as intelligent, sometimes dark, sometimes even a little experimental, but always human in scale. For instance, she came into one meeting spouting off the results of her research based on reasons people bring chickens in to see the vet. Every once in a while, an egg gets stuck inside a chicken. You can see it in an X-ray. Kendra found the situation to be hilarious. She went off on a tangent, spitballing soothing things a vet would say to a chicken. Assuming the role of the vet, she put herself in the mindset of a chicken. Next thing you know, she's acting out a scene between a chicken and a shrink, doing both voices. "I can't let go. I was separated from my mother when I was but an egg. You never get o-o-over the sense of abandonment." And then the egg comes out. The shrink reaches for it, asking, "Are you going to eat that?" All Shatsky said was, "May we move on?"

Kendra Lewis-Frost

I'm not going to lie: until we had actors reading our lines, I wasn't feeling the magic of writing the series. I continued to write with Stephen. When we'd present our scripts to the rest of the writers, they would tear our work to shreds. Elvin sat at the head of the table, enjoying the show. Besides having the tendency to be demoralizing, his process was less than efficient. Each deadline loomed larger under his leadership than they had in my previous writers' room experiences.

Elvin Shatsky

We had seven solid scripts once the filming began. Being ahead of the game is the hallmark of a seasoned showrunner.

Austen Hughes

After the network picked up the series for a second season, I moved in with Bronwyn and sublet my room. With my newfound success came access to a kitchen where the fridge didn't come fully stocked with ninety-two strains of homegrown penicillin. Yet we rarely used it because Bronwyn wanted to go out every night. The network had made me sign a document promising I wouldn't gain or lose weight or change my hairstyle— I'm sure actors on every series sign the same thing. But I was a fat guy trapped in a fairly trim body confronting a food and alcohol-doused lifestyle. If I reneged on my promise, I wonder who would have dropped me first, the network or Bronwyn.

Bronwyn Davies

We were trying to be seen as the *it* couple. I had a little bit of a following before *Pet Peeves* aired. Austen was the new guy on the scene. And he was so good looking. It would have been a shame to keep him locked up at my apartment.

Austen Hughes

Bronwyn is one of those people who diets by not ordering the food she wants to eat. Then she makes her companions order it, and she'll nibble on their food instead. Stupidest thing to fight about, but the first fight I remember having with her was about me refusing to order onion rings. I started to bring Wade along with us. He can eat anything and not gain a pound.

Wade Hanson

We had tons of fun that summer on set and off. I'm not sure if Austen ever noticed, but I spent a lot of time studying him to learn how to be funnier. I never saw him stress out. If you're angry or sad or repressed, your outer layer is too tough for the jokes to come out. Or they come out all brittle and calculated. Austen didn't have a protective layer. Everything good he had inside him flowed out nonstop. He's one of the few people I've ever known who could make my outer layer more porous, more malleable.

Season 1 had established the rivalry between the two animal clinics, providing a reason to prevent Felicity and Peter from dating. Peter didn't take part in the dispute between the Quinns and the Copelands. He was the peacemaker, or at least he attempted to bring peace to Califon. His crush on Felicity had the unintended consequence of threatening his partnership with Trip. In the season 1 finale, Felicity's resolve to resist her feelings for Peter began to wither. With romance in the air for season 2, Davies and Hughes continued to let life imitate art.

Bronwyn Davies

I've dated actors who played the romantic lead opposite me before, but we were always getting to know each other while having to make out in front of the cameras. Austen and I had been together for over a year before we shot the episode where our characters began dating. I think I matured both as an actor and as a girlfriend because of the lag between our real and fake relationships. I was pretty sure I had started to fall in love with Austen.

Austen Hughes

From what I heard from the writers, Peter and Felicity were going to remain a couple for the duration of the show. Maybe they'd break up in a later season for a short while, but their coupledom was a done deal. Having one relationship—albeit a fictional relationship—fated to endure, I let myself believe Bronwyn was my one true love.

Elvin Shatsky

One thing I hate is when my actors date within the cast. Oddly enough, the sex scenes become less steamy, and if the actors split up, the only one who's getting screwed is the executive producer. You try dealing with an actress whose costar boyfriend just got caught *in flagrante delicto* with the wig master. And you wondered why *Gopher!* wasn't a success.

Moishe Bronfman

Moira O'Shea, who played my wife on both *Another Day* and *Pet Peeves* is simply terrific. I didn't see it in her when she played the dramatic version of my wife, but given the right part, she had a touch of Catherine O'Hara in her. She played my wife the second time around with this ditzy yet prideful studied mannerism. The vein of pathos running through her performance made it brilliant. You saw this microscopic shred of self-awareness that underneath her Chanel suits, Claudia was terrified her Park Avenue counterparts would determine her to be a fraud. My hat is off to you, Ms. O'Shea!

Kendra Lewis-Frost

Duke and Claudia lived in Manhattan, an hour and a half away from Califon. After helping the boys open the clinic in season 1, they were back in the City, leading their own lives. How often could we send Trip home or have his parents visit him in the country? I loved scenes with the Quinns, but weaving them into the story became a greater challenge in our second season.

Blaine Carson

In season 2, my role expanded out of necessity. So it didn't always make sense to write Moishe into an episode? I'm not complaining.

Elvin Shatsky

As it turns out, rival veterinary clinics in a small town is a lousy premise for a sitcom. And with Carson's dull-as-a-button-convention portrayal of Felicity's father, the less we saw of the Copelands' clinic, the better.

Kym Gifford

The fall 2006 season was far more successful for the network—and by extension, I was more successful—than the previous year. Three of our new shows had legs. One of the comedies, *Making Lemonade with the Lemons*, was doing well even in a terrible time slot. We made the decision to do a little rejiggering of the schedule in the winter.

Elvin Shatsky

Friday nights at eight o'clock? Are you fucking kidding me? The network had given up on us. We still had a few scripts left to write and shoot. Let Kendra wipe her dirty paws all over them. If they canceled the show, which I was sure they would, better its demise be associated with her.

Kendra Lewis-Frost

I was honored when Elvin gave me a chance to oversee the last scripts of season 2. We had to maintain consistency, of course. But the viewers were familiar enough with my voice for me to be confident in bringing it to the fore.

The third to last episode of season 2, "The Comfort Room," showcased the looser, more daring side of Pet Peeves. *Filming began in mid-February on the episode that aired on April 27.*

Bronwyn Davies

Oh, my God, "The Comfort Room." Give me a second. Seriously, I can't talk about that episode without losing it. So friggin' funny! No, don't worry about me. I can still breathe.

Wade Hanson

I figured you were going to ask what my favorite episode was. It's hard to pick one because I love so many of them, but "The Comfort Room" was definitely my first favorite. I bet our blooper reel for it was longer than an entire season's worth of outtakes.

Kendra Lewis-Frost

"The Comfort Room" earned me my first Emmy nomination. I don't deserve full credit for its success.

Well, the idea behind it was mine. But Austen definitely shares the credit. His improv during rehearsal led to script changes. And then he went off script during the shooting. The finished product was absolutely brilliant.

Elvin Shatsky

I didn't find the episode to be particularly funny. It came as no surprise when Kendra didn't win an Emmy for it. And no one could have convinced me then it was for the best of the show to change its voice. I gave her control of the script, and look what happened.

Moishe Bronfman

Going back to the beginning, when Duke helped Trip and Peter design the clinic, he had suggested they make one of the exam rooms considerably larger than the other three, sort of an executive suite, as you will. It had the usual sink, cabinets, and stainless steel exam table of your typical examination room. But instead of a pair of plastic chairs, it had a taupe suede couch. Claudia added a host of ridiculous decorative touches to the room, or at least details that were ridiculous when you consider it was an examination room at a veterinary clinic.

So, anyway, early in the first season, Trip and Peter had an argument about who should lay claim to the exam room. Since the two vets didn't need four exam rooms, they resolved their conflict by converting the largest exam room into a comfort room, a place where they would see pets that were about to be euthanized. The grieving families would have a homier environment in which to say goodbye.

"The Comfort Room" begins with an early morning exam of a dying dog in another room. When the decision to put down the dog has been made, Wade ushers the family and their pet into the comfort room only to stumble upon a sleeping Duke. Mrs. Quinn had kicked him out the night before, a common, insignificant occurrence between the two.

It had not previously occurred to Trip and Peter to use the room for personal matters. Starting that morning, the room became a haven to a host of non-veterinary pursuits.

Austen Hughes

We hadn't filmed any scenes in the comfort room after its purpose had been established in season 1. Putting down beloved pets is not exactly sitcom fare.

I thought Moishe was phenomenal in the episode. His acting set the tone for the rest of the scenes in the story arc. He captured Duke's overblown self-importance, unbowed by the fact that he was selling his status to people who were saying goodbye to a cocker spaniel all while wearing nothing but a pair of boxer shorts and a too-small top covered in pink poodles borrowed from a set of a vet tech's scrubs.

Bronwyn Davies

Of course, Peter's first idea for how to use the room was to sneak Felicity in for a nooner. Why not? The room's equipped with a couch and ambient lighting. At the table read, Austen said he didn't believe Felicity would want to lie naked on a piece of furniture that had perhaps absorbed a bit of, we'll call it history, from the end moments in the lives of dogs and cats.

Kendra Lewis-Frost

This is why you'll never find any textiles in an exam room. In rehearsal, Austen and Bronwyn carried on an improvised conversation laying out her arguments against having sex on the couch and his lack of issues with lying in whatever biomatter the couch harbored. He rattled off more positions than are in the Kama Sutra, assuring her that with a little ingenuity, she wouldn't have to make contact with the couch. Ultimately, the couple ends up in the back seat of his car, which, incidentally, was visibly far less sanitary than the couch.

Wade Hanson

I've never laughed so hard at work. We filmed a bunch of short scenes to make a montage of Trip, Peter, the vet techs, the receptionist, and even the UPS guy sneaking into the comfort room to use it for increasingly weird purposes. And of course, the sillier the scene, the more takes we had to shoot after one of us would start giggling.

Trip and Peter hooked up a video console to the TV in the room. While they were playing a violent game, a vet tech relocated a family with a dying cat to the comfort room. The second the little girl walked into the room, Austen went off script, yelling, "Die, you freaking alien, die!"

Emma Bates, actor (KellyAnne Hurley)

They stuffed my character into the saddest rip-off of a Minnie Mouse costume you've ever seen and had her engage in some cosplay with someone online when she was alone in the comfort room. Austen was in a penguin costume, appearing on the computer monitor via CCTV. Thank God for my mask! If I could keep from laughing out loud or garbling my lines, I knew I could make it through the scene.

Kendra Lewis-Frost

Elvin has a penchant for potty humor. I figured I'd throw him a bone in the script. Once the novelty of having a comfortably appointed spare room wore off for the staff, they each independently settled on a single reason to go into the room alone. It became the clinic's fartorium.

Austen Hughes

Please tell me I'm not the only one who actually farted while filming their scene.

Bronwyn Davies

Felicity, like me, is very private about certain matters. She would come to the clinic to see her boyfriend, a visit when she would have been doing her best to charm him into spending quality time with her. While she appreciated having a safe place to float an air muffin, so to speak, even when she was alone in the comfort room, she would have been too self-conscious to use the room according to its new functionality. Of course, I wasn't alone on set when we shot my scene, what with the director and the crew being there and all. I only pretended to poot.

Lucy Hernandez, editor

Here's a fun fact I stumbled on while working with the sound editor on the episode: all the actors supplied their own sound effects during the fart room takes.

When Pet Peeves *returned after the winter break, it had lost its Tuesday night time slot, exiled to the primetime equivalent of Siberia, Friday night at eight o'clock. Its ratings, while never strong, slid throughout the winter. Initially,* Making Lemonade with the Lemons *had thrived in its new time slot on Tuesdays.*

With six episodes left to shoot following the schedule change, Making Lemonade *received a devastating blow: its star was five months pregnant and had been ordered to bed rest for the remainder of her term. Without the star power of its lead actress,* Making Lemonade *began to hemorrhage viewers. The slide in the show's rankings did not reflect well on Entertainment chairman, Kym Gifford.*

Kym Gifford

While not stellar, my second year as Entertainment chairman had begun stronger than my first. We had ordered pilots from about sixteen of the scripts we read over the winter break. It had been my hope that the early success of *Making Lemonade with the Lemons* plus an exciting crop of pilots for the next season would pave the way for my third year to prove to the network I was the right woman for the job.

Thelonious Trout, chairman of ABS Television Network

HBO was ascendant when we had promoted Kym. That year, they received double the number of Emmy nominations as NBC, which was in second place. And, well, I don't want to do the math. It hurts my head. Let's just assume NBC had at least double the number of Emmy nods as ABS. The ABS Network appeared weak, a little flabby, even. It was crunch time for us. We had to find a way to compete with HBO.

Kym Gifford

We were losing the ratings war. When I received my promotion, ABS had been clinging to third place overall in weekly ratings. In my second year, we slipped to fourth place and threatened to fall lower. It would be callous of me to wish Alexandra Collins [the star of

Making Lemonade with the Lemons] hadn't gotten pregnant in the first place. Or if she had to get pregnant, that she would have carried the baby to term and given birth to a healthy baby after they finished filming their season.

Everything turned out fine for the child in the end, but with a preemie to care for, she opted out of signing a contract for a second season, and we had to cancel *Making Lemonade*, the only successful show I had brought to the lineup.

Kendra Lewis-Frost

With *Pet Peeves* sitting in the TV equivalent of the fifth circle of Hell and with the ratings to match, our head was in the lion's mouth. Yet my level of delusion was on par with Don Quixote's. I hoped the network would switch our show back to Tuesdays when Alexandra Collins left on maternity leave, and I even dared to dream we stood a chance of ABS picking up *Pet Peeves* for a third season.

Elvin Shatsky

Even without that lemonade show in the lineup, I didn't like our chances for a third season. I had considered using my charm on Kym to save *Pet Peeves*. She didn't exactly get my motor running, but it was a sacrifice I would have been willing to make had I actually given a rat's ass about saving the show.

Kendra Lewis-Frost

Pet Peeves had come into its own halfway through its second season. Elvin was all about putting the situation in sitcom. I strove to write character-driven episodes. We had found a synergy and created situations to highlight the essence of the characters, all of whom had become real people to me. Peter straddled the line between being an exceptionally gifted vet and an otherwise ignorant, goofy farm boy. Trip was a snob, never adjusting to being stuck out in the country. Felicity had a heart of gold and a brain of mush. One always held their breath when she handled a complicated case. While I tended to take the humor to dark places, I never let her dizzy tendencies lead to the harm of an animal, mind you. Her mother and Trip's father were natural rivals, both prideful and stubborn. We had such fun writing stories for these disparate personalities.

Without question, meanness will always play funnier than kindness. What I sought to capture in my scripts was a veneer of hostility masking warmth and humanity. You saw this quality come to life in Moishe's scenes.

I'm rambling now. Sorry. Revisiting the second season will always make me emotional. By the end of the second season, I no longer thought of myself as an imposter. I took great pride and joy in my contributions to the sitcom genre. I had become fiercely protective of what we had created.

With twenty-two episodes compared to six, shooting the second season presented more challenges for the cast and crew than the first. Coupled with low ratings, the stress seeped into their personal lives as the season came to a close.

Bronwyn Davies

Austen is definitely different from my other exes. He's this nice Midwestern boy, the kind of guy girls should marry. He brought me home to meet his mom. I bet I hadn't met a boyfriend's mother since I was in high school. We lived together; we worked together. At the end of a long day, we'd go home and decompress together. It surprised me how much this version of dating initially suited me. Maybe I didn't feel a big, romantic love for Austen, but the cozy, comfy life we had sure was like being in love. And I definitely loved seeing the pictures of us in the gossip magazines.

Austen Hughes

I guess I wanted more out of the relationship than Bronwyn did. I was in it to fall in love, get married, grow old together. She, on the other hand, loved the happy, sparkly side of dating an actor.

Bronwyn Davies

To produce the second season of *Pet Peeves*, we shot one episode a week for our twenty-two week season. That's nothing compared to the schedule for a daytime drama where we'd shoot five or six hour-long episodes every week for a yearlong season. I put in about a year and a half at *From Boardroom to Bedroom* before they wrote me off the show. Though, unlike *Pet Peeves*, I wasn't on set every day.

But anyway, starring on a sitcom left me with more free time than I was used to. I sort of thought Austen and I would go out on the weekends when we were shooting, but he was always running off to some boring town to do one measly comedy set. I did the dutiful girlfriend thing and traveled with him a couple of times. That didn't last long. No offense, Kalamazoo, but life's too short for me to go watch another comedy show at your local VFW hall.

Austen Hughes

I had been cast to play a small role in a movie. After the second season of *Pet Peeves* was in the can, I flew out to Vancouver for the movie shoot. I invited Bronwyn to come with me.

Bronwyn Davies

I hadn't been up for a role in whatever movie it was Austen went to shoot in Vancouver, not that it matters. Even though he wanted me to come with him, I decided to stay home because I thought it would be awkward to have an actor not in the cast hanging around the set. Also, I didn't want to give the impression I was available to hang out on my boyfriend's movie shoot because I couldn't get a job of my own.

Austen Hughes

Do I think she was jealous when I started to receive offers for roles in films? I've never thought about it. Hmm. No. I don't think so. It's not like we would have been competing against each other for a part. Except for the role of short, blonde best friend in a rom-com, the one who has a crush on the lead's brother. I would be, like, oh my god, so cute and totally perfect for it, she wouldn't have stood a chance against me in an audition.

Kendra Lewis-Frost

I had been in a long-term relationship since about a year before I began working at *Another Day to Live*. We fought a lot; pugilism was our dance of seduction. Each of us was driven; each of us had reached new heights in our careers at about the same time. But without job security, my emotional pendulum swung between disparate moods. I couldn't have been easy to live with. Neither of us was. We fought more often, but we made up less and less frequently. It made for a great plotline for a TV show, but as for how to lead one's life for real, I wouldn't recommend it.

Bronwyn Davies

To be honest, I don't remember if I thought it was a big deal to be apart from Austen for the three or four weeks he was off in Vancouver. One of my friends kept telling me I should be jealous of the other actresses in his movie. Is it weird I wasn't? I was having fun in New York without him. Being in a serious relationship turned out to be less of a thrill than I thought it would be.

Austen Hughes

Before I had left for Vancouver, I sensed that Bronwyn might not have been as committed to our relationship as I was. I alternated between trying harder to prove my love to her and ignoring the problem altogether. Man, is it hot in here, or am I just burning up from the embarrassment of owning up to my total case of love blindness?

Kendra Lewis-Frost

One bright spot from that spring: one of our online fan groups, Everything Pet Peeves, had its review of "The Comfort Room" go viral and get picked up by BuzzFeed. For the first time, I recognized what a loyal fan base our show had gained. You forget about individual people when you obsess over how many millions of viewers were or weren't tuning in to watch your show. Low rankings don't tell you the whole story. I must say, seeing the viral review and reading the comments from fans helped me through the personal crisis I was facing.

Blaine Carson, actor (Harold Copeland)

Wrapping up a season is tough, even when playing a smaller role. You've been working your tail off and leading this intense life. And then it stops. You need a break, that's for sure. I suppose if you have the security of knowing you'll be back on set in four or five months to shoot the next season, you can enjoy it. We didn't have such a luxury. Actors always say they don't read Variety and the other Hollywood rags, but we all do. We track ratings and reviews the way someone else does The New York Times crossword puzzle every day. We knew things were dicey for *Pet Peeves* as the season drew to a close.

Kym Gifford

When the network fired me in early May, I wasn't surprised. Highly disappointed, but not surprised.

Thelonious Trout, chairman of ABS Television Network

My job as chairman of the ABS network is to ensure we remain strong and air programming that appeals to our core demographic. When you hear someone like Bradford Ellis, the executive vice president of programming at HBO, is searching for a new position, you sit up and take notice. We lured him to ABS in the spring of 2007. I believed in Kym to a point, but she hadn't provided the strength the position required. The opportunity to bring in Ellis was one we couldn't pass up.

Kym Gifford

Only two of the shows I had added to the schedule were still airing in the spring of 2007. And one of them had already been canceled for the following season. It was easy for the network to erase every trace of me from their fall lineup once I had been fired.

Kendra Lewis-Frost

Not everyone on the show received the news of our cancellation directly from their agents. A few of them heard the news from a third party who had read about it in Variety or Deadline or wherever the story first broke.

Blaine Carson

Here's what a habitual reliance on Variety to start your day gets you. You shouldn't have to go online to learn you've been canned. I fired my agent the minute I read the news that I was out of a job.

Austen Hughes

I heard about our show being canceled from Bronwyn while I was in Vancouver. I offered to fly home early—or at least to fly home on my days off—to be with her, but she told me not to bother.

Bronwyn Davies

By the time Austen came back home after his movie shoot, I had adjusted to being alone. Well, maybe not quite alone.

Austen Hughes

Bronwyn wasn't the one to tell me she had been cheating on me; I heard it from Wade.

Wade Hanson

I'm not exactly clear about the bro code. I figured if I was in Austen's position, I'd want to hear that my girlfriend had cheated on me from him, so that's why I told him.

Austen Hughes

When I got over the initial shock about what Bronwyn had done to me, I forgave her. The last thing I wanted was to break up with her. I was so into the security of having a serious girlfriend, I would have done anything to save the relationship.

Bronwyn Davies

It was for the best, ending things with Austen. Besides, our breakup and my new relationship received more coverage than the story of *Pet Peeves* not being picked up for a third season. See? He didn't have to worry about everyone talking about how his show had failed.

Kym Gifford

A rival network invited me to interview for an executive position out in California. I've always thought of myself as a New Yorker even though I grew up in Kentucky. Screw it. When they offered me the job, I jumped at the chance to get out of Dodge.

Kendra Lewis-Frost

My relationship didn't survive the cancellation of *Pet Peeves*. I took an elongated holiday back in Stoke Poges to sulk over my failures.

Austen Hughes

I didn't want to kick out the guy subletting my room before the end of the month, so I slept on the couch in my old apartment for a couple of weeks. Because nothing says single and out of work better than curling up in the fetal position on a stained couch, using your housemate's balled-up dirty gym socks as a pillow.

Chapter 6
The One Where I Said We're not Friends

With the cancellation of Pet Peeves, *the cast and crew moved on — or not.*

Elvin Shatsky

Pet Peeves being canceled didn't mean anything to me. *Grab Your Hat* got picked up for the fall season, and they needed a production studio to make it. Spent six seasons with them — enough for the show to go into syndication — and I've been writing and producing *Major Regrets* ever since. Some of us in this business are built to survive.

Kendra Lewis-Frost

A friend of mine was co-producing the show *Gumbo Gumshoes*. She recommended me for the position of story editor on the show. Now, mind you, story editor is several steps down from executive producer, but it kept me busy during those early months.

Austen Hughes

One perk of doing a sitcom for two seasons was they gave me better time slots at the comedy clubs because I was a "name." Having my heart broken was good for my sets, too. I didn't have to labor over creating new material. Here, you try it. Stand up on a stage. Make sure you're wearing an ugly, wrinkled shirt. Take a moment before going on stage to ask the lighting guy to direct the spotlight on you in such a way to bring out the bags under your eyes. Now, with flat inflection, say, "So, my girlfriend cheated on me. I guess that means we're done." People will laugh every time.

Bronwyn Davies

I had only one big guest-starring role — on a legal drama — that fall. I'm not going to kid you; it was kind of a bummer not being on the air every week. But the lead of the lawyer show, Thad Powers, didn't hold it against me. Well, he did for most of the summer if you know what I mean.

Wade Hanson

I got a good tan that summer but no new roles. It doesn't cost anything to lay on the grass in Central Park. I made new friends, but I missed hanging out with my former colleagues, Austen especially. He and I met up once. It was a blast.

Austen Hughes

I spent an afternoon with Wade, but seeing him reminded me of Bronwyn. I told him I was too busy to do it again when he asked me the next time.

Kendra Lewis-Frost

It dawned on me, having been the co-creator/executive producer of a sitcom, what someone else in my position would do would be to come up with an idea for a new series. However, writing the occasional episode of a show based on someone else's premise better suited my speed at the time. I was no more motivated to abandon Peter, Felicity, and the rest of the *Pet Peeves* characters in favor of a new gang than I was to fall in love again.

Bronwyn Davies

Austen texted me in August. I deleted it without responding. I didn't want to encourage him to continue to send me texts.

Austen Hughes

My agent regarded the cancellation of the show as an opportunity to promote me. He had lined up a mess of auditions. I was doing okay in the clubs. My material was funny. I wasn't going as big as I used to, but the low-energy persona matched the material. Sad sack guy wasn't an asset on the audition circuit, though. It hadn't been my intention to blow the auditions, but I had developed a superpower that allowed me to transform every joke into a gesture of sniveling despondency.

Moishe Bronfman

I caught one of Austen's sets at a club after we were canceled. He wasn't the same guy I knew from our days of working together. Funny as he was, I felt bad laughing at his jokes. Bronwyn really did a number on him. I intended to stay in touch with him, but I didn't keep my promise. I was still a newlywed then, off in my own world.

Kendra Lewis-Frost

If you had asked me which was harder, ending a relationship or having my show canceled, it would have been an easy question to answer. Definitely much harder to lose the show. When the Emmy nominations came out in late July, receiving one hadn't been on my radar. I wasn't in a place where I could even appreciate the recognition I received for writing the comfort room episode.

After a couple of weeks of ego boosting, courtesy of my amazing friends and colleagues, it hit me: simply because one network canceled a show doesn't mean the show is dead. A handful of great shows earned a second chance on a new network: *Taxi* and *Gilmore Girls*, for starters. I ran across a website committed to trying to persuade the ABS Network to bring back *Pet Peeves*. If strangers were making the effort to save my show, shouldn't I make a similar commitment, too? I'm a bloody Emmy nominee, for fuck's sake!

Elvin Shatsky

Kendra called me with her harebrained idea to resurrect the damned show. I wasn't interested. If she wanted to knock on every door in New York and Hollywood, be my guest.

Kendra Lewis-Frost

With Elvin's blessing, I got to work putting together a pitch for the revival of *Pet Peeves*.

Lewis-Frost polished her elevator pitch on the plane to Los Angeles for the Emmy Awards presentation. Bolstered by the courage of representing Pet Peeves *at its finest moment, she pledged to approach every network executive in attendance. Top of her list had been Kym Gifford. Ultimately, her courage did not extend in Gifford's direction.*

Rex Braithwaite, chairman of IBS Television Network

Kendra cornered me at the Emmys. I respected her for earning an Emmy nomination, and the fact that Shatsky was no longer involved in her project added a certain appeal, but the premise of the show didn't interest me. I invited her to come see me if she had any new ideas.

Kendra Lewis-Frost

I toned down my pitch at the Emmys after receiving a rejection from Rex. With each network head I ran into, I basically pitched the idea of me pitching my show at a later date. The softer pitch went over a little better. I booked five meetings, including one with Kym's replacement at ABS.

Bradford Ellis, ABS Entertainment chairman

My intention for scheduling the meeting with Kendra was to hammer home the point that the network was not going to get back in bed with *Pet Peeves* under any circumstances. I admired her talent and her passion. It was only fair to spend a minute or two with her woodshedding the initial premise of the show, which was actually two separate premises: generational and workplace. Had she and Shatsky jettisoned one of those things in development, the show would have been stronger, in my opinion.

Kendra Lewis-Frost
The meeting with Bradford had been the last of my pitch meetings. My emotions were all over the map when it was through. He had given me a clear reason why the show had not succeeded. I had thus far put my energy into fighting for people to change their minds about a failed show. But the show held a certain appeal. Until I understood exactly where its appeal lay, I was wasting my time—and the networks' time—beating a dead horse.

Ursula Fletcher, head of Everything Pet Peeves Fan Club
I totally fangirled when Kendra Lewis-Frost contacted me. OMG!!! The executive producer of my favorite show knows I exist!

Kendra Lewis-Frost
The people who decide what we watch focus solely on making a profit. They give you advice about scripts and actors not because they're amazingly talented writers but because they're business people. If I needed meaningful insight about *Pet Peeves*, wouldn't dedicated fans of the show be a preferable community to approach for their opinions? Ursula and I set up a video conference between a handful of the top contributors to her site and me.

Ursula Fletcher
Seriously, it was one of the most exciting projects I'd ever worked on. Ms. Lewis-Frost actually listened to what we had to say. Of course, we told her everything we loved, but we totally felt com-

fortable saying what we didn't like about the show, too. None of us were fans of Felicity's father, for instance. But not in a good way, like if he was the kind of guy we loved to hate. He creeped me out a bit. It was fun when Duke would come visit them, like to deliver puppies. But the scenes with just him and his wife made it seem like we were watching a different show.

Kendra Lewis-Frost

What an astute bunch of young people! I'm not sure they shed light on any new points, but they validated the doubts and concerns I had harbored about the show. What was clear was how they felt about the actors and their roles.

Ursula Fletcher

Okay, so I'm totally team Peter, but we also had a few Trip heads in our group when we met with Ms. Lewis-Frost. They wanted Trip to have a will-they-or-won't-they thing going on with a woman. I begged her to keep Peter and Felicity together forever. OMG, I loved them!

Kendra Lewis-Frost

From the start, we knew the day would come, if we were so lucky as to remain on the air, when we'd have to cast a love interest for Trip. Being familiar with Wade's lack of chemistry with Bronwyn, I had hoped we wouldn't have to cross that bridge for seasons to come. Trip's snobbishness against anyone in Califon made his continued bachelor life plausible.

You may wonder why I even entertained the thought of revamping *Pet Peeves* rather than creating a new vehicle for Austen, et al. based on what I knew would appeal to viewers. I'm stubborn. I'm a perfectionist. If something doesn't go right the first time, the second time, the third time, I'm a dog with a bone, determined to figure out what went wrong in order to fix it. I suppose I've just described what I had done for years in my defunct relationship. Admittedly, my track record is questionable. But you'll never know if you don't try, right?

Lewis-Frost understood that her revised concept for Pet Peeves *alone would not make a compelling enough pitch to persuade one of the network executives with whom she had already met to reverse their decision. She needed an ally on her quest.*

Austen Hughes

The first thing I wanted to do when Kendra called me was to hang up. I was in the "revisiting happier moments" stage of grieving. She caught me when I was rewatching season 2, episode 2, the one where Felicity finally gives in to her feelings for Peter. There may have been some ugly crying involved on my part. I'm not talking about me in the role of Peter here. The phone rang, and I was sure whoever was calling could see me and the pigsty I called home. I pushed a pile of dirty laundry off my bed and used a blanket to cover up the food wrappers and empty beer cans strewn about my room.

Kendra Lewis-Frost

Of course, protocol dictated my manager should reach out to Austen's, but having eschewed professional assistance to develop a new pitch, I saw no reason not to continue the human-to-human contact.

Austen Hughes

On a scale of one to ten, my ambition level was hovering somewhere around visiting the site of a nuclear meltdown without wearing protection. Kendra could have been enlisting my help to develop a brand-new series, and I can't say I would have jumped at the chance to do it. But resurrecting Peter's relationship with Felicity? I wanted it to happen so desperately in real life, but I had finally come to the conclusion Bronwyn didn't want to get back together with me. The seventeen unanswered texts may have helped me to figure this out. I politely declined Kendra's offer, hitting the rewind button on my DVD player when I hung up.

Kendra Lewis-Frost

I had no idea Austen had been suffering to such a great extent from his breakup. We should have commiserated together during the summer. He alone would have best understood exactly what I had been going through, and I would have had the same understanding of where he was. When I hung up with him, I determined it to be my mission to help him heal.

I was at a loss for how to engage Austen. Without giving away any details about why I wanted to gain Austen's attention, I enlisted Wade's help, but he, too, lacked the magic touch to lure Austen out of his cave. I thought of one person whose call Austen would not let go to voicemail. I approached Bill Cantor [his agent] for advice.

Bill Cantor, Austen's agent

With Austen's star on the rise and him being available for other gigs when his show ended, I had been able to send him out on a lot of auditions. The feedback we were getting from the casting directors disappointed me. My job is to find him work opportunities. His job is to land a gig in order for me to receive my cut. If he's not going to try, why should I? Outside of a couple of calls that came in specifically for him, I hadn't sent him on an audition in a few weeks. I didn't know what to make of Kendra's idea, but anything was worth a try.

Austen Hughes

My agent called me to set up a lunch with a casting director. Smart man, luring me out of my home with the promise of a free meal. I showed up, and there was Kendra. It was an ambush. I left before ordering anything.

Kendra Lewis-Frost

Well, that was a disaster.

Austen Hughes

Bronwyn had made a guest appearance on a legal drama in the fall of 2007. I guess her role was sort of a big deal for primetime. She played a paraplegic lesbian who shot her would-be rapist. It was one of those ripped-from-the-headlines stories. The real woman had served two years in prison. Anyway, Bronwyn and the woman she portrayed appeared on a morning talk show. I, being a lovesick puppy, watched it. The host asked her about me, and she said, "Austen? I haven't thought about him in ages. I blame my acting skills for whatever went on between us. My commitment to remaining true to the role of Felicity led me to forget to be Bronwyn when I was out of costume. Next thing I knew, I was dating a guy I had never planned on dating."

Kendra Lewis-Frost

Austen called me in early October, suggesting we meet to discuss the future of *Pet Peeves*. He took me by surprise, quite frankly.

Austen Hughes

And the Emmy for best impersonation of a girlfriend goes to… I laughed so hard when I heard Bronwyn's description of her feelings toward me, I had to change my sheets. Because I was sick of playing the role of the slob with a broken heart.

In contrast to the earliest stages of developing a pitch with Shatsky, Lewis-Frost and Hughes quickly established a strong working relationship.

Austen Hughes

We met at Kendra's apartment, a huge-ass prewar apartment on Riverside Drive. I remember thinking, *If this is how someone can live after being an executive producer for two seasons, I want in.*

Kendra Lewis-Frost

In the event Austen told you anything about my flat, don't believe a word of it. It belonged to my ex. You know your ex clearly resents you when they move out of state right after the breakup. I lived like a squatter in the nearly empty apartment until it sold later that year.

Austen Hughes

Granted, the apartment lacked furniture. She had decorated it mainly with a bunch of cardboard boxes in various states of fullness. Don't quote me on this, but the dining table in my old apartment might have cost a few dollars more than the folding table standing in the center of her dining room.

Kendra Lewis-Frost

Oh, he was a sight for sore eyes! He had lost the pasty, grayish pallor in his cheeks. His shirt lacked the wrinkles and stains I had noticed on the one he wore to our previous meeting. He had even gotten himself a Dr. Gluck-inspired haircut.

Austen Hughes

The apartment was a metaphor for where we both were in our lives. She was a cheap card table, and I was an unmarked cardboard box filled with who knows what. Turns out, I make a good chair, metaphorically speaking.

Kendra Lewis-Frost

We collaborated well right from the start. Why didn't we invite Austen into the writers' room earlier? Well, Elvin hadn't believed in him, for starters. He thought Austen and Peter were interchangeable; two mild-mannered doofuses from fly-over country who existed solely to make us laugh at them.

Austen and I began by examining whether each character in the first two seasons helped or hurt the story's premise. Best to go straight for the parents, I had suggested.

While I loved Duke and Claudia, we had to say goodbye to them, at least as regular characters. The concept of a mother, father, and daughter practicing together at a veterinary hospital could have stood on its own. But it was unrealistic to continue with the rival veterinary clinics. We needed to eliminate one of them, and obviously, it couldn't be Trip and Peter's.

Austen Hughes

Blaine never had warmed to me. He warily sized me up out of the corners of his eyes like he expected a mammoth spider to jump out of my mouth and attack him. He certainly wasn't going to develop a case of the warm fuzzies when we wrote him off the show. We came to the decision to have Felicity's parents sell their animal hospital and open a new one in Florida.

Blaine Carson

That was cold to have all but left me out of the new show. Doesn't matter. I've done okay without them. You've seen my work the last few years. I'm still a big get for any show, I'll have you know.

Kendra Lewis-Frost

Austen and I broke down the remaining characters to evaluate potential changes to the cast.

Austen Hughes

Kendra shot down each of my ideas for Felicity's storyline. I suggested Felicity could lose her medical license after one too many mistakes. She could become horribly disfigured, and viewers would beg us to write her off the show. She could move to Florida with her parents and have a freak accident involving a manatee, ending her career.

Kendra Lewis-Frost

What I meant by cast changes was, "Do we have characters from the previous seasons we underutilized? What personalities will be missing from the cast without the parents?" The one thing I knew to be true was Peter, Trip, and Felicity needed to form the core of the cast.

Austen Hughes

I guess I was stuck with Bronwyn. I took to referring to her as Dr. Copeland during our meeting to keep her at an arm's length.

As far as the other characters I felt were worth keeping, I thought KellyAnne, the cosplaying vet tech from the comfort room episode, had potential. We had used a few actors in the role of the re-ceptionist throughout the first two seasons. One who had impressed me was this scrawny guy who played it kind of campy. He showed loyalty to Trip, but not to Peter. Trip's patients got taken care of right away, but he was kind of dismissive for no explainable reason of anyone who came in to see Peter.

Kendra Lewis-Frost

We had to address the elephant in the room: Trip was in want of a love interest. We could stretch it out over many seasons, put off the need for Wade to have to play a love scene for as long as possible, but fall in love he must.

While lamenting his lack of onscreen chemistry with Bronwyn, neither of us had discussed whether Wade was gay, by the way. His sexuality was none of our business.

Austen Hughes

I hadn't considered Wade's sexuality. During the first two seasons of *Pet Peeves*, he always brought a beautiful woman to big dinners and events. He appeared to be perfectly comfortable with each of them. So I never saw him making out with his dates. So what? I've never thought of him as a PDA kind of guy. He's a true Southern gent.

Wade Hanson

I had never heard the rumors about my sexuality. I can't even imagine how they had begun.

Kendra Lewis-Frost

One thing we knew: for a character to have any chance with Trip she needed to be A: a princess and B: a bitch. A likable, funny bitch, that is.

Austen Hughes

We created sketches for the principal characters on separate pieces of paper. Next thing you know, we have six pages. Three women, three men. What, so we're *Friends* now?

Kendra Lewis-Frost

Of course, we weren't *Friends*. Our show would be about two couples: one together, one not.

Austen Hughes

See? *Friends*. Ross and Rachel. Monica and Chandler.

Kendra Lewis-Frost

But ours was a workplace comedy. And we had two additional members of the office staff who would have their own storylines.

Austen Hughes

Exactly. We added a Joey and a Phoebe to the cast. And then sent the whole mess of them to work at *The Office*.

Kendra Lewis-Frost

How many times do I have to say it? We're not *Friends*!

Lewis-Frost and Hughes continued to develop their pitch throughout the month of October. Meanwhile, the drumbeat of a potential writers strike grew ever louder. When members of the Writers Guild of America went on strike in November, Lewis-Frost, a WGA member, could not meet with network executives until the issues precipitating the strike had been resolved. Had Pet Peeves *aired for a third season, the cast and crew, like their counterparts on the other scripted shows, would have suffered throughout the strike. Lewis-Frost marched in solidarity with her fellow WGA members.*

The Writers Guild members voted to end the strike on February 12, 2008. Lewis-Frost and Hughes flew to LA immediately afterward to pitch the new version of Pet Peeves *to Rex Braithwaite, chairman at the IBS Network. Armed with a short pitch, a draft of one episode, an outline of the full season, an overview of additional seasons, casting suggestions, and a map to find the holy grail (I'm kidding about the holy grail, folks), they commanded Braithwaite's attention. Their efforts paid off. In early March, IBS gave Lewis-Frost an order for a twenty-four-episode season. The network brought in Bruce Leibowitz to be the showrunner. Lewis-Frost and Hughes would both be executive producers. Neither could share the news until the upfronts in May.*

Kendra Lewis-Frost

To this day, I haven't the foggiest notion regarding who had blabbed the story to Variety the following week. I learned about it after Bronwyn's agent called my manager to ask if we would be casting her as Felicity. Quite frankly, it was a relief to be out in the open about *Pet Peeves'* second life. We had to nail down both Bronwyn and Wade ASAP.

Bronwyn Davies

Who did Kendra have to sleep with to get the show back on the air? I'm teasing, of course.

Rex Braithwaite, chairman of IBS Television Network

I had heard the insinuations. Recently divorced man, beautiful woman, unlikely resurrection of a show. People are so jaded by whatever incestuous machinations define business in Hollywood, they no longer have any idea of what the concept of merit means. Kendra's pitch was better than any others I heard that year. She earned it. Period.

Kendra Lewis-Frost

It's odd how this incident was the one to get the tongues wagging. No one said a peep when ABS gave a failed daytime drama a chance to reinvent itself as a sitcom, rewarded said show with a slot in prime time, and put a breakdown writer in the position of executive producer. Then again, these were the same people who showed zero curiosity as to why Kym, the well-salaried Entertainment chairman, and me, an executive producer of a sitcom remained roommates for five years. I'll chalk it up to the patriarchy. No one assumes a female executive would wield power like a man, down to granting her lover favors. While I stand by the script and pilot we offered ABS back in 2004, I'm sure my chances would have been close to nil that they would have invited me to pitch *Pet Peeves* in the first place had it not been for my relationship with Kym.

Hughes, Davies, and Hanson signed their contracts, committing themselves to the series. Bruce Leibowitz (the new showrunner), Lewis-Frost, and Hughes decided to introduce a new character: the clinic's surly receptionist. She would become Trip's love interest. In addition to the cosplaying vet tech, they determined the office would need a second vet tech. The actor who played the campy receptionist was no longer available. Another actor, Robert Chang, dazzled the casting director with an improvisation during his audition on how much he loved fluffy bunnies, cold, wet doggy nosies, and deceitful little kitty cats. The only animals he feared were human. He got the gig. The producers had one character left to cast: the receptionist.

Rex Braithwaite

I flew out to New York for the final round of casting. As we were building an ensemble cast, I felt it imperative the would-be receptionists each read scenes with the three leads. I had asked Leibowitz, Lewis-Frost, and Hughes to line up a half-dozen actresses to read for me.

Austen Hughes

The last day of casting was the first time I had seen Bronwyn since I had moved out of her apartment nearly a year earlier. She has such a power over me. If you get hold of the receptionist audition tapes, you'll see rivulets of sweat on my face. Oh, and my eyes were rolling around like ball bearings on an uneven floor in my efforts never to look directly at her.

Bronwyn Davies

I hadn't given much thought to how I would be reconnecting with Austen when I went back to the studio. I guess I should have. I was going back to being his onscreen girlfriend. It was just a job. I couldn't let it bother me.

Austen Hughes

The scenes we were reading were incredibly funny, but Bronwyn never let loose that laugh of hers. If she didn't want to be a part of the show, she should have turned down the offer. You wouldn't have heard me complain if she had.

Wade Hanson

I can't tell you how marvelous it was to be reading pages with Austen and Bronwyn again. The chemistry between the three of us! I almost forgot they called us in specifically so Rex Braithwaite could see if our magical bond would extend to include a new actress.

Austen Hughes

I picked up on another weird dynamic in the studio when we read with the would-be receptionists. Bronwyn had been the only young female lead on our show. With the revamped version, she was going to have competition. Not regarding Peter's affection for Felicity, but in general, with the screen time and all. She circled each actress at the audition like a prizefighter assessing an opponent in the ring.

Maria Rivera, actor

Yeah, I read for the part of the receptionist on *Pet Peeves*. It's tough to be the new face in a cast where everyone knows each other already. Austen was easy to work with, I'll say that. Bronwyn took one look at me and decided I wasn't a threat to her. They told me my character would hate Wade's character until she fell in love with him in a later season. The guy sure is handsome. I was game. But interacting with him? No one would believe our characters secretly had a thing for each other. I knew I didn't get the part before the first scene ended.

Wade Hanson

The producers put way too much pressure on me. I think they brought Austen and Bronwyn to the reading only as a ruse. Their m.o. was to find some-one to play opposite me. I may have blown it for the first two actresses who auditioned. If you're reading this book, I'm sorry. Y'all did great. It was me.

Rex Braithwaite

I was having difficulty believing in Wade as Trip while we were casting the receptionist. I was familiar with his work, of course. He and Austen acted in some great scenes together during the first two seasons. He had the right bearing for his character, too. I had heard that Trip and Felicity were supposed to be the original couple. Whoever had told me about the original script had described Wade's sexual energy in the pilot as being on par with a moldy dish sponge.

Austen Hughes

It was bad enough that Bronwyn and I couldn't stand to be in the same room. My man had to come through for us. I took Wade aside and went through a round of improv exercises with him to loosen him up. I may have been overly personal, asking him about what turns Trip on in the bedroom. Come to think of it, I probably sounded like I was a phone operator at 1-999-SEXYVET.

Wade Hanson

I can't say this enough: I love Austen. I swear I owe my acting career to him. The entire run of first *Another Day to Live* and then *Pet Peeves*, he was something of a personal acting coach for me. Acting turned out to be harder than I thought it would be. But he pumped me up for the remaining auditions. I knew one of the women would play well opposite me if I put myself into the role.

Bronwyn Davies

This one actress stood out from the others. You just know when you see some people before an audition, they will get the role. There was no way I was going to let her outshine me, though. I mean, Peter's supposed to be in love with Felicity. I wanted to make sure Austen didn't flirt with her. You know, for his sake during the audition. I wouldn't want to make things confusing for anyone.

Wade Hanson

I found the essence of Trip's relationship when I read opposite one of the actresses. Honestly, reading with her was almost as easy as reading with Austen. She played her character so cutting, so mean. She intimidated the crap out of me, but Trip could handle her. The challenge of being Trip, not Wade, inspired me.

Austen Hughes

We clearly had a winner. I can't imagine the other producers or Braithwaite having any deliberations about whom to hire. She was spot-on perfect. The one thing I found odd, though, was when this particular would-be receptionist read her lines, Bronwyn suddenly couldn't pay enough attention to me. We, or at least our characters, found our missing spark.

Madeline Puri, actor (Kerani Flynn)

I loved, loved, loved my final audition! If I hadn't been offered the part, I think I still would have floated away on a happy cloud. How rare is it for the right actors and the right script to unite? I was sure I didn't deserve such a wonderful opportunity, but I set out to make the most of it and to savor every minute as a part of the *Pet Peeves* team.

Chapter 7
The Golden Years

Filming for season 3 of Pet Peeves *began in June 2008. Showrunner Bruce Leibowitz, sober for three years and a devotee of loving-kindness meditation, brought a quieter, more generous energy to the set than his predecessor.*

Wade Hanson, actor (Trip Quinn)

The daily meditations Bruce ran at the start of each day at the studio were a little weird to me. I'm a Southern Baptist. When we want to demonstrate kindness, we give people casseroles.

Madeline Puri, actor (Kerani Flynn)

The meditations provided a lovely means of connecting the cast and crew members to each other. While I loathe saying anything even a little negative about my experience with my colleagues at *Pet Peeves*, I do recall thinking Bruce had put me in an awkward spot before the first rehearsal, inviting me to lead a meditation. I assumed he did so because of my Indian heritage. But I was raised a Catholic.

Austen Hughes, actor (Peter Gluck)

I kind of dug the meditation sessions. It was a chance to quiet my body and mind. I wreaked a lot of havoc on set in the role of Peter, but Peter isn't a super high-energy character. His mayhem surprises in part because it seemingly comes from out of nowhere.

Emma Bates, actor (KellyAnne Hurley)

I couldn't quiet my mind like Bruce was telling us to at the first rehearsal. Madeline freakin' Puri was standing next to me! I have totally had a girl crush on her ever since I saw her in *What's in Your Locker?* She stole every scene she was in. I'm two years older than her and was already a working actor when the movie came out. It may have been her first role—and it was only a small part—but her performance was a master class in comedic acting. I've watched her in every movie and TV show she's been in ever since to learn from her. She might have been typecast in each of her roles because she's Indian. But she never plays the same part twice. The girl has range!

Bruce Leibowitz, executive producer and showrunner, *Pet Peeves*

I couldn't get a handle on Austen at first. Peter, his character, is this easy-going bumpkin. He's a whiz at his job, but with everything else in his life, he's a bumbling goof. When he chooses to apply himself, when he gets a little intense, that's when things blow up. Always funny stuff. Austen is similar to Peter when it comes to being chill. It's easy to forget he is a guy with a brain.

Kendra Lewis-Frost

Bruce has an aura of being unflappable. He lifts himself above the swirl of emotions others may be exhibiting. One of the few occasions when I saw him struggle to contain his reaction was during the first reading of the reboot. We had done his Zen activity; we were loose and ready to go. Everything went along swimmingly for the first few minutes. We reached the page where Madeline's character, Kerani, introduces herself to Peter. Now, it was our habit to add pronunciation guides in first drafts. It usually applied to whatever vet-speak our scripts required. Page two of the season 3, episode 1 draft included a pronunciation of Kerani: ke-RON-ē. Austen, reading as Peter, repeated her name back to her: KĒ-rin-ē. He made it rhyme with *tyranny*. Bruce stopped to correct him. Austen mispronounced it a second time. Bruce corrected him a second time.

Bruce Leibowitz

I couldn't help but wonder, *Is this asshole testing me*? My temperature rose each time I had to correct his pronunciation. Meanwhile, Austen never broke a sweat.

Kendra Lewis-Frost

Each person seated at the table froze in place, heads bowed down as if they were studying their scripts. Madeline alone remained engaged. Her head slightly tilted, she studied Austen with an ever-so-slight smile on her lips.

Madeline Puri

Outside of the scene we had read together at my audition, this was my first day working with Austen. I wasn't able to guess what was on his mind, but from his body language, I gauged he had a reason to mispronounce my character's name. When I asked him about it at the table read, his reasoning was because Peter grew up in a small town in Ohio, it would have been out of character for him to be adept at assimilating a foreign name. What an amazing introduction into the depth of his intelligence and commitment to the craft of acting he provided with one simple answer!

Bronwyn Davies

It was unsettling to be back at *Pet Peeves*. A lot had happened since we had gone off the air in 2007. Austen and I breaking up, for instance. Having new cast members like Madeline upset the balance, too. She comes across so sweet, so unlike the character she plays. Don't we all bring a little of who we are into each of our roles? Kerani couldn't spring out of nowhere, could she?

Austen Hughes

Season 3, episode 1 ran kind of like a pilot. We had to explain to our viewers that the Copeland Animal Hospital had shut its doors, thanks in part to the success of Duke's schemes. And then we're introducing two new characters, Kerani and Robert, a vet tech.

I hadn't yet warmed to the notion of working with Bronwyn again or to us having to play a happy couple. I still stand by my idea of utilizing the plot twist about the career-ending injury she sustained during an attack by a rabid manatee.

Bronwyn Davies

The opening Felicity/Kerani scene got me fired up. It's Felicity's first day of practicing at the Califon Small Animal Clinic. And in blows this hurricane of a character carrying a constipated Chihuahua.

Madeline Puri

Kerani's backstory: She married for money. Her prenup prevented her from collecting a significant alimony settlement if she asked for a divorce before their ten-year anniversary. Her louse of a husband cheated on her on their ninth anniversary and moved to a horse farm in Kentucky with his mistress. She tried to hold out for another year, but her husband forced her hand. Now she's broke, divorced, and living alone in their mansion in Califon, which she has to vacate in a few days' time. On top of everything else, her beloved pooch needs an enema.

Bronwyn Davies

Trip, viewing Felicity as the low doctor on the totem pole, tasks her with getting the dog's train to leave the station. Kerani walks all over Felicity during the appointment. Felicity was generally the nice one in the cast in the first two seasons. She knows when to stand up for herself, though. I was supposed to be feeling insecure about being on staff at a new clinic—my boyfriend's clinic—which is why Felicity didn't defend herself against Kerani. Knowing that later in the script Kerani would win over Peter's sympathies—he'd offer her a receptionist job and then recommend she move in with Felicity—I added in another layer of insecurity by assuming Felicity would be jealous of Kerani, worrying Peter might be attracted to her. I mean, have you seen her? Madeline is gorgeous. No amount of makeup renders my eyes half as huge as hers even when she isn't wearing mascara.

Austen Hughes

Words can't describe what an asset Madeline was to our cast. She owned every one of her scenes starting with the first table read. I found her mesmerizing, but at the same time, I had to contend with a certain distraction. By the time we shot the scenes where Peter and Felicity were doing their boyfriend/girlfriend cuddling stuff, Bronwyn had found the inspiration to add a little heat to the action. It kind of messed with my head. And my body.

Before the first episode aired on Tuesday, September 23 in the nine thirty time slot, Bronwyn and Austen had gotten back together, a fact they flaunted at the premiere party. Hanson and Puri, both single, attended the event together.

Wade Hanson

I was so pleased when Madeline asked if I'd go with her. She didn't make a big romantic overture or anything. She told me flat out Bronwyn had put her up to it. Since I wasn't involved with anyone at the time, having her as my date meant none of the reporters would get too deep with their questions about my love life. I mean, we had just met each other and all.

Madeline Puri

I don't date actors.

Bronwyn Davies

Wade and Madeline made a stunning couple. It felt right to me, setting them up together. It's always a matter of time on any show or movie before the entire cast couples up. I had Austen, she could have Wade.

Madeline Puri

Let me make this perfectly clear: I do not date actors. I know, I'm dooming myself to a lonely existence because it's difficult to meet people outside our field. And of course, there are some very attractive specimens right at our fingertips on set. But acting is a terribly intense endeavor. We're not faking the emotions you see on the screen; we're experiencing them, at least through the eyes of our character. I'd hate to confuse my onscreen emotions with my true feelings. When a show or movie wraps, couples are bound to experience heartbreak when they no longer have to adopt their characters' points of view as their own. Best to avoid hurting a fellow castmate, I've always believed.

Kendra Lewis-Frost

I was dateless for the premiere, which was a shame. The network hosted an event for us at a restaurant in Midtown. We had a proper red carpet, unlike our event up in the Bronx. Even still, had I walked the red carpet in front of fans at our first premiere, Kym and I wouldn't have been able to attend the event as a couple. She was the one who had set up the condition that we never reveal our relationship publicly. Funny how she made the decision to come out when she began dating a supermodel four years ago.

Austen Hughes

I've always been skeptical about exes getting back together. But, as I've said previously, I am powerless around Bronwyn. A part of me—a sliver, really—maintained a practical stance on the whole Austen/Bronwyn 2.0 situation. While the romantic in me threw a parade when we reunited, my rational side gave my heart the stink eye. I guess the stinkiness was unavoidable; I had made the decision not to move out of my ever-ripe apartment this time.

Early reviews of Pet Peeves *indicated the show stood a chance of proving the naysayers wrong. The network, producers, and actors endeavored to keep* Pet Peeves *on viewers' minds before its airdate. The efforts paid off.*

Bruce Leibowitz

I guess it can be said now: when I received the call to take the helm of a show another network had canceled, I had my doubts. Reviving a show on a new network is usually a just-one-more-season affair. I've never been the sort who likes one-night stands.

We had over nine million viewers for the *Pet Peeves* premiere. The numbers put us about even with *Two and a Half Men* and *The Office*. Nice numbers. The ratings and reviews we received made me think this little lady and I would bed each other for some time to come.

Bronwyn Davies

Did you read what The New York Times' critic wrote about my performance in the premiere? Wait. I'll find it.

Kendra Lewis-Frost

For anyone who had doubted the show's merit, the welcome *Pet Peeves* received justified my ambition to put it back on the air.

Bronwyn Davies

Here it is. "Davies adds a nuanced layer to a role I had previously written off as one-dimensional. One can imagine that the changes to the show both onscreen and behind the scenes are responsible for bringing out a touch of vulnerability formerly missing from her performances during the first two seasons. She is funnier and more likable in the current season." I can't figure out why he thought Felicity was one-dimensional. It's probably because we didn't have as strong a team of writers in the early seasons.

Elvin Shatsky

I was happy for them. Really. Look closely at the credits. You'll see my name listed as co-creator on every single episode of the show. Cha-ching!

Kendra Lewis-Frost

The numbers declined for the second episode, but not by a lot. And they remained steady throughout the season. I didn't want to jinx it, but I was sure we had found the secret to making our show a winner.

Stephen Burrows, writer

I considered declining Kendra's offer to come back to *Pet Peeves*. But what else did I have going on? Not enough to turn down the gig. Thankfully, the writers' room was totally different under Bruce. He split up Kendra and me—we were to write the scripts alone. It was cool to see my name up on the screen all on its lonesome after having shared a credit with Kendra in seasons 1 and 2.

D'Wayne Curtis, writer

Bruce had a touch of the hippie in him. He was big into community. He used the analogy about how one single writer births a script while the rest of the writers on the staff were the midwives. And the wet nurses. Maybe not exactly the way I would have worded it, but you get the gist.

Kendra Lewis-Frost

Under Bruce's leadership, we avoided the hungry vulture approach to editing a script I had grown used to with Elvin. He believed in each individual writer and gave us each equal opportunities to succeed, a favorite quip of his. For those of us who stayed on through the series finale, the writing credits were rather evenly distributed amongst the writers.

He wouldn't tolerate unkind attacks on another writer's script in the writers' room. We nourished each other, he often said. Like wet nurses. So there was that with Bruce as well. You'd almost be in sync with what he was saying, and then he'd take it somewhere a little, hmm. You'd leave a meeting with the desire to take a bath in a tub of bleach.

The ratings and reviews may have bolstered confidence for those involved in the production of Pet Peeves, *but the ultimate sign of success is measured in awards. In December, Hughes and Puri both received their first Golden Globes nominations.*

Bronwyn Davies

Oh my God, oh my God, oh my God! I died when Austen was nominated. I'm going to the Golden Globes, baby!

Austen Hughes

The nomination caught me by surprise. I hadn't paid much attention to the award shows before *Pet Peeves*. And isn't this the big message in the whole Exodus story, not worshipping golden statues? Maybe that's why Charlton Heston didn't win a Golden Globe for his performance in *The Ten Commandments*.

Bronwyn Davies

I swear I was more excited about Austen's nomination than he was.

Austen Hughes

Before I had digested the news, Bronwyn was online, gown shopping. Mind you, I hadn't invited her to be my date yet. Maybe I wanted to bring my mom.

Madeline Puri

I was sure the powers that be had made a mistake. Me? Nominated for Best Performance by an Actress in a Television Series – Musical or Comedy? I would have been less surprised had it been for Best Supporting Actress, not that I was expecting any nomination.

Bronwyn Davies

Was I disappointed I didn't receive a nomination? If I can be humble, I hadn't yet truly earned a nomination. I was surprised Madeline made the cut, though. Not that she wasn't good in those early episodes. But she was new. I saw her more as a supporting actress.

Kendra Lewis-Frost

I was chuffed when I heard about Austen and Madeline's nominations. I so hoped Bruce would invite me to represent the studio at the awards ceremony, but why should he?

Bruce Leibowitz

And thus it begins. I'm not saying I was head-over-heels ecstatic for the recognition of our actors, though. Until the show itself receives a nomination, it isn't yet a true success. But to be on hand to represent the studio—and the show, of course—and maybe be on camera when one or both of our actors head to the stage to collect an award, well, it's a start.

Bronwyn Davies

I was in heaven at the awards. I saw Brad Pitt and Angelina Jolie. Leo, too. Sigh! He's twice as handsome in person than he is on screen. I had put meeting Meryl Streep at the top of my wish list for the award ceremony. She had been nominated for both *Doubt* and *Mamma Mia!* I didn't see *Doubt*, but I heard it was good. I could only see the back of her head from where I was sitting. Once, when she was turning around to wave to someone, I totally thought I could catch her eye. I had my hands cupped together, ready to press them to my chest when our eyes met, but she didn't face my direction. Oh, you asked about how it felt to watch my boyfriend accept his award? I was proud of him, of course. It was especially cool when he mentioned my name in his acceptance speech.

Pet Peeves *concluded its third season with strong ratings and a spot on the network's fall lineup. At the same time the cast and crew headed back to the studio in July, Hughes and Puri received their first Emmy nominations, Lewis-Frost her second, and Leibowitz his first for writing an episode of* Pet Peeves.

Bronwyn Davies

In hindsight, I preferred the dress I wore to the Golden Globes to the one I wore to the Emmys. Tangerine is a good color on me, but it kind of clashed with the red carpet.

Kendra Lewis-Frost

How different this was from my first nomination! The previous one had been an asterisk, of sorts, coming on the heels of our cancellation.

Rex Braithwaite, chairman of IBS Television Network

The network was pleased with the four nominations the show received. Would I have liked to have seen the series itself garner a nomination? Hell, yes. Just between you and me, do you really believe *Flight of the Conchords* deserved its nomination?

Kendra Lewis-Frost

The spirit of invincibility from being nominated and having my show still on the air made me do something crazy: I called Kym to invite her to be my date to the Emmys. She said it would not be prudent for her to sit anywhere near me as my show was competing against shows on her network. Oh, and she was in a relationship.

Bronwyn Davies

Where did Madeline find her date? He was so basic.

Madeline Puri

On a lark, I attended my ten-year high school reunion that May. My parents still lived in Pittsfield, Massachusetts, the town where I grew up. I was due to pay them a visit, anyway. At the reunion, I reconnected with Brad Connelly from my AP History class. He worked in the Greek and Roman curatorial department at the Met. I've mentioned to you before that I don't date actors. It can be a challenge to meet people when I'm knee-deep in a show or movie. It was a no-brainer to start dating Brad, compatibility issues be damned. He is the studious type, not the sort of guy who's cut out for the glamorous life of attending black tie events. He was even out of place at the airport in LA. But we stayed together for nearly two years. He's married to a librarian now.

Bronwyn Davies

The *Pet Peeves* contingent attended the Governors Ball after the ceremony. I had my heart set on attending the ET/People Magazine party, but I wasn't a nominee, so who cares what I wanted, right? Austen was all gaga for getting to meet Bob Newhart. It wasn't my kind of crowd. No one paid any attention to me.

Austen Hughes

Madeline and I had a fake saber fight with our statues at an after party. The tip of the wing on Madeline's award caught a loose piece of fabric on Bronwyn's dress.

Bronwyn Davies

She tore a huge hole in my dress. As if waving her award around in front of me wasn't enough of an insult.

Madeline Puri

Oh, I had forgotten about the dress incident. I felt horrible! I didn't even see her standing behind me. Austen and I were having a bit of fun. I offered to pay to have her dress repaired or replaced, but she graciously declined my offer. I sent her a basket of some of my favorite lotions and scents instead.

For most of the cast and crew on Pet Peeves, *the success the show attained in its third season provided a long-awaited (and for some, first) taste of stability. Each settled into the new reality in their own unique way.*

Austen Hughes

The timing was right for me to make a change to my housing situation. I know, who wants to give up living with a bunch of guys in a three-bedroom dump in Washington Heights? I had to make a couple of sacrifices when I bought my condo. For instance, I couldn't find a single place redolent of swampy feet and desperation and had to settle for one that smelled of fresh paint and little else.

Kendra Lewis-Frost

After moving out of Kym's old apartment, I rented the teensiest studio in Murray Hill. Certainly, by the summer of 2009, I could afford a space where I wasn't in danger of flushing the toilet when I rolled over to turn off my alarm, but I stayed put for the time being.

It's rather sad, I suppose, how intrinsically united I imagined home and relationship to be. I felt somehow that to buy a proper apartment without being in the position to make a home with another person was pointless. My friends pushed me to view properties. Even still, it wasn't until we had finished shooting the season 4 finale when I finally signed a contract for a two-bedroom co-op in the West Village.

Bronwyn Davies

I told Austen to wait until I had a free day to go house hunting with him. Maybe we'd find a place to buy together. He went without me. The first day he looked at properties, he put a down payment on a condo. In Brooklyn. Not even Williamsburg or someplace hip. Greenpoint. It may be all artsy and trendy now, but it wasn't back then.

Austen Hughes

The neighborhood was still unpretentious and the market user-friendly when I bought my place in the summer of 2009. It suited me. Now? Forget it. How many artisanal chitlin bars does the average person need within twenty feet of their front door? I could get a lot of money for my condo if I sold today, but I'm too lazy to move.

Bronwyn Davies

I wasn't crazy about visiting him in Brooklyn, but the commute was a lot easier from his place to the studio than from mine.

The combination of one year's experience with new producers and characters under its belt plus the glow from the two Emmy figurines transformed an already happy workplace into one of the best production studios in which to work the following season.

Stephen Burrows, writer

The writers' room at *Pet Peeves* had to be the most awesome place of employment on the planet. I can't believe they paid us to sit around and tell jokes.

Bruce Leibowitz

I had the honor of sitting around the table in the writers' room with as talented and likable a group of people as any producer could possibly desire. Each brought a special gift to the table. Stephen was a workhorse when it came to churning out story ideas. Kendra, with her loopy, twisted mind, gave us our distinct voice. And I could always count on Austen and D'Wayne, for instance, to take a funny joke and turn it into a gut-buster. You could say collectively, we made for one sexy beast. The jokes were like perfume or a revealing little dress, the storylines the pheromones, and Kendra's tone brought the kink.

D'Wayne Curtis, writer

Writers—even successful writers—live in fear they will never have another good idea. It's hugely stressful to have to come up with three storylines per episode, twenty-four episodes per season, for years on end. Bruce minimized the pressure the suits put on us to write episodes guaranteed to make money for the network. You hear about shows where an executive producer always rides the writers, cast, and crew hard. Elvin hadn't been the worst boss in the business, not by a long shot, but Bruce, even in his creepy moments, was the best boss I've ever had.

Moishe Bronfman, actor (Duke Quinn)

I returned to the set after an absence to shoot a season 4 episode. What a wonderful studio environment they had created! I would have been surprised to find it otherwise. I had followed the show through the whole third season. Their achievements, what I saw onscreen, filled me with *naches*.

Blaine Carson, actor (Harold Copeland)

Kendra and company conveniently forgot about Felicity's parents. I didn't make it back onto the show until the season 5 finale, and that was for one scene—a phone call, no less—between Felicity and her parents, down in Florida. Duke had his own storylines from time to time. Me, I was just an extra.

Even the few minor disruptions to the harmonious life on set could not alter the mood, serving instead as inspiration.

Bronwyn Davies

Felicity had grown up in the country, leaving home only to attend veterinary school. She wasn't particularly fashion-conscious. My costumes were pretty boring, nothing like what I wore off the set. And then Madeline shows up. She wasn't into fashion, but her character was a slave to designer labels. About all she retained from her marriage was an extensive wardrobe filled with Prada, Dolce & Gabbana, Stella McCartney... Hmm. The show was supposed to be on a tight budget our first season on IBS, but somehow they came up with the funds to buy her a full wardrobe of fabulous costumes.

Madeline Puri

Kerani and I did not have the same taste in clothing. I love textures, fabrics I can feel. I prefer a neutral palette and simple pieces of jewelry. Kerani favored bold colors and patterns. A lot of her wardrobe was difficult to wear for all of its hardware and fit-tab-a-into-slot-b (conveniently located on the opposite side of the body from tab a) construction. And then we have the accessories. Heels long and lethal enough to be classified as weapons. Necklaces large enough to have a gravitational pull.

Bronwyn Davies

The irony was that Felicity wore a white lab coat over street clothes to work while Kerani, who sat behind the receptionist desk the whole day, wore scrubs. Felicity barely tried to dress like a grown-up with a good job. Meanwhile, Kerani came to the clinic accessorized within an inch of her life. And in the scenes shot outside of the clinic, she was always ridiculously overdressed.

Austen Hughes

I guess we were at the Emmys in 2010 when Bronwyn gave me an idea for an episode: Felicity would "borrow" a piece from Kerani's closet—they were still housemates—and wear it to work, suffering the inevitable consequences.

Bronwyn Davies

I loved buying new gowns every time Austen received another award nomination, don't get me wrong. The 2010 Emmys were the third award show I had to attend with him that year. Designers were now hip to Madeline when she received her second Golden Globe nomination. They were falling all over themselves to entice her to wear their clothes to the ceremonies. Austen commented about how amazing she looked at the Emmys. Who wouldn't look fabulous while wearing a borrowed Armani Privé and half the stock from the Beverly Hills Harry Winston store? I had to do my own hair and makeup. Did he compliment me on how I looked? Well, he probably did. But still.

Madeline Puri

Awards ceremonies were terrifying for me. Not because of the anticipation of whether I'd win but because of what I wore. I was sure I was doomed to put a heel through the hem of my borrowed designer dress or to drop a priceless earring down the toilet.

Bronwyn Davies

Austen wrote an episode in season 5 where I could wear a decent pair of shoes. He didn't get it, though. Felicity tries on a pair of Kerani's Louboutins when she's alone in the house. Mind you, they were mine IRL, a pair of medium blue, sky-high pumps with a peep-toe, covered in silver studs. Those shoes make me feel fierce. So Felicity had her moment of experiencing the power the shoes gave her and decided if she wore them to the clinic, Trip would take her more seriously.

Being the sort of woman who thought fashionable footwear meant matching her Crocs to her outfit, Felicity was undone by her choice of footwear. She did a lot of teetering and foot rubbing throughout the episode. Kerani, who had the day off, finds the shoes missing, correctly assumes Felicity has stolen them, barrels into the room where Felicity is performing surgery on a guinea pig, and takes the shoes from Felicity's feet. The final scene is Felicity trudging home barefoot save for the gazillion Band-Aids covering the mess of blisters she had gotten from her shoes. Like a pair of Louboutins in the correct size would ever give you blisters.

While Pet Peeves *had yet to have received a nomination in the best comedy category of any of the major television awards, Hughes and Puri continued to receive nods. In December 2010, the nominations for the SAG awards came two days after those for the Golden Globes.*

Bronwyn Davies
It's an honor just to be dating someone who is nominated, my ass. This was getting old.

Bruce Leibowitz
I'm not going to lie to you. Proud of my actors as I was, the lack of recognition for the show was beginning to trouble me. We simply needed to embrace our opportunity to succeed a bit harder.

Rex Braithwaite, chairman of IBS Television Network
Pet Peeves remained a quality show, no question. We had the advertisers we wanted; the ratings were solid. I'm not saying we would cancel the show if it went

another season without being nominated, but we have to take notice of these things.

Kendra Lewis-Frost

I had finally won an Emmy the previous September. But ours was an ensemble show. I could not wait for the day when the whole team received a nomination.

Madeline Puri

Brad, my boyfriend, had never grown comfortable with the extended duties associated with dating an actor. He declined my invitation to attend the Golden Globes with me. My brother nearly ruptured his spleen when I invited him to be my date. Zach is a man who would make a living attending black tie events, given the chance.

Austen Hughes

I know this may come across sounding disingenuous, but I promise you, it's the truth. I was not particularly jazzed about being nominated. I had won, hmm, I can't come up with the number offhand, a bunch of statues by season 5. I felt bad for Bronwyn. Her performances deserved recognition.

Bronwyn Davies

I actually debated sitting out the SAG awards in January. My manager talked me into going. She said the exposure was important. Do I think it would have been better for everyone had I stayed home? We don't get do-overs in life. What's done is done.

Chapter 8
The Kiss

Kendra Lewis-Frost

I tuned in for the SAG Awards broadcast, starting with the red carpet coverage. I'm such a sucker for watching the actors swan in front of the paparazzi. Yes, I did notice a bored and distracted Bronwyn standing beside Austen during his red carpet interview. She missed a great interview—he managed both to show poignant regard for being a SAG member and to give viewers a dose of his comedic self, all in the span of about thirty seconds.

Bronwyn Davies

Natalie Portman was being interviewed right next to us. I had to turn around to check her out because I didn't have the chance to see her baby bump at the Golden Globes. Could she have been more radiant? Meanwhile, Austen was rattling off stock answers about how being honored by his peers is such a big whoop because it's so hard for an actor to receive a SAG card, blah, blah, blah. I caught the tail end of him making a joke about him wondering if someone who is colorblind would get lost trying to find the red carpet. Typical Austen interview bullshit.

Madeline Puri

My brother Zach attracted quite a bit of attention at the Golden Globes. He's gorgeous if it's okay for a sister to say so about her brother. I didn't have a pat answer at the ready for when I had to field questions about where Brad was—we had broken up the previous week, but it hadn't been reported. Zach swooped in, laughed off suggestions about him being my new beau, and charmed everyone into forgetting to ask about Brad. He was a real lifesaver.

Zach Puri, Madeline's brother

Dude, I gotta tell you how much I love award shows! I'm so glad Maddy didn't let the teasing about her being a drama geek back in high school deter her from becoming an actress. I never would've gotten to pretend to be a Hollywood star if it had. Who teased her? Well, mostly me.

Bronwyn Davies

So, yes, I missed the part about Zach being Madeline's brother.

Austen Hughes

Just as they were announcing my category, Bronwyn left to use the ladies room. Not that she missed anything. Alec Baldwin won.

Bronwyn and I were past our expiration point by then. Because she had cheated on me back in 2007, when we started dating again, I wasn't all in. One small, wary part of me prevented me from falling back in love with her. I found her to be amusing company, almost likable at times. I really enjoyed the physical side of our relationship. And, for all the drama that comes with being around Bronwyn, it still beat the drama of being single on the media circuit when you're kind of famous.

Zach Puri

I remained with Madeline for a few minutes after she didn't win in case she needed my sympathy or something. She didn't, so I left to take a leak. On the way back, I ran into Bronwyn. I figured we'd walk back to the table together.

Bronwyn Davies

I had kind of been gawking at Zach throughout the evening, thinking Madeline might actually have good taste in men after all. The guy she dated before him? Anyway, I was in a pretty crappy mood. The cast of *Modern Family* was sitting at a table together, having a blast. Why hadn't *Pet Peeves* been nominated for the ensemble category? I started to have the teensiest inkling that maybe it was my fault. Wade and I hadn't yet been nominated for any awards. Maybe we were the reason the show wasn't getting any notice. Self-scrutiny always messes me up.

Anyhow, I ran into Zach on my way back from the ladies room. I was mad at Madeline for her award nominations and mad at Austen for no reason whatsoever. I decided to find a way to make myself happy, even if it was at their expense. I wanted to kiss Madeline's boyfriend, and I didn't care who saw me. Oh, my God, his lips were begging to be kissed!

Madeline Puri

I went to say *hi* to a few friends. I noticed a couple going to town with each other's faces off to the side. I continued to talk with Mila only to do a double take. I belatedly recognized my brother's hair on the guy making out off to the side. Hollywood people have great hair, but Zach's is in a class of its own. And he knows it. That's why he wears it at a length just beyond the point where a sensible person would go get it cut. But I digress. I thought, *Good for you, bro, getting lucky with a star tonight!* He pulled away and I saw whom he was with. Luckily, no one else was paying attention. I walked over to the pair of them and talked to them as if they were puppies who had made on the carpet. All I was missing was a newspaper to swat at their noses.

Bronwyn Davies

I finally figured out Zach and Madeline were siblings when she started to yell at him. So, it turned out, the only person I was hurting was Austen. Madeline promised she wouldn't tell him. I decided, once we were back in New York, to suggest to him in a neutral way that we should break up. He agreed with me, and we ended things in a civilized manner. To this day, I don't think he ever knew what happened that night. I have to say, Madeline was way cool not to say anything. Oh, wait. He's going to find out now, isn't he? Shit.

The mood in the writers' room, and then on set, changed when the last few episodes of season 5 went into production. Bronwyn and Austen's break up in no way impacted the coupledom of Felicity and Peter onscreen. Writers and actors alike dedicated themselves to producing the highest quality show possible, aiming specifically for the Emmy Award for the Best Comedy Series. The finale of season 5, during which Peter proposed to Felicity, received the highest ratings of the season. The finale was also the one-hundredth episode of the series, a milestone marked by the show being picked up for syndication.

Elvin Shatsky

This was the moment I had been waiting for. I was glad to have washed my hands of the show, but I had to root for it to make it into syndication. My contract entitled me to residuals as I was the show's creator. Being paid without having to contribute time or energy? Imagine if Phil Mickelson was your caddy, and he took the tricky shots for you to keep your handicap down. This was twice as good.

Bruce Leibowitz

Signing a syndication contract was a delightful bonus, but I was playing the long game. Why collect residuals for three seasons when I could collect them for six? We just needed that elusive Emmy nod. I found myself repeating the Serenity Prayer several times a day to counter the anxiety swallowing me while I waited for the Emmy nominations.

Kendra Lewis-Frost

Reaching the one-hundredth episode had been a dream of mine. Considering the trouble we had getting the first episode on the air, and then the twenty-ninth, I had to stop for a moment to bask in what we had achieved.

Bronwyn Davies

As an experienced actor when I signed my contract in 2005, my base fee per episode was a little above scale plus it included a minuscule share of the residuals. Of course, I was earning plenty of money compared to the average American. The thing is, they had roped me into signing a contract covering six seasons, which is pretty standard. I knew I deserved a better contract. I would have my first opportunity to renegotiate my contract in June of 2012. The time to formulate a plan for a better deal was now.

Wade Hanson

Bronwyn had made a good suggestion about the cast of *Pet Peeves* trying to do a collective bargaining thing like the cast of *Friends* had done when they renegotiated their contract. We'd need Austen and Madeline to take the lead, of course, since they were the de facto stars of the show. Did I believe we stood a chance of getting a million dollars an episode as they did on *Friends*? A million bucks was a long way off from what they were paying me in season 5. Maybe?

Emma Bates, actor (KellyAnne Hurley)

Bronwyn approached me with her renegotiation plan. I told her I'd be game to do whatever everyone else was doing. My one concern was she was throwing around numbers so high, I got a nosebleed.

Robert Chang, actor (Thomas Huang)

Because the show had been on the air, albeit on a different network, for two years already when I joined the cast, meaning some of the actors were already a couple of years into their contracts, my lawyer negotiated a better starting salary for me and stipulated for my contract to be up at the same time as Bronwyn, Austen, and Wade's. I was already ahead of the game.

Also, I pointed out to Bronwyn and Wade that Austen was a producer. I figured he might not want to negotiate with us.

Bronwyn Davies

It was best for us to keep our plans to ourselves. We needed heftier bargaining power, anyway. An Emmy win under our belt would do the trick.

Obviously, I was mega-excited about the nominations in 2011. I threw a super-early brunch the day they were going to announce the Emmys. Here's another reason it's better to pursue an acting career in New York rather than in Hollywood: the announcements were made at five thirty in the morning, Pacific Time. Can you imagine being in hostess mode in LA that early?

Austen Hughes

I hadn't been to Bronwyn's apartment since the very beginning of the year. Like a nightmare, it all came back to me: the doorman who always tested material on me for a comedy set he would never perform, the snooty residents who took a step away from me waiting for the elevator because they considered TV fame to be as desirable as an STD...

Wade Hanson

When I ran into Austen in the lobby, he was buzzing with nerves. I figured it was because of the nominations. Next thing you know, I'm nervous, too.

Austen Hughes

...and the daytime drama ingénue who ate the romantic dreams of Midwestern boys. If Wade hadn't spotted me, I would have been halfway to Missouri before the elevator doors opened.

Madeline Puri

Despite having no real friendship with Austen outside of the studio, I resented what Bronwyn had done to him and the secret she made me carry. But to avoid her off the set wouldn't help matters.

Kendra Lewis-Frost

I was rather pleased to attend Bronwyn's Emmy nomination party. The pessimist in me didn't believe the show would receive any nominations. It can be quite lonely receiving disappointing news when you're by yourself in your apartment.

Bronwyn Davies

I can still see exactly where everyone was sitting when the live stream began. One of the cater waiters picked that exact moment to shove a platter of French toast kabobs in my face.

Austen Hughes

Bronwyn was unusually invested in the presentation. Maybe even more so than she had been when we were dating. I very much doubted she cared whether I received another nomination.

Bronwyn Davies

Oh, my God. Did we really need a minute-long introduction from the CEO of the Academy? Just get on with it!

Madeline Puri

Bronwyn held onto the laptop, and the rest of us crowded around to watch. I suppose I prefer a quieter atmosphere when I'm a little tense. I stepped off to the side where I could still hear the presentations even if I couldn't see the screen.

Bronwyn Davies

When they started off with Best Drama, I figured Best Comedy would come up right after it. They made us wait forever, through the Best Miniseries or Movie, the reality shows, and the late night categories. Joshua Jackson had a weird little giggle he kept doing after every nomination. It started to get on my nerves. I was under the impression Melissa McCarthy, his co-presenter, found it annoying, too.

Austen Hughes

Bronwyn had reached "meat cleaver in a microwave" on the energy-level chart well before they got to the comedy nominations. I chose to join Madeline in the safety of the dining area, away from the scrum around the laptop.

Bronwyn Davies

Finally! Lead Actress in a Comedy Series. Melissa McCarthy was the next-to-last person nominated. At first, she acted humbled and surprised to hear her name. But it grew old. I mean, she's delaying the broadcast now. I kind of thought this would have been my year. I was dying to hear who the last actress would be.

Madeline Puri

I nearly missed Joshua announcing my name because of Bronwyn's dialogue about the hosts.

Austen Hughes

A big cheer went out in the room when Madeline's name was mentioned. Bronwyn hushed us immediately. No one dared to congratulate me beyond flashing a thumbs up when I received my nomination.

Wade Hanson

I held one side of the laptop, and it was tilted between my hand and Bronwyn's a few inches lower than mine. She grabbed the other side from me and drew the laptop closer to her face. I don't know if anyone could see it by that point. I noticed Austen and Madeline were watching it on his phone off by themselves, oblivious to the rest of us.

Kendra Lewis-Frost

I pressed my head right up against Bronwyn's to watch the Best Comedy announcement. We held our collective breath when John Shaffner [chairman and CEO of the Academy] returned to the stage for the last big category.

Bronwyn Davies

And then he congratulates Melissa for her nomination. Shouldn't they have picked hosts who weren't likely to be up for nominations? Sheesh! So he announces, *"Big Bang Theory. Glee. Modern Family."* He barely had the first *P* out of *Pet Peeves* when my living room erupted in a jubilant roar.

Wade Hanson

All our phones went off simultaneously and kept buzzing the rest of the day. I had never been nominated for anything. And now my show was up for an Emmy!

Kendra Lewis-Frost

I never understood why we were all watching the nominations on a single laptop. The entire ceremony was broadcast on *Good Day America*, after all. Bronwyn shut the laptop despite the list of awards yet to be announced. I spent a minute fiddling unsuccessfully with her remote trying to call up the show on her TV. We missed hearing Moishe's nomination as a guest actor. The director of the season finale also received a nod, I later learned. I first heard about my nomination when I called Bruce to congratulate him on the series nomination. When I was back home by myself later that day, I watched the video of the ceremony online. It would have been lovely to have shared the occasion with another being.

Bronwyn Davies

Once the major nominations had been announced, I wrapped up the party. I couldn't sit around all day patting everyone on their backs. I had work to do like making sure I booked the right stylist before every other actress in Hollywood beat me to it.

The joyous mood from the party spilled into the studio during the production of the first few episodes of season 6 in advance of the fall premiere and the Emmy Awards.

Blaine Carson

I didn't need Kendra to remind me that since I wasn't a regular cast member, I wouldn't be attending the Emmys. At least the writers would be keeping me busy in the next season, what with Harold's daughter getting married.

Kendra Lewis-Frost

We had coalesced into a family. A family where everyone gets along, of course. Am I terrible to say I preferred having Austen and Bronwyn split up? It eliminated any sense of tribalism backstage. Bruce strove to make sure we didn't separate ourselves between producers and actors, directors and crew, and so on. When Bronwyn and Austen were dating, they often ate by themselves in the commissary, laughing at their own private jokes.

Austen Hughes

You would have thought Bronwyn was planning her own wedding, the way she threw herself into the scenes related to her onscreen nuptials. She had this chipper little bounce in her step. It kind of reminded me of the person she had been way back when on the set of *Another Day to Live*. I'm not saying I was thinking fondly of her and planning for a third go around. I, too, had a bit of the chipper bounce in my step, being single again. The world is full of women worth knowing, and I had been enjoying getting to know a few of them. And now it has happened: after nine years together, I've begun to sound like Bruce.

Bruce Leibowitz

The success of *Pet Peeves* was a shared success. I believe an observant boss deduces when to reward his underlings, and I've since learned it is best he does so before they come at him with their grubby little hands extended.

Bronwyn Davies

It was too early to get the contract negotiations rolling, but I began my preparations, dropping hints to

Bruce about how valuable we all were now that the series had been nominated for an Emmy. Despite my subtlety, I assumed he understood what I left unsaid.

Madeline Puri

I couldn't believe it at first when Bruce invited me to be an executive producer. I'm not a writer.

Bruce Leibowitz

I had a host of reasons to offer Madeline an executive producer position. She is an actor's actor, adept at understanding the inner workings of a character's mind. It was only a matter of time before she tried her hand at directing, but I wanted to tap into that brain of hers at the script-writing level, get her feedback on how to keep our characters from becoming caricatures of themselves.

Austen Hughes

When the three EPs met to discuss adding a fourth executive producer, I thought Bruce meant bringing in someone new. Kendra and I both were poised to reject anyone not already connected to the show.

Kendra Lewis-Frost

I loved Bruce's idea. And I so looked forward to collaborating with Madeline.

Madeline Puri

Even after three seasons on the show, I still felt like the new kid at school when I attended my first producers' meeting.

Austen Hughes

It was kind of adorable how timid Madeline was in the early EP meetings. The polar opposite of Kerani. I had never thought her to be an anxious or shy person. She has a quiet confidence. She doesn't impose herself on people or dominate a room, yet you'll always be aware of her presence.

Madeline Puri

I haven't a clue as to what I could have been scared about. I already had such a strong working relationship with Austen. These are three of the kindest, most supportive people I have ever had the pleasure of calling colleagues. Added bonus: I now knew every last one of the secrets of the coming season!

Bronwyn Davies

I was pretty pissed when I found out Madeline was a producer. Her promotion meant she got a raise before her contract was up. So, now it was four of us bargaining together. The four actors who hadn't won any awards.

The entire cast of Pet Peeves *plus the producers eagerly anticipated attending the Emmys together in September 2011.*

Emma Bates, actor (KellyAnne Hurley)

I couldn't wait for the Emmys. Besides being stoked about our nomination, I was psyched to dress in girly clothes. And not having to wear any part of an animal costume while appearing in public. I seriously can't remember if I ever shot a scene when my character wasn't dressed in scrubs she had embellished with tidbits from her cosplay costumes.

Madeline Puri

Zach was super excited to dust off his tux. I made him swear to keep his hands off of Bronwyn or I'd never invite him to another awards ceremony.

Austen Hughes

I love the way my mother handles herself on the red carpet when she's my plus-one. She pulls off the wholesome, humble, Midwest-housewife routine, all the while vamping for the camera. While she tells whoever is on the other end of the mic how she feels like a fish out of water at these fancy events, she's swishing her earrings and striking poses like a pro. I knew she was as eager to attend the Emmys as any of us in the cast.

Wade Hanson

Most everyone from *Pet Peeves* who was up for an award brought a family member. Except for KellyAnne and Robert, none of us were married or even dating anyone seriously. I had struck up a conversation with one of the cater waiters at Bronwyn's party. We were still dating in September, so I brought her to the Emmys.

Delia Johnson, cater waiter

I had hoped passing around trays of food at a party thrown by Bronwyn Davies would lead to my big break. Honestly, I had been hoping to flirt with Austen, now that he was single. But Wade started joking around with me, and I figured even though he might not be as big a star as Austen, he was still a lead actor on a hit TV show. And he's so handsome. We didn't last very long—there wasn't any chemistry between us. Ultimately, dating him didn't lead to me getting any parts anyhow. But I did get to go to the Emmys that one time.

Bronwyn Davies

It was such a big night for us. We walked away with four Emmys, including best sitcom. Oh, sorry. Five. Yeah, Madeline got one, too. I was sort of hoping to hook up with her brother again to celebrate our big win, but I couldn't find him at the after parties. I struck out with a second guy that night, come to think of it. No, I'm not going to say who it was.

Bruce Leibowitz

The night was nearly a total success. We went in with seven nominations and walked away with five awards. I was very happy for Kendra. She and I had a pattern of hopscotching wins from one year to the next.

In a brief moment of weakness, I considered celebrating our wins at a very exclusive after party, but I caught myself from making a mistake I'm sure would have haunted me a few months down the pike.

The cast of Pet Peeves *received the SAG Award for Outstanding Performance by an Ensemble in a Comedy Series, bolstering their ratings and the machinations behind the actors' impending contract negotiations.*

Bronwyn Davies

Our contracts were up about four months after the SAG Awards. Wade, Emma, and I were fired up with our wins. I wasn't sure if we could count on Robert, though. I'm not saying he was a snitch or anything, but Bruce made a couple of seemingly offhand comments about recognizing one's value and resisting the urge to inflate it. I didn't know for certain what he meant, but it came across like a warning. I can't explain how he would have been onto us unless Robert had said something.

Bruce Leibowitz

I had been keeping a close eye on the contract calendar since day one. An executive producer needs to make sure he has happy actors. Everyone has his or her price and value. The trick is to anticipate who might not be happy, who might channel her unhappiness into a bit of a mess come negotiations. I'm not a fan of messes.

Madeline Puri

I had been waiting since July to shoot the season 6 finale. Of course, we had a beautiful wedding planned for Felicity and Peter. Which Peter nearly ruins when he agrees to perform emergency surgery on a possum Duke had hit with his car. Trip takes over the later stages of the surgery to give Peter the chance to put on his tux. Kerani stops at the clinic on her way to the church. I'm getting ahead of myself. The tone of this script gave me the idea Austen should direct it, not that he had ever expressed an interest in directing. I thought a certain quality he has, how his uproarious humor springs from such a quiet exploration of human emotions, would be the right touch for the episode.

Kendra Lewis-Frost

Madeline's suggestion made perfect sense to me. She, too, understood Austen's sensibility. It's interesting to note that, even by this point in the show's history, various cast and crew members continued to underestimate the depth of Austen's intellect and emotion. Bruce knew the quality of his work, yet he was on the fence about handing him additional responsibilities.

Austen Hughes

It surprised me when Madeline made her suggestion for me to direct the season finale. At meetings, when Bruce asked her who she thought should write which script, she didn't usually volunteer me for the job. I immediately had ideas about what I wanted from the script for the finale if I got to direct it, but I figured they'd hand it off to an experienced director.

Bruce Leibowitz

Never in a million years had I considered reaching out to Austen to direct. He was professional as they come, but he's not one of those go-get-'em types. I wouldn't have thought he'd want me to burden him with additional responsibilities. But when I looked into his eyes, really took a good look, I saw the flame burning in them. While I gave him the episode to direct, I planned on keeping him on a short leash.

Bronwyn Davies

So right away, I had issues with the wedding episode. The Copelands had the money to throw a big shindig at a fancy hotel. But instead, my wedding reception was going to be a simple affair at some local restaurant. And then I saw the dress they picked for me. So basic. I didn't care if Felicity was a country vet. Let a girl glam it up! I was stuck having to wear the dress they picked, but I did manage to get them to give me an updo. Originally, they wanted me to wear my hair down with a flower tucked in here or there. Who am I, Taylor Swift?

Austen Hughes

I hadn't thought it through. I'd be directing my ex-girlfriend.

Blaine Carson

Someone had gotten a little big for her britches. I don't remember Bronwyn asking for so many retakes back when I was a regular on the show.

Robert Chang, actor (Thomas Huang)

Bronwyn is the type of actor who doesn't claim responsibility for her errors. She forgets a line? It's because another actor didn't hit his mark. When she faced the wrong camera during one of our scenes in the finale, she blamed me for it, saying I had taken a beat where I hadn't taken one during rehearsal. I pitied poor Austen.

Austen Hughes

Most of the scenes were straight ahead. I didn't need to reinvent the wheel to shoot them. I just had to be patient with Bronwyn.

Madeline Puri

So we get to that scene at the clinic. My heart was racing a little. Kerani couldn't stand blood and gore. On a normal day, she always stayed behind her little desk, turning a blind eye to any reminder of what went on in the exam rooms.

Austen Hughes

In her first season, Madeline had come up with the idea of putting in little outbursts from Kerani anytime she had to confront a stitched-up wound or a pile of dog puke on the floor. It got me every time. She had this way of scrunching up her face and an endearing squeak in her voice no matter how nasty her reprimand was to whichever vet or tech had forgotten to warn her before sending out the pet sporting shaved fur and a row of stitches.

Wade Hanson

I was in my tux for the possum scene. While I waited for them to ready everything on set, I was doing a little routine. "It's Quinn. Dr. Quinn. I like my possums shaken, not stirred." I thought it was funny.

Austen Hughes

Wade's acting had been undergoing a change during our sixth season. He had always done a good job, but a subtle difference emerged. You began to believe the emotions his character expressed. And I had the impression he enjoyed acting more than he had at the beginning.

Madeline Puri

Trip had been assisting Peter during the surgery. Once Peter left the clinic, Trip had to close up the incision. He needed a hand and called in Kerani to help. She surprised both of them by not freaking out on him. They're dressed to the nines. They've shared a bonding moment, helping out a wounded animal. After four seasons of being enemies, they have this moment.

Kendra Lewis-Frost

Do you remember the Trip-Felicity kiss from the pilot? I sure did during the filming of Wade and Madeline's scene. I chewed my nails down to the quick while they shot it. We had added extra time to the schedule to accommodate any issues. That is how little faith we had in Wade handling his scene.

Moishe Bronfman

I watched the episode when it aired. Something caught my eye: the lighting. It's daytime; they're in a room with a window. You can't do mood lighting in a daytime scene. If you're paying attention, you'll notice the faintest beams of light enveloping Madeline and Wade. The light is discernible mainly because of the dust motes shimmering within the beams. We weren't witnessing the effect of natural light, of course. We were in a windowless studio. It took an artist to paint the light.

Wade Hanson

Honestly, I wasn't thinking too hard about the end of the scene. Madeline and I just read our lines, and everything felt perfectly natural.

Austen Hughes

We needed one single take for the kiss. Trip and Kerani convinced me they had wanted to share a kiss for a long time.

Bronwyn Davies

For a second, I was happy for Wade and Madeline. The tender way he cradled her head, how wide her eyes were when she pulled away. I held my breath at the moment where they nearly had a second kiss. But when they ran to opposite sides of the exam room in disgust for what had gone down, I snapped out of it. If Wade and Madeline hooked up, we could no longer count on him to be part of our collective bargaining plan. It was time to call my lawyer.

Chapter 9
The Seven-Year Itch

Madeline Puri

The whole sixth season was one extended fireworks display for me. From coming on as an executive producer to the show's Emmy win to the emotional content of the finale, I was oohing and ahhing the whole year.

Wade Hanson

Yeah, the season 6 finale was a fun one to shoot. I was kind of sad it meant we were done working together until July. Austen and I were still close friends on the set, but we had stopped hanging out together in the real world when he and Bronwyn started dating again. And it stayed that way when they broke up. Life gets in the way. But I felt closer to him after the finale. To Madeline, too.

Madeline Puri

The success of a show like *Friends* was not simply based on its premise, the writing, and the acting. The cast members were actual friends, which showed in their acting. I genuinely cared for each and every one of the actors in our cast. It was a shame we went our separate ways at the end of a day on set.

Bronwyn Davies

When we wrapped the season in April, Madeline had this idea of getting the regular cast members together for brunch dates. I hesitated in agreeing at first, but when everyone else in the cast said they wanted to do it, they kind of forced me to accept the invitation.

Wade Hanson

Madeline hosted the first brunch the following week. She established one rule: no one besides the six of us could attend. Which meant no significant others or caterers.

Austen Hughes

Well, there goes Wade's dating pool.

Madeline Puri

For the record, I wasn't making a dig at Wade for dating the cater waiter from the Emmy-nomination party. I wanted to create a safe environment for us to be ourselves. My decision to ban staff from our gathering kind of bit me on the heinie, though. Here I was, hosting the first gathering, and I can't tell the difference between a sauté pan and a bottle of Pepto Bismol except that I know both are necessary at different points during my culinary experiments. What had I gotten myself into?

Wade Hanson

I had been a server at Aureole when I first moved to New York. Sometimes I would hang out in the kitchen before my shifts to watch the chefs prep for the dinner service. A few of them saw what I was up to and always answered my questions. They gave me pointers about knife work, ingredients, the heat of a pan. Anyhow, I picked up a few skills.

Madeline Puri

Wade was a lifesaver! He showed up an hour and a half early for the first brunch, bearing foil-wrapped pans and with bags of groceries cascading from his shoulders. I'm not sure my kitchen had ever gone through such a workout. Or smelled so divine!

Bronwyn Davies

My driver picked me up way too early. I made him go around the block when we got to Madeline's. Wade was the only one who had shown up before me. Because he was settled in, wearing an apron and taking command of Madeline's kitchen, I figured he might have arrived a whole lot earlier than me, like maybe the night before? I knew something was up with their kiss!

Austen Hughes

I had never been to Madeline's even though she lived in Brooklyn Heights, not far from me. Mismatched flowerpots brimming with plants and flowers lined the steps up to the front door with cheeriness. I had an impression that, had I walked down this block without knowing she lived nearby, I would have instinctively stopped in front of her brownstone and entertained some random thought about her.

Bronwyn Davies

Dang! Everyone else brought her flowers or wine. I didn't think it was that sort of party.

Emma Bates

I had assumed the four main actors were always going out without Robert and me. If I can be honest, this is the reason why I tended to be kind of aloof in the studio. I didn't want to crash a party I hadn't been invited to.

Robert Chang

My boyfriend was super-jealous I was having brunch with Wade without him. Not jealous like something would go on between us, just a FOMO thing 'cause he's always had a mad crush on Wade.

The only time we had encountered Wade outside of the studio was at the awards shows. You should have seen Jeremy fawn all over him! I'm the one who should be jealous.

Austen Hughes

For people who had worked together for years, we had more than our fair share of awkward silences at that brunch before the mimosas kicked in. It must have been a sign of me growing up because I didn't feel compelled to liven things up by acting the fool to get everyone to laugh like I used to do.

Bronwyn Davies

I'm sure I wasn't alone in thinking we were crashing a romantic brunch between Madeline and Wade. I could usually count on Austen to break the ice with one of his dumb jokes, but he didn't say anything. Instead, he kind of sussed out everyone else's demeanor, Madeline's especially.

Wade Hanson

I was a little nervous about how my shrimp and grits

were going to go over. I doctored up my mother's recipe, adding in a little truffle oil. She'd kill me, accusing me of putting on airs with those fancy northern ingredients. But the grits fired up the conversation.

Emma Bates

None of our characters talk like we do when we are back home. I had forgotten that Wade was from the South because he has a newscaster accent. Until you get him talking about grits and collard greens and the like.

Bronwyn Davies

Everyone was going on about Madeline's home. She was humble-bragging about owning an entire brownstone in Brooklyn Heights. The one thing that caught my attention was she said Zach lived on the top floor. I knew he'd be better company than Madeline et al., so I excused myself at one point to "use the restroom."

Madeline Puri

I felt closer to my castmates by the end of our meal. We began to make plans to meet again in two or three weeks, but we couldn't complete our plans until Bronwyn returned.

Wade Hanson

While we were waiting for Bronwyn, I headed upstairs. I needed to use the facilities and after the hearty meal, I was looking for a little privacy, if you catch my drift.

Bronwyn Davies

Zach wasn't home. On my way downstairs, I passed through the floor where the bedrooms are. I couldn't help myself from snooping around a bit. Madeline had converted one of the rooms into an office. And then it hit me: maybe I could find her contract in her office. Hopefully, I'd uncover a bit of information to bolster my upcoming renegotiation bid.

Wade Hanson

I peeked into the master bedroom. You can't help but be curious about how someone lives, can you? I figured it would be rude to use the master bath, choosing instead to use the one in the hallway.

Bronwyn Davies

I had just found a manila folder that hinted I might have hit pay dirt. Then I heard a toilet flush. I moved away from the doorway leading back into the hall and stood stock still, hoping whoever was in the bathroom wouldn't come into the office.

Wade Hanson

The bathroom had a second door in it. *No harm continuing my tour*, I thought.

Bronwyn Davies

Shit! I held the folder behind my back and then dropped it on the desk before I had a chance to learn anything. I'm pretty sure Wade didn't see it when he came through the second door. All he said was, "If you were waiting for the bathroom, I'd suggest using one on a different floor."

Madeline Puri

After the first few brunch gatherings, I began to suspect that perhaps Bronwyn would have preferred not to spend time off the set with me. Austen volunteered to host the fifth brunch. When Bronwyn mentioned she might not be able to make it, I suggested everyone check their availability for either the week before or after the original date. I fibbed about me not being available on either of those dates and implored them to go ahead without me. I didn't want Bronwyn to miss out on the fun simply because we hadn't yet forged a bond. She did appear to be considering joining the group on a different date.

Wade Hanson

As soon as Madeline suggested another date to accommodate Bronwyn, a date Madeline couldn't attend, everyone protested. How could we continue the brunch tradition without her? Yes, when I asked her to crack the eggs to make French toast, she managed to get more eggshells than eggs into the bowl. So she can't cook. But she was kind of the heart of our group.

Emma Bates

Don't tell anyone, but I enjoyed our brunches better when Bronwyn didn't show up. I may not be alone in my opinion.

Robert Chang

Bronwyn and I get along—we've stayed in touch since the show wrapped, actually. When it's just the two of us away from the cast, we have a blast. If I were a drag queen, she would totally be my drag mother. But she wasn't feeling it with Madeline's bonding brunches. Oh, well. More of Wade's cooking for me!

At the end of June, Davies entered her contract negotiations on her own a few days before the cast returned to the studio to begin filming season 7.

Austen Hughes

I wish I had had an inkling of what Bronwyn was up to, not that I could have talked any sense into her. First things first, she had the cast of *Friends* to thank for the fact that her original contract even included residuals in it because earning residuals hadn't been an option available to most actors before *Friends*. Second, their cast renegotiated before season 3, not season 7. And third, the whole idea behind collective bargaining was the highest paid actors—actors like Bronwyn—would have to take a pay cut in order to bring their salary down to the level of the lowest paid actors—I think Emma was at the lowest tier. In essence, she'd be setting the clock on her salary back a few seasons in hopes of a big payout a few seasons into the future. Can you imagine her reaction if the big boost in salary wouldn't come until season 9, but the show was canceled after season 8?

Bruce Leibowitz

As I've said, I had begun mentally preparing for the contract renegotiations the day I took the job. I fancy myself a Phil Jackson, Zen-master type. Always be in control, but never make people suspect you're bossing them around. It's a gentle kind of manipulation I practice. I had worked on Bronwyn when we began shooting season 6. While I had learned what I needed to learn, I discovered the limits of my ability to alter her point of view.

Robert Chang

The process of renegotiating my contract was painless. I hired an entertainment lawyer, she did her homework, and we struck a deal pretty quickly.

Emma Bates

I can't guess if I got the best deal possible, but I believed the process had been a success. I've read online what lead actors on the big shows get, and sure, I'd like to be super-rich like the big stars. But I still got paid a shit-ton to be a part of a great show.

Bronwyn Davies

I didn't agree with the advice my lawyer was giving me, so I found a new one. He and I went into the meeting with guns blazing.

Rex Braithwaite, chairman of IBS Television Network

Bruce sure called it. Bronwyn came in with a list of demands I can only describe as laughable. Forget the numbers she quoted us for her salary. She was after meaningless little perks like having her lunch brought to her dressing room. And which dressing room she would use. We had given her the biggest dressing room back when the show moved into studio space in Brooklyn. Yet she came to us asking for a better dressing room.

Bruce Leibowitz

One detail about the show that was important to me from my first episode and remains important to me to this day was ours was an ensemble show. No stars. That means we listed the actors in alphabetical order in the credits. On this point I would not budge.

Bronwyn Davies

I had considered changing my name during the negotiations. It was such an insult for Emma and Robert to be listed before me in the credits just because their last names came first in the alphabet. Something like Aniston would have worked. Maybe people would have thought I was Jennifer's baby sister.

Bruce Leibowitz

We ended the first day of negotiations without a contract. It was right before the Fourth of July. None of us stayed in town for the holiday.

Kendra Lewis-Frost

Bruce had moved the start date of filming earlier and earlier each season. His reasoning was we could produce additional episodes in the summer to reduce our workload during the back half of the season.

Bronwyn Davies

I didn't have a new contract the day of the first table read. They didn't actually expect me to show up for it, did they?

Kendra Lewis-Frost

While we figured missing a table read would hurt Bronwyn more than it would the rest of the cast, I did entertain troubling thoughts about rewrites in the event Dr. Copeland would not be on staff at the clinic for an episode or two. Hmm, perhaps she fell overboard from her cruise ship whilst on honeymoon? A small fishing vessel finds her. Unfortunately, due to a slight bump from hitting her head on a shark during her fall, she is now suffering from a case of amnesia. Her return to Califon depended on her regaining her memory.

Bruce Leibowitz

I often forgot about Kendra's prior experience writing daytime dramas. But every once in a while, she'd provide a little reminder.

Bronwyn Davies

I had instructed my lawyer to use every resource available to find out the terms of Madeline's contract. I wanted to base my salary on hers, plus ten percent. I figured the billable hours would be worth it if the numbers were right. It took him several days to track down the information.

Madeline Puri

She hired a lawyer to track down my salary? If I'm not mistaken, the details of my per episode fee structure were posted on the *Pet Peeves* Wikipedia page shortly after I renegotiated my contract a year earlier.

Bronwyn Davies

I blew a gasket when I learned that both Madeline and Austen had renegotiated their contracts before they expired. If I hadn't fired my old entertainment lawyer already, I would have canned him the second I realized I could have taken care of renegotiating my contract years earlier.

Bruce Leibowitz

We were back in the negotiation room the afternoon of the table read. I let Kendra bring up the possible plots we were considering to explain away Felicity's absence. I couldn't allow Bronwyn to surmise that missing a table read had gained her the upper hand.

Rex Braithwaite

Her lawyer was chickenshit, the sort of guy who starts a negotiation with his aggressive meter set to eleven. He ran out of steam fast. We had no trouble getting him to agree to our numbers. He accepted our offer to pay Bronwyn the same six-figure per episode fee we had offered Madeline; it still represented a healthy raise, after all. We also persuaded him to agree to another six-year contract with basic annual pay raises. Just to show Bronwyn that we're nice guys, we sweetened the deal with a slight increase in her residual percentage.

Bronwyn Davies

I guess they didn't consider me to be worth one million dollars. But at least they didn't think Madeline was, either. In order to reiterate my value to the show, I asked them to give me her dressing room.

Madeline Puri

I would have gladly swapped dressing rooms with her at any time. She only needed to ask.

Bronwyn Davies

Madeline's dressing room turned out to share a wall with the laundry. The churning and dinging drove me mad. I traded rooms with Emma a week later.

Bruce Leibowitz

The contract negotiations behind us, we welcomed Bronwyn back to the studio on day two as if we had actually missed her. I had assumed the drama was over.

Austen Hughes

Bronwyn owned a car, but she never drove herself to the studio. I would drive to the studio for the sole purpose of avoiding having to find a parking space near my home on street cleaning days. So, at the end of the day maybe a week or two after we had started filming, Bronwyn comes up to me in the parking lot, hysterical.

Bronwyn Davies

Someone had stolen my car!

Austen Hughes

I walked with her to where she said she had parked her car, expecting to find nothing save for a pile of shattered glass.

Bruce Leibowitz

We each had assigned parking spaces at the studio. Even though not everyone used their space, anyone driving in would know better than to park in a space with, oh, say, "Bronwyn Davies" painted in it.

Austen Hughes

Her assigned space is right next to mine, the closest space to the front door any actor on *Pet Peeves* had. Anyhow, Bronwyn led me away from our section of the parking lot to another one, the lot in front of the next studio over where they shot *Girls*. She stood facing an empty spot—the best spot, mind you—right in front of the entrance to the studio. Again, not a shard of broken glass lay on the pavement. But there, in bold yellow paint, was Lena Dunham's name.

Bronwyn Davies

Oh, my God! How petty did Lena have to be to have my car towed? It's not like she ever used her spot. Do you have any idea what a pain in the ass it is to rescue your car from the pound?

In contrast to the energy that had motivated the cast and crew in season 6, a lull descended on the set the following season.

Kendra Lewis-Frost

The writers had long ago learned to work in synchronicity. We churned out script after script like clockwork. And our cast brought the words to glorious life week after week. How lucky we were to come together to produce this wonderful show!

Stephen Burrows, writer

Yawn.

D'Wayne Curtis, writer

We'd managed to marry off Felicity and Peter. And four years after bringing in Kerani to be Trip's love interest, they kissed. Yay. Throw them a parade.

You know how sometimes cruise lines have these repositioning cruises? Say a ship has been in the Mediterranean throughout the summer but now it's going to sail around the Bahamas. A ship that always does these short hops to local ports suddenly is offering a one-way, trans-Atlantic cruise from Barcelona to Miami. That's what it felt like in the writers' room in season 7. And seasons 8 and 9, come to think of it. We had to cross an ocean to get from kiss number one to kiss number two.

Madeline Puri

We had built up such great chemistry between us actors, and I believe I can speak for all of us when I say the on-camera quibbles and squabbles crackled with such fun energy because of it.

Bronwyn Davies

Getting married meant I got to kick Madeline, I mean Kerani, out of my house because Peter moved in with Felicity after the wedding. Unfortunately, it also meant Felicity lost access to Kerani's closet. Instead, Peter and Felicity were always throwing dinner parties for their coworkers. Boring.

Wade Hanson

Trip and Kerani were at each other's throats with renewed vigor after their little smooch. They fought with passion, which I guess was the whole point. To prove he didn't have a thing for Kerani, Trip doubled down on his playboy reputation, having an endless string of women spend the night at his bachelor pad.

Austen Hughes

Something we've never explained, kind of the *Twilight Zone* of *Pet Peeves*: where did Trip find all those gorgeous, well-dressed women to date? He lived and worked in Califon, New Jersey, eligible female population: zero.

Kendra Lewis-Frost

Trip may have had a lucky streak with the ladies, but I sure as hell didn't. Seriously, I dated exactly one woman in the five or so years after Kym and I broke up. My nesting urges were so strong, no twig or scrap bit of string lying about was safe around me.

Austen Hughes

People always want to learn about the similarities between Peter and me. The differences are easier to discern. I don't share Peter's sense of wonder. I have a healthy dose of cynicism clouding my eyes. I'd love to experience everything the way he did, feel his spark of excitement. The thing I envied most about him, though, was how he fell in love and made it stick.

Madeline Puri

Despite the rumors to the contrary, Wade and I did not date. The kiss was acting, nothing more. He's such a good friend, but I hope I can speak for the two of us when I say we never, not even for a second, thought about taking our screen kiss to the next level. I'm sure I sound like a broken record—is that even a thing anymore? Do kids today know what a broken record is? Sorry. As I was saying, I don't date actors.

Austen Hughes

I had a little of the Trip, post-kiss, in me. Having missed out on dating in high school and college, when Bronwyn and I broke up the second time, I was like a fawn discovering an open field after being confined to walking through a dense forest for most of its life. I played the field, reveling in the fact women actually thought I was attractive. The greater my desire to fall in love, the less appeal these flings had for me.

An image of my ideal woman had begun to develop in my mind, and none of the women I met outside of work came close to matching her. I knew such a woman—one who was at ease with herself, allergic to artifice, and above all, funny—existed, but without making the connection to her, my love life definitely stagnated in the later years of the show.

Kendra Lewis-Frost

Accolades-wise, we were also in a bit of a dry spell. While we interrupted *Modern Family*'s streak with our

Best Comedy Series win in 2011, they became invincible at the Emmys. At least we continued to receive nominations in the category.

Wade Hanson

We still had a bunch of awards shows to go to, so all the single cast members and producers were trotting out family members and friends instead of boyfriends and husbands. It would have been nice to bring someone special with me, but that wasn't possible.

Madeline Puri

I put any thoughts about still being single as I approached my thirties out of my head. I had so much to be grateful for.

Bronwyn Davies

It's convenient to date men you meet on set. You don't have to remind me I had totally denied my history of dating coworkers when you first started interviewing me. But when I'd date another actor not on my show, he'd always pick up a role in another show or movie and end up with his lead actress. We needed new blood on the set.

Bruce Leibowitz

Perhaps I first noticed Bronwyn's restlessness in the months after she signed her new contract. I didn't give it much thought, though. Collectively, we all suffered from sagging libidos. I needed to massage the cast and crew, get those juices flowing again.

Leibowitz invited the executive producers and staff writers to a three-day weekend retreat in the Bahamas in February 2013.

With a third of the lead actors already on the guest list, he extended the invitation to the four non-executive producer/actors.

Bruce Leibowitz

I booked us into my favorite boutique property on Andros. I had spent my first month sober at the Blissful Andros Resort and Spa several years earlier.

Austen Hughes

Did anyone else consider the irony of a guy drying out at a hotel whose acronym happened to be his no-fly zone?

Emma Bates

It was a charming hotel. Unfortunately, it was a hotel with only six guest rooms. Each of the eleven people in our group had arrived expecting to have their own room.

Kendra Lewis-Frost

Bruce is nothing if not an egalitarian. He wouldn't abide one of his executive producers getting their own room. I certainly saw his point, but I vehemently turned down his offer to bunk with him.

Bronwyn Davies

Don't look at me. I share beds, not rooms. And there was no one at our retreat with whom I cared to share a bed.

Wade Hanson

Me and Austen paired up. And then Madeline and Emma did the same. The four of us left to check into our rooms while the rest of them figured it out.

D'Wayne Curtis

I've known Stephen long enough to be okay sharing a room with him for three days. He needed to allow me to go up to the room first, though. Traveling always does a number on my stomach.

Kendra Lewis-Frost

I'd be out of line to say it was Bruce's intention to share a room with an eligible woman. Just in case, though, I reached out to Melanie Keep, a writer and one of the two remaining women in our group, inviting her to be my roomie. I noticed Bronwyn and Bruce standing at opposite ends of the lobby from each other, avoiding eye contact. Hmm. Very interesting. And poor Robert, stuck in the middle.

Robert Chang

Bronwyn had unsuccessfully tried to manipulate Bruce during the contract negotiations. You can probably guess how she wanted to do it. I'm not sure she had recovered from him turning her down and ultimately gaining the upper hand. One of them would be sleeping on the beach if I didn't step in to save her.

Bruce Leibowitz

Probably best I ended up with my own room. I snore like no one's business.

Bronwyn Davies

God, I needed a drink after our little French farce at check-in! The mini bar in our room only had coconut water and chia seed snacks. I'm not too proud to admit that I was the first one downstairs for the cocktail reception. A staff member shooed me outside to the beach where a waiter held a tray of daiquiri glasses filled with pastel-colored concoctions. Yes, please! It was all I could do to resist grabbing two at once.

Austen Hughes

Lots of people don't consider themselves on vacation until they have their feet in the sand and a frosty blender drink in their hand. I've never been a beach guy, what with coming from Missouri and doing the world a favor by not donning swimming trunks in my youth. And you can have your fruity, slushy drinks. Make mine a beer. Only thing was, they didn't have any beer at BARS. Or rum. The hotel was as dry as Bruce.

Bronwyn Davies

Are you kidding me? Robert and I checked ourselves into the resort next door. I kid you when I say the word *resort*. It was a three-star lodge. But they had booze.

Kendra Lewis-Frost

Bruce had prepared a detailed schedule for each of us. At six o'clock the first morning, the writers were to meet for a tantric breathing class. No, it wasn't an actual tantric class. They called it a yoga breathing session. Bruce came up with the cockamamie idea that to find our voices as writers, we first had to find our breath. Basically, we sat in a circle on the beach and held our hands against our stomachs and chests. I can't say it was my breath I found so much as I found I became hungrier when I pressed on my abdomen.

Madeline Puri

Those of us who remained on the property made our best effort to be like Bruce. He obviously derived great joy from yoga and meditation. It wouldn't do us any harm to follow suit.

Wade Hanson

My mother had warned me about yoga cults when I first moved to New York. I've met lots of people who swore by their hot yoga or whatever, but I never got the impression they participated in the religious side of yoga. One more way my mother had overprotected me.

Bruce is the one person I know who gets into the spiritual side of yoga. I have to admit that some aspects of the retreat kind of disturbed me a bit. By Sunday morning, I had to go and find myself a church, a Christian church, for balance.

Kendra Lewis-Frost

Saturday night, Madeline and I made a pact to join Bruce for his sunrise swim the next day. We had no expectations the other actors or writers would choose to join him, and we didn't want him to feel unloved. I was living on my own in Bronwyn and Robert's old room when Madeline knocked on my door at an ungodly hour on Sunday morning. It did surprise me to see Emma behind her, clutching a beach bag.

Austen Hughes

And then there were five. Not that I'm a big drinker, but between the lack of booze, meat, and sugar in my system during our retreat and the early end to our evenings, I actually had no trouble waking up early on Sunday morning.

Madeline Puri

Bruce should have warned us about the bathing suit situation.

Austen Hughes

Dude was hung. I say that as your run-of-the-mill straight guy, just to be clear.

Kendra Lewis-Frost

Oh, dear. Emma took one glance at Bruce's glistening white bum mooning us from the surf and headed back to bed.

Bruce Leibowitz

My intentions of freeing my team from their inhibitions had clearly failed. If they needed to cling to the security they experienced within the confines of the Lycra and polyester woven into their swimsuits, who am I to judge?

Kendra Lewis-Frost

I took Bruce aside after breakfast. Perusing the rest of the schedule, I realized far too many of the remaining activities would give your average head of HR heart palpitations. I had to draw the line at the massage extravaganza he had planned for Sunday afternoon. In its place, Austen and Madeline led the actors in an improv session while the rest of us worked out the kinks on the next script. Ack! See how even reminiscing about the retreat has corrupted my vocabulary?

Chapter 10
The Gnome Home Massacre of 2014

Despite Leibowitz's best efforts, the writers, directors, crew, and most of the cast of Pet Peeves *remained united in their efforts to produce quality television. Questions remained, however, about whether individual personalities might have the power to disrupt the harmonious atmosphere.*

Kendra Lewis-Frost

Douglas Adams said it better, but the thing about Bruce you need to remember is he is mostly harmless. The #MeToo movement came to the fore a few months after the final episode of *Pet Peeves* had aired. It is possible that my—or another *Pet Peeves* alum's— description of Bruce offers a picture of a man whom one would expect to exhibit predatory characteristics. Such a vision could not be farther from the truth.

Austen Hughes

It's easy for a guy to say he never suspected Bruce to be the same kind of dude as, oh, say Harvey Weinstein. Yes, I saw his dick. No, I never saw him doing anything with it.

Madeline Puri

Did Bruce ever cross a line? Heavens, no! While he was not one to hide his interior life from the outside world, it's safe to say what any of us saw from him in public reflected his private behavior. His thing was to meld his subconscious existence with the natural world, free himself from the restrictions the conscious self places on the corporeal self. Oh, dear. I'm sounding like him, aren't I?

Let me try to put it in my own terms. He wanted to write freely, for us to act freely, to avoid overthinking anything. That is where art resides, he has said. On a personal level... The thing is we all have active libidos. When Bruce was feeling sexy, yes, I guess everyone knew about it. But I only needed to decline his advances once, and at no point did I feel threatened for having rejected him. He presided over a safe, nurturing work environment.

Bronwyn Davies

Of course, you're asking ME about Bruce. Fine. You got me. Yes, I tried to seduce him after we won our Emmy. It wasn't the other way around. Bruce has the aura of someone who may be a bit, mmm, deviant, which kind of turns me on. He appears to be constantly staring at you, and you assume he has sex on the brain when he does. He has this look. His face kind of goes slack, but his eyes are laser-focused on you. Truthfully, it surprised me when he declined my overtures. He must not be as horny as he makes himself out to be.

Bruce Leibowitz

Bronwyn once presented me with an exceptional invitation, yes. I had considered how a carnal encounter would offer me an opportunity to connect to her, perhaps to head off any brinkmanship she might have employed during the contract negotiations. But were I to succumb to her charms, I would have had to have played my hand very differently during the contract negotiations to have avoided any impropriety. I won't lie: of course, I was tempted, but my better angels were watching over me that night.

Austen Hughes

I had witnessed a lot of odd behaviors from Bronwyn over the years. While she has many sides, one thing I can say for certain is she is reliably superficial. When she acts up, it's because she wants something. Well, specifically, what she wants is attention. I learned to tune her out whenever she got her knickers in a knot. Which is why I probably was the last of us to figure out she was heading down the rabbit hole once the contract issue had been resolved.

Madeline Puri

Austen had talked me into asking Bruce for the chance to direct my first episode. If he hadn't suggested it, I may never have had the courage to ask on my own behalf. Come to think of it, I'm not sure I had valued the friend Austen had become to me. Sorry, I drifted off on a tangent. Back to your question. Thanks to Austen's encouragement, I received Bruce's approval to direct the season 8 episode entitled "The Book Club."

Bronwyn Davies

The thing with Bruce's vision of an ensemble show was we rotated who got the big storyline each week. You'd have one major plot and two smaller plots in an episode. So every few episodes, I'd be at the center of the story. Of course, now that Felicity and Peter were married, they always shared a storyline. But, whatever. In between the big episodes, there'd be weeks where I'd have the lead in a subplot and a week or two where I sort of faded into the woodwork. We had shot one of my off-week scripts the week before it was my turn to star. When it's my big episode, who do they let direct it? Madeline friggin' Puri.

Madeline Puri

At the end of the day, whether I'm acting or directing, I want every actor to be proud of their work. It does the show no good to keep a take in which I knocked the scene out of the park if another actor needed us to do another take. As a director, it's important to me to listen to each and every actor to help them to achieve their desired goals. I never protest when someone asks to redo a scene. I strive to nurture my fellow actors, to allow them to find their best performances.

Emma Bates

Bronwyn was kind of outdoing herself in the first episode Madeline directed. Mind you, no one was asking her to do anything unusual for her character. "Felicity gets in over her head in this week's episode." When doesn't Felicity get in over her head? Bronwyn could make her character really cute in those moments, all flustered and such. But in "The Book Club," it was Bronwyn who was flustered. We heard her say, "I wasn't ready" a lot that week.

Austen Hughes

I missed the worst of it since I wasn't in the book club scenes.

Madeline Puri

Bronwyn has stall tactics, but then again, I suppose I do, too.

Wade Hanson

Oh, yeah! I know what you're talking about. If she forgets a line, she'll burp when it's time to say her line, and then she is laughing too hard to continue.

Austen Hughes

"He stepped on my line." You'd hear that excuse whenever she tripped over her tongue.

Madeline Puri

Because Kerani was a member of the book club, I had to be on set during the book club scenes. Otherwise, I would have been in the booth. Maybe the presence of the director on set made her nervous.

Emma Bates

I'm pretty sure if anyone else had been directing, the episode would have gone a lot smoother.

Wade Hanson

We had a lot of late nights that week, but the episode turned out okay once the editors did their thing.

Bruce Leibowitz

While it wasn't one of our stronger episodes, I gave Madeline a few additional opportunities to direct later episodes. I knew the path to success for her rested on me making certain the scripts I handed to her in the future were not quite so Felicity-centric.

Davies' antics aside, the bonds between the cast and crew members gave Pet Peeves *a reputation as being one of the friendliest television productions. One particular friendship led to an episode likely to remain on everyone's top ten lists of favorite episodes.*

Madeline Puri

I had fallen on lean times, romantically. Rather than let my single status torment me, I put my energy into developing my existing friendships. I became especially close to Kendra later in the show's history.

Kendra Lewis-Frost

I have never had a large circle of friends. In fact, so many of the friends I've made over the years had been friends I borrowed from my girlfriends, friends I invariably lost after the break-ups. Madeline was the first close friend I had made on my own in years.

Bruce Leibowitz

I don't know how I could have missed it, but it wasn't until our Bahamian getaway that I learned of Kendra's Sapphic nature. When I realized she and Madeline had become such good gal pals, I shared a mantra with them to ensure they have a long and happy love life together.

Kendra Lewis-Frost

Bruce!

Madeline Puri

Kendra and I had a lot of shared interests: wine, knitting, hiking. Oh, did I mention wine?

Kendra Lewis-Frost

I hadn't been back to Califon since we had shot the pilot. Between the wrap up of season 8 and before we were back in the studio to film season 9, Madeline and I decided to spend a day visiting our show's hometown. A hiking trail runs through Califon—the Columbia Trail—and I had been meaning to visit it for years.

Madeline Puri

It had been forever since I enjoyed a simple walk in the woods. Kendra and I alternated between chatting and not, taking moments to commune with the hushed sounds along the trail. When you're quiet, you can observe the world without distraction. We found a treasure on our outing, although I don't remember which of us spotted it first.

Kendra Lewis-Frost

Madeline stepped off the trail, stopping in front of a tree. It grew in such a manner, a hollow had formed near its base. Covering the hollow was a small wooden door, shaped to fit the contours of the space. Someone had attached it to the tree via three wee leather straps.

Madeline Puri

I delicately grasped a tiny doorknob between my thumb and middle finger and pulled. The door opened to reveal, well, not much at all. Just a bit of moss and a rock or two.

Kendra Lewis-Frost

I delight in random occurrences of the inexplicable. My job is to tell a story no one has ever heard. Our tiny door fired up my imagination. Madeline, on the other hand, could not rest until she learned the real reason why the door existed. We walked back into town in search of an answer.

Madeline Puri

The explanation was better than I could have imagined. A saddle maker named Sue had built a gnome home on the trail in order to pull a young friend away from his computer games and encourage him to play outside. She put a toy inside a hollowed-out tree stump, built a door for it, and sent the boy on a gnome hunt. Over time, she installed doors farther and farther from home to lengthen the nature walks the two would take together. Hikers, entranced by her gnome homes, built additional dwellings. Soon gnome homes dotted the length of the entire Columbia Trail.

Kendra Lewis-Frost

Not everyone used natural materials. To some who walked the trail, the man-made additions to the woods resembled litter, not whimsical gems. And after a while, the wooden doors fell into disrepair. People complained, as they're wont to do. One fateful day—not long before our visit, in fact—park rangers removed most of the gnome homes and their plastic residents.

Madeline Puri

I'm thinking, *Who would do such a thing, complaining about a source of such delight?* And it hit me: Kerani. Kerani would be exactly the type of person to incite a massacre against gnome homes.

Kendra Lewis-Frost

The two of us volleyed story ideas back and forth on our way home.

Madeline Puri

As had happened in real life where people on both sides of the issue attended a parks advisory committee meeting a few days after the gnome home purge, in our story, Kerani tried to rally the troops from the Califon Small Animal Clinic to speak out on behalf of banning all gnome homes from the trail forever more. The thing that cracked me up about the premise of the show was the fact that I couldn't for one second believe Kerani would ever have stepped her Manolo Blahnik-clad feet upon even an inch of the Columbia Trail.

Kendra Lewis-Frost

"The Gnome Home Massacre" was the only episode during the Bruce era to give credit to a pair of writers. And it represents Madeline's only official writing credit.

Madeline Puri

Now, whenever I find a gnome or gnome merchandise, I think of Kendra and have to buy it for her.

The drama Davies brought to her contract negotiations and her disruptions on the set under Puri's direction presented the earliest signs of Davies' growing discontent.

Bruce Leibowitz

A showrunner needs to keep the big picture in sight at all times. We aired twenty-four episodes during each of the nine seasons for which I was at the helm. That amounted to approximately, hmm, let me do the math. We must have come up with about six hundred fifty different plots. We needed seven regular members on our writing staff plus a few extras to handle the workload. I didn't want to get bogged down with plotting each and every episode. But the shows have to work together to tell an extended story. The characters have to behave in an immediately recognizable manner. I had a plan for each season of *Pet Peeves*, but more important, I had a plan for the entire run of the show before the season 3 premiere, my first episode as executive producer, aired.

Kendra Lewis-Frost

Peter and Felicity married in the spring of 2012. Bruce wanted to have Felicity knocked up by the middle of season 9, about two years later.

Austen Hughes

Bronwyn and I weren't getting along by the end of season 8. I didn't have a clue what was going on with her, but then again, I didn't care. Well, I'm not being entirely truthful. She could snub me all she wanted to in the commissary, say snide things to me when we were off set. But once the cameras were rolling, we had to behave like newlyweds. I'm no expert on such matters, but I did believe, for instance, a wife should look at her husband's face when handing him a mug of coffee rather than regard his crotch with devious intent as if she were contemplating dumping the scalding liquid onto the family jewels.

Wade Hanson

Having a steady acting gig for eleven years gave me a huge opportunity to learn everything I could about being an actor and then put it into action. By the series finale, I wasn't the same guy who blew the love scene in the pilot way back when. And I owe a great deal of what I've learned to the amazing actors on *Pet Peeves*. You can't help but do your best when you're going head to head with either Austen or Madeline. I used to admire Bronwyn's acting, too, but at some point, she stopped trying to do her best. Except for one scene where she had to stand in front of a mirror for a bunch of lines. I wouldn't be surprised if, given the chance, she would have preferred to play her scenes opposite her reflection instead of any of us. She and her mirror image made a cute couple.

Bronwyn Davies

I stand behind each and every moment I appeared on camera. If anyone has a different opinion, they should read the scripts—they weren't always great—or check out the work of my castmates. I think everyone's efforts became uneven after our big Emmy win. Really, I had outgrown the small screen by the time Austen, I mean Peter and I got married.

Austen Hughes

I went back to behaving like fat Austen/Peter when Bronwyn would shut down on set. I resorted to antics like the attention-grabbing stunt I pulled my first day on set at *Another Day to Live*. Or the version of Peter Kendra had written into the pilot before they cast the role. I wasn't flinging cat heads around, but I found that playing the doofus kept the energy positive on set.

Kendra Lewis-Frost

Bruce and I had a meeting, just the two of us, after we had shot the second episode of season 9. It was hard to let go of our dreams for Peter and Felicity's future family, but given the situation, we felt we should back away from the affection and introduce a little conflict between the lovebirds.

Bruce Leibowitz

The Felicity they wrote into the first two seasons was a sweet, not exceptionally logical country girl who had the occasional feisty moment. While we retained hints of her feisty spirit into season 3 and beyond, we relied on it less when we added Kerani to the cast. With the combative nature of Kerani's relationship with Trip and her bullying tendencies toward Thomas and KellyAnne, to have gotten Felicity riled up too often would have upset the balance between aggressive and passive characters. We had previously planned to tone down the war between Kerani and Trip in season 9. I saw the problems going on backstage as a gift. With a subtle push on one end of the seesaw, we tilted the battles from one pair of actors to another.

Bronwyn Davies

Finally! They gave me some good lines when Felicity and Peter started heading toward Splitsville.

Kendra Lewis-Frost

Bruce and I had a plan for our couple to reconcile by the end of the season. Bruce sure wanted to get Felicity pregnant! Erm—

Austen Hughes

It was cathartic to fight with Bronwyn on camera, not that either Peter or Felicity went for the jugular. Felicity mostly griped to Peter about whatever he had done wrong. And whenever she'd attack him, he practiced avoidance techniques like enthusiastically volunteering to clean up the explosive diarrhea left behind in the waiting room by a skittish husky.

Bronwyn Davies

I asked my agent to solicit movie scripts for me. And I let everyone in the studio know it.

Kendra Lewis-Frost

I'm not quite certain anyone took Bronwyn's movie aspirations seriously.

With no roles in upcoming movies being offered to her, Bronwyn explored additional ways to demonstrate her frustrations.

Austen Hughes

Ask any TV star about going to work ill, and I guarantee they all have at least one story involving projectile vomiting. Because everyone knows that vomit stories are the best.

Madeline Puri

I bet when you asked Austen the same question, he regaled you with puke jokes. Typical.

Wade Hanson

One of my better acting efforts came when I had the flu. I was in the fever, achy stage; no snot issues until we finished shooting, thankfully. I focused my brains out on every line, inflection, gesture, getting everything right on the first take. I couldn't mess things up for the other actors, especially since I exposed them to my germs like that Mary chick. Who am I thinking of? Typhoon Mary?

Bruce Leibowitz

I prefer to film episodically—one episode per week—as opposed to shooting scenes from a couple of episodes at once on the same set. It's highly unusual for an actor to call out sick, but in the event it's un-avoidable, I will have the actors present read future scripts, block scenes that don't involve the missing actor, or what have you. We'll film a later scene if we're ready. Flexibility from all involved in a production is key.

Kendra Lewis-Frost

I guess it was late March 2015, near the end of filming for season 9. We had done the table read the day before. Day two is basically revising the scripts and rehearsing. No live cameras. Anyhow, call time for the actors had come and gone. We had five of our principals and our guest stars at the studio, but not Bronwyn.

Bruce Leibowitz

I get a call from Bronwyn's manager: she's sick. The next day, she's still home in bed. By now, I'm the one who's feeling sick. We shot a couple of scenes without her and went home early. Guess what? No Bronwyn the next day, either. We'd finished filming what we could and got through a couple of scenes for the next episode. I had to call it. I gave everyone a paid day off for what should have been our final day of the week. Now you know why shows carry insurance.

Madeline Puri

Bronwyn went AWOL during the week I directed my second episode, a fun one called "The Day Off." Needing an escape from his marital woes, Peter spends his day off by himself. We had done a couple of location shoots the preceding week—oh, I wish we had saved filming them for the following week! It would have made valuable use of our downtime.

There was a Mr. Bean-like quality to Austen's performance. He floated in and out of other people's experiences like a balloon. Like a self-destructive balloon. He winds up in Manhattan, enjoys a vigorous episode of day drinking, watches children playing with boats in Central Park—of course, he fell into the pond—and ends his day disheveled and dripping wet at Duke and Claudia's penthouse. His performance was so strong, and directing him was a blast. These were the saving graces for what was otherwise a frustrating week.

Kendra Lewis-Frost

Bruce does not lose his cool. Back in his drinking days, I understand the opposite was true. But in our nine years on the show, I witnessed his rage exactly once: the day of the table read the following week.

Austen Hughes

I was in my dressing room going over my lines when Bruce received a call from Bronwyn's manager. I heard a roar, an eruption of obscenities ricocheting off the metal ceiling of the soundstage.

Kendra Lewis-Frost

I went flying out of the office to find him. I made it to the set in time to hear him shout threats of suing Bronwyn for breach of contract. He hung up and threw his phone against the wall of a set. A stethoscope he had picked up off a countertop nearly clipped my ear. I was able to hide behind a sofa before he lobbed a chair in my general direction.

Bruce Leibowitz

Anger brings me back to dark days. The sight of Kendra cowering behind the couch snapped my rational behavior switch to the *on* position. Chastened, I sat crossed-legged on the studio floor and invited her to meditate with me.

Wade Hanson

I left my dressing room to see what the commotion was. For a minute there, I had a flashback to our retreat in the Bahamas, seeing Bruce and Kendra do that hippy-dippy stuff, ohming and all. But I guess it was better than Bruce tearing up our sets. And at least he was fully clothed.

Austen Hughes

Thanks to the best legal minds the network could hire, they managed to bring Bronwyn in the next day. She was surprisingly well behaved. Healthy, too.

Rex Braithwaite, chairman of IBS Television Network

Bruce and I had a long chat on the phone after our diva pulled her little stunt. The ratings were acceptable, the show was making the network money. I didn't necessarily see a reason to end the show, but I needed Bruce to convince me he had things under control out there in Brooklyn.

Bruce Leibowitz

Getting called into the principal's office made me want to give up. Any producer would kill to have what we had had with *Pet Peeves*, but I wondered if it was worth it.

Kendra Lewis-Frost

I'm going to be honest here. My biggest concern for Bruce was Bruce. Someone close to me has been through recovery. When life becomes difficult, it takes his entire support system rallying around him to reinforce his belief he is strong enough to prevent himself from making regrettable choices.

Bruce Leibowitz

Kendra talked me down. What a blessing! She reminded me we had expended so much time and energy building up to the moment when Kerani and Trip would become a couple, it would have been devastating for us and the show's fans to walk away now.

The two of us made the decision to sit down with Bronwyn and her representation to get to the bottom of what had led to her walkout.

Bronwyn Davies

They made such a big deal out it! I'll tell you a little secret: I wasn't actually sick. I had flown to LA for an audition the previous weekend, and when I came home, I decided I needed a few days off.

Kendra Lewis-Frost

Remaining patient during our meeting was quite the ordeal. Bronwyn wanted our attention, and she had it, all right. Bruce, thank goodness, is an excellent communicator, and soon we were exploring ways Bronwyn would be happier when she was on the set. I'm not sure she spoke a single truthful word to us, but the truth wasn't what we were after; we were looking for a viable working relationship.

Bronwyn Davies

It was about time the executive producers listened to my ideas for a change! I figured viewers must be sick of

Felicity and Peter as a couple. Real relationships don't last as long as ours did. I wanted a divorce. And I didn't want to act in any scenes with Madeline.

Bruce Leibowitz
I can sympathize with Bronwyn in how undervalued she must have felt. My show without stars in actuality had two, both of whom served as executive producers and directors. We offered Bronwyn the title of co-executive producer. Interestingly, she never inquired who the other co-executive producer was. Technically, yes, co- implies at least two, but who's counting? It did the trick, quieting her down.

Blaine Carson, actor (Harold Copeland)
I owe Bronwyn a huge debt. I can't say for certain whether she had gone to bat for me or not, but I'd like to think that after all those years of playing my daughter, her request for Felicity to move to Florida to practice in her parents' animal hospital was in some way motivated by her desire to gain me additional screen time.

Kendra Lewis-Frost
We rejiggered the script for the season 9 finale to include Felicity's farewell to Califon.

Bronwyn Davies
So long, bitches!

Tempering the shock of Felicity and Peter's divorce was a moment fans had been waiting for: a second kiss between Trip and Kerani

Ursula Fletcher, Everything Pet Peeves Fan Club
Oh. My. God. Their kiss was everything! It almost made up for the fact that Peter and Felicity were getting

a divorce. If Peter had been the one to ask for a divorce, I would have stopped watching the show. I totally had to know the real reason why the writers made them get a divorce. I searched online for any dirt about Bronwyn leaving the show, but I couldn't find anything. And then when she was back on the show the next season but living in Florida, I thought, "Okay. The writers totally played a trick on me but in a good way." This is why it was the best thing on television. You knew what plots they'd do, but sometimes they went the totally opposite direction.

Wade Hanson

I never minded Austen getting to play the romantic lead in our show. I've been typecast as the romantic hero since I played the prince in my middle school production of *Cinderella*, but my heart wasn't in it when I had those roles. That said, once Trip and Kerani admitted to their romantic feelings after their second kiss, I felt almost like I was playing a new character. In a good way.

Madeline Puri

Season 10 was FUN! Falling in love with Trip gave me yet another angle to work for Kerani. Don't think for a second she'd soften up or anything. She had an opening for a new sparring partner now that she was batting her eyes at Trip instead of batting his balls around like a maniacal cat with a toy.

Austen Hughes

Yes, Peter needed a heavy-duty cup in season 10. I guess nothing cured him of his broken heart quite like having a love-struck, materialistic Indian-American receptionist have at him day in, day out.

If you go back and flip through seasons 3 through 9, you'll discover that Peter and Kerani rarely had shared plotlines, which means Madeline and I hadn't spent nearly as much time on set together as I had spent with either Wade or what's-her-name. That's a shame. Playing against Madeline brought me back into the game after the acting difficulties I faced during the whole Peter/Felicity debacle. Don't get the wrong idea or anything, but working with Madeline may very well be my favorite part of the *Pet Peeves* experience.

Kendra Lewis-Frost

Kerani and Trip radiated when they were being all lovey-dovey. And Kerani and Peter radiated in their contempt for each other with equal heat. When it came down to it, Madeline simply radiated no matter whom she played against. I—and I'm sure half the actresses in Hollywood—have uttered the same curse to the heavens more times than I care to count, but, "Damn you, Julia Louis-Dreyfus, for being so talented!" Really, how many Emmys does one woman need? If only *Pet Peeves* had remained on the air for a twelfth season. Madeline would have stood a fighting chance of walking home with the statue in 2018.

D'Wayne Curtis, writer

Producing season 10 was relatively drama-free. One additional agreement the producers had struck with Bronwyn was she wouldn't appear in every episode. Save for a few *And now a word from our Florida vets* scenes and the occasional call with Peter (always split screen, never shot with the two of them on set together), we focused on getting Trip ready to pop the question.

Bruce Leibowitz

You could have asked me at any point during the run of *Pet Peeves* when it would be time to say goodbye, and I always answered, "The characters will tell me." But I'll let you in on a secret: I always knew they would tell me it was time to end the show when Trip and Kerani walked up the aisle as husband and wife.

At the upfronts in May 2016, the IBS Network broke the news that season 11 would be the last one for Pet Peeves. *And there was much rending of the clothing and inconsolable sobbing. Not everyone took the news quite so hard. One imagines every other network with a show on Tuesday nights at nine thirty popped a champagne cork the day of the announcement.*

Chapter 11
The Eleventh Season

The cast and crew returned to the studio in the summer of 2016 filled with emotion. Determined to savor their remaining time together, they also grappled with thoughts of the ways their lives had changed because of the show and how their lives would change again when the series came to an end.

Kendra Lewis-Frost

Twelve years before the start of our final season, I had been a breakdown writer on a daytime drama. It still boggles the mind to evaluate where my life has taken me. Facing the impending end of my show left me with some big questions to answer: how does one follow being the executive producer of a sitcom when one had never set out to write a sitcom? Should I take another huge leap, reinvent exactly whom Kendra Lewis-Frost is? Will I be able to take a nap in my next life?

Madeline Puri

My agent receives scripts for me to read fairly frequently. I had been turning parts down because I couldn't make another commitment while the show was on the air. When *Pet Peeves* wrapped, I knew, at the very least, I would be able to choose a role in a movie or two. Part of me wanted to put aside ambition in favor of taking the time the following summer and perhaps beyond to be me for a little while. And maybe, just maybe, to find someone nice to date.

Austen Hughes

One thing I definitely wanted to do was do a big comedy tour, maybe even pitch the idea to HBO or another network to film one show. I had new material I was itching to try out. Thank you, Bronwyn, for yet again supplying me with the inspiration!

Moishe Bronfman

My schedule on *Pet Peeves* allowed me to keep a few balls in the air over the years. I made my Broadway debut in the role of the Rabbi in the 2015 revival of *Fiddler on the Roof*. At this point, I plan to continue to pursue stage roles rather than to look for a role in another series. I've had more fun in the theater than a man should be allowed. And my mother would die happy if I were cast as Tevye in the next Broadway revival of *Fiddler*. Just putting it out there for any would-be producers.

Bronwyn Davies

I definitely had planned on building my film career even before *Pet Peeves* wrapped. It's kind of funny how the news about the show coming to an end affected me. I changed my mind about the number of episodes I wanted to appear in during the final season. I knew the show would receive lots of media buzz in the last season, and I didn't want to miss out on the publicity by not starring in every episode.

Bruce Leibowitz

The outline for the final season all but wrote itself. Bronwyn may have thought she had the power to change the outcome, but I was two steps ahead of her.

Austen Hughes

Bruce had warned me Felicity would be coming back to Califon for several episodes, meaning she and I would be in scenes together again. Bring it. I had my comedy set notebook and a pencil at the ready.

Wade Hanson

Getting to plan my TV wedding put a bounce in my step. Being unmarried myself, it sure got me thinking about how maybe it's relationships that stay with us through life, not things or jobs.

Madeline Puri

I was pleased for Kerani, getting a second chance at her happily-ever-after. I will admit that her wedding forced me to contemplate what I had sacrificed for the show. I was thirty-three when we shot the first episodes of season 11, hardly over-the-hill romantically, but I had to wonder if perhaps my rule about not dating actors had exerted excessive influence over my prolonged singlehood.

Austen Hughes

It made me sad for Peter to have his marriage end. Here's this guy who wanted nothing more than to have a wife and two point five kids. He came from a small town where childhood sweethearts grew into couples who celebrated golden anniversaries together. Failing in his own marriage short-circuited his brain. He wasn't built for divorce. And Califon wasn't built to endure an untethered Peter. Not with big plans to celebrate its centennial on the horizon and a river for him to fall into when all eyes were on the town.

My parents had split up when I was in junior high. I still managed to grow up dreaming I would settle down with a woman who wouldn't mind being married to the world's greatest stand-up comedian. I knew, realistically, my career choice fated me to a lonely life. But then my career took an unexpected path, and here I am, leading the pretty normal life of a guy with a mortgage and an eleven-year stretch of steady work. Obviously, the stable lifestyle hasn't been a boon to my dating life.

Kendra Lewis-Frost

Madeline set me up on a blind date with a woman who owns a shop in her neighborhood. Alice and I began dating in June 2016. She's a fake taxidermist. Well, she's a real person, of course. And she creates animal sculptures in traditional taxidermy poses. The animals she sculpts are fake. She fabricates them from wire and plaster skeletons covered in felt and faux fur. They're quite expensive and quite popular. Isn't it interesting how we've both found animal-adjacent career success?

Bronwyn Davies

Because I hadn't been around the set much in season 10, I felt a little like an outsider when I came back to the show full-time. It was weird having to do scenes with Austen again. I was sorry for how I had treated him. He didn't deserve any of it.

Austen is totally the guy you're supposed to marry. When I look back at what bothered me about him when we dated, I realize he was doing normal couple things like wanting to stay home with me. Part of me still wants what he offered me back then, but part of me understands it would never be any different between us. One of these days he'll meet a woman who will never grow tired of him cracking himself up when he makes fart noises. I'm just not ready to watch him fall in love with another woman.

Two relationships heading in opposite directions had bookended season 10. While Kerani and Trip sped toward their future together and Peter and Felicity prepared to divorce, the writers and actors milked the final season for every drop of fulfillment in the relationships they had with their coworkers and the show.

Kendra Lewis-Frost

From July into early fall and again from March until we shot the series finale, I walked into the writers' room each day with a hyper-conscious mindset as if willing myself not to miss a moment. At some point, the demands of the job took over and I simply walked into the room because I had to go to work. It's just as well; worrying about what was to come had kept me from experiencing life to its fullest.

Madeline Puri

Do you remember your last summer before going off to college? Being eighteen, every little bit of being alive is amplified. My friends and I clung to each other as if we'd never be together again. We were onto something, although it was something less obvious than what we could comprehend. We're still friends to this day, but we've spent far more time shaping our own lives apart from each other than we had spent together in our youth.

Maybe a better way to say it is we parted at the point in our lives when we were beginning to be responsible for what our lives were to become. Our separation happened at the true start of our lives. That is kind of what the last year on set felt like. Being somewhat wiser than I had been at the end of high school, I knew what we stood to lose when we were no longer creating a show together. We would go on to form new families on the next set. But my *Pet Peeves* family will always occupy a large section of my heart, no matter where I wind up.

Austen Hughes

I directed two episodes during the final season. The first of them was "The Postnup." For better or for worse (apt choice of words, I know), Peter and Felicity's signing of their divorce papers brought up a lot of sentimental issues for me. I'm supposed to be the clown on the set, but I have a maudlin streak about a mile wide running through me. I wanted to explore what kind of pathos and regret I could wring out of the scene where Peter and Felicity would begin their lives no longer legally connected to each other.

Bruce Leibowitz

I wrote the script for "The Postnup." As I see it, marriages can end one of three ways: with full-on acrimony, with apathy, or in that weird middle ground where the former spouses wonder if they made the right choice. Only one of these scenarios makes a compelling story. I may write sitcoms, but the drama behind a good "What if?" is powerful in any kind of script.

Madeline Puri

I don't think I'm alone in saying how nervous I was when we rehearsed and shot the third episode of the last season. It was Bronwyn's first time back with the full cast. It ended up being one of her strongest performances. She truly deserved the People's Choice Award she won that season.

Austen Hughes

The years melted away during the bedroom scene. My best moments as an actor are when I forget I'm acting. I go to what I call the *real zone*. Even though I've memorized lines someone else had written, when I deliver them, it's as if I'm saying whatever pops into my head at that moment and feeling whatever my character feels.

The scene began with Felicity and Peter sitting on the edge of the bed, taking a little breather before getting naked and down to business. They compare the desperation with which they had lunged for each other's lips down in the kitchen minutes earlier to a sex scene back at the beginning of the second season.

Bronwyn Davies

It took a bit for me to remember what it had been like to shoot the episode when Felicity and Peter did it in the back room of the clinic, the room where the animal patients are hanging out in their crates. The sound editor had a ball with that episode. Listen closely, and besides hearing cats meowing and dogs barking, you'll hear ducks, sheep, and even an elephant. The sounds are subtle, a barely perceivable presence in the background. Oh, sorry. Back to your question. Anyway, Austen and I were all hot and heavy in the second season, so it was pretty easy to get in the mood for the scene.

Austen Hughes

Peter's desperate to get his ex-wife ex-clothed. She, meanwhile, is blabbing away, using their conversation as a stall technique. He figures maybe what would put her back in the mood was a soundtrack. I went through my catalog of animal noises, making the moves on her while honking and bleating away. It had been a long time since I had been able to make Bronwyn choke and bray with laughter. In an instant, I forgot about the later version of Bronwyn. I reconnected to her, to the charming version of the woman I had known for over a dozen years.

In addition to strengthening their bonds, the cast and crew shared the set with a parade of bold-faced names throughout their final season.

Wade Hanson

A really cool thing about being on a hit TV show is big-named actors want to be guest stars on it. As awesome as it was to be a part of the best cast in television, it was also tons of fun when someone new came around. And in the final season, everyone wanted to be on our show. Some came on to play cameos, usually in the roles of pet owners. But on occasion, they'd portray a character connected to one of the leads. Barry Bostwick ended up playing my grandfather in the wedding episode, for instance.

Moishe Bronfman

Barry's about ten years older than me. I kept my teasing to a minimum about having such a young dad. I'm sure he was already sick of our non-stop choruses of "Dammit, Janet!" Best not to scare away the stars.

Madeline Puri

The casting director had set up an audition to cast someone to play my cousin in two episodes: the one about my bridal shower and then at the wedding itself. Then she gets a call from Mindy Kaling's agent, asking if we had a spot for her client.

Mindy Kaling was not available for comment.

Kendra Lewis-Frost

We needed a madcap script for "The Bridal Shower," which meant we turned to Austen. Between the content of his script and the energy coming out of Mindy and Madeline, we were strapped to a meteor during their scenes, one veering toward explosive destruction. I suspect the blooper reel from this episode is second in length only to "The Comfort Room" outtakes.

Emma Bates

If you've ever imagined how fun it is to work on a TV show, you've probably imagined an episode along the lines of "The Bridal Shower." The days on set can be long and sometimes kind of boring until they're crazy intense. But acting in a scene like the bridal shower scene is why I'm convinced I'll never find a cooler job. The cast members of *Pet Peeves* were such amazing colleagues, but then Mindy Kaling or another guest star comes in and makes the experience ten times as good.

Bronwyn Davies

Felicity was one of Kerani's bridesmaids, so she came back to Califon for the bridal shower. She wanted to host it, and Peter had agreed to let her use their house. When I read the script, I thought maybe it was a bad idea to have agreed to reconnect with everyone at the show. I had a sneaking suspicion Mindy's character was sort of Austen's imagination gone wild, a caricature of how he saw me.

Madeline Puri

Mindy's character, Sarita, was a few years older than Kerani and obviously had played a major role in shaping Kerani into the lovely, mild-mannered woman we knew her to be. Not. Sarita out-Keranied Kerani. Sarita had never married, though not for a lack of trying. And attending a second bridal shower for her cousin brought out every ounce of her insecurity.

All it takes to get me to laugh myself silly is to conjure an image of Sarita leaving the party, a paper plate topped with ribbons tied onto her head and a partially unwrapped gift meant for Kerani sticking out of her oversized handbag.

Bronwyn Davies

Working with Madeline, et al. ended up being better than I had thought it would be. I suppose I was paranoid before we shot the episode. I never would have unwrapped Madeline's gifts or bossed her around at her own party. And Mindy was so awesome to work with, too. Here, let me show you a selfie she let me take of the two of us.

To demonstrate that Pet Peeves *could surprise its audience even at the end, Leibowitz made the decision to film the hour-long series finale before a live studio audience.*

Bruce Leibowitz

Craziest thing I could have done, inviting an audience into a studio after shooting an audience-free show for the past nine years. Logistics were a nightmare. Cameras would only be shooting from one angle—from behind the audience—which changed the look of the sets from our normal multi-camera shots. We had to rebuild the sets in order for the live audience to be able to see the action while it played out on different sets. And now we had to shoot scenes in the order viewers would watch them. It would be akin to having sex with the lights on for the first time with a new partner.

Kendra Lewis-Frost

I lived in terror of our final episode throughout the entire season. Bruce must have been in a deep Zen state when he dreamed it up, immune to the effect of chaos. He wrote the episode, brought in a director who could handle the stress, and rehearsed the crap out of cast and crew, convinced it would be nothing to pull it all off.

Wade Hanson

I had gotten used to our sets being empty when the studio was quiet, so anytime I'd be in there, everything was normal like when you walk around your own house when you're alone. Before the final episode, it was different. A lot of the action was in Trip and Madeline's apartment, as usual. But they had to change where the walls were and eliminate one of them for the audience to be able to watch the action. It was familiar and unfamiliar all at the same time. One new addition to the studio was the rows of chairs up on a platform facing the sets. I hadn't done theater since back when I played Qaddafi ages ago, but it evoked the memories I had of being on stage. The empty chairs gave me a sense of anticipation like I had felt before opening night. It totally got my nerves going.

Bronwyn Davies

The wedding sets killed me! Trip's parents offered to pay for the wedding, and Kerani made sure no expense was spared. The ceremony was at St. Patrick's Cathedral, and they held their reception at a private club in Manhattan. The crew built both sets for just this one episode. For Peter and Felicity's wedding, the crew temporarily repurposed the Copelands' veterinary clinic set for our wedding reception. They sure know how to make a girl feel special!

Austen Hughes

It would be impossible for an audience to see action on all the sets during a live taping. We filmed live on the sets where multiple scenes would be shot. The other scenes had been pre-shot and were shown to the audience in sequence on monitors set up in the studio. Of course, since we'd now have what amounted to a laugh track during the live scenes, the editors had to drop a laugh track into the pre-taped scenes.

Elvin Shatsky

It took them eleven years, but they finally came around to my point of view on the laugh track.

Austen Hughes

We didn't have the room to welcome a huge audience. The people in attendance were connected to the show somehow, people who had sacrificed for the show because of their loved ones' crazy schedules. Bruce opened up the seating first to guests of the camera operators, the boom operators, the lighting crew, and so forth. These folks were the heart and soul of our show. We'd go home at seven at night; they'd be in the studio until three in the morning, getting the equipment ready for the next day. Except for Dave, one of the lighting guys. Dude's a real slacker.

Bruce Leibowitz

He said what about Dave? Wait a second. We didn't have a lighting guy named Dave.

You can talk to a man like Tank Watson, one of our camera operators, and learn a little about him over the years. I knew he was married, knew the names of his kids. But after all the time we had worked together, I had never met his wife. *Pet Peeves* was first and foremost about family. Meeting the real families behind my work family meant a great deal to me.

Bronwyn Davies

I had all sorts of people I figured I could invite, but they limited the cast members to one guest each. I kind of regret not bringing someone with me for whom the experience might have meant more. I don't know who that would have been, though. I ended up bringing a guy I had started dating the previous weekend. Blake something?

Austen Hughes

Biggest surprise of the finale didn't have anything to do with a cat head. It was Wade's guest. Dude got married behind our backs.

Wade Hanson

I'm a pretty private guy. And I was brought up not to think kindly on people of my ilk. I'm not talking about actors, by the way. I had spent years wrestling with a realization: I'm gay. I came out to myself just a few years ago. Justin is only the second guy I dated, but we knew right away we would fall in love. It was after they had announced the show was ending that I realized he, like the show, represented happiness and stability for me. Justin made me the happiest man on the planet when he agreed to be my husband. We had a small ceremony at a friend's home up in Hudson, New York last December. We're interested in buying a house up in the area.

Kendra Lewis-Frost

I can reflect on it now and marvel at how Bruce managed to take a show on its deathbed before its third season and make it look brand new. It's no wonder why the show not only won its second Emmy in 2017, but for the first time, it won the best director and writer Emmys the same year. Of course, those were both for the final episode.

Beyond the logistics of filming a live show, the format presented hurdles for the cast, as well.

Austen Hughes

Ours was not a "live in front of a studio audience" kind of cast. While most of us were typically on our best professional behavior, striving to get a scene right on the first take, we all had our moments when we needed additional takes. You don't want to move onto the next scene too quickly; maybe you'd end up leaving something on the table if you settled for the first take. Sometimes your head isn't in the game and it takes longer than usual to shoot the scene. And sometimes, when the humor gets out of hand, well, the harder we try not to laugh, the likelier one of us is going to blow it.

Wade Hanson

I'm probably the first to start giggling. Madeline is usually the last. Austen can hang in there longer than most of us, but when he loses it, you might as well send us home. He doesn't even try to stop himself. He'll repeat whatever made us laugh, adding in an even sillier element the next take.

Madeline Puri

One of the first scenes in the finale was the gang hanging out in the clinic. Since we would be shooting a single scene on the waiting room set, it was one of the scenes we had pre-taped, thank goodness.

Bronwyn Davies

It was just the six principals in the scene. Madeline was sitting at her desk, Wade stood right behind her, Robert and Emma were in front of the desk, I was a couple of feet off to the side. Austen comes into the waiting room with a wedding present for Trip and Kerani. It's wrapped in this gorgeous silver moiré paper. They're supposed to unwrap the gift, a fancy silver bowl a local artisan had crafted specifically for them. Wade lifts the top off the box, peels away the tissue layers, and reaches inside the box to pull out the gift only to withdraw his hand and squeal.

Austen Hughes

I'm quite sure I've never heard a baritone transform so quickly into a shrew with an attitude problem.

Bronwyn Davies

The sound Wade made! And people make fun of me for the way I laugh.

Wade Hanson

I expected to feel the cold metal of the prop bowl. Instead, my fingers grazed on a clump of damp fur. Instinctively, I grasped for whatever I had touched, and it was kind of mushy. It freaked me out big time.

Madeline Puri

The cameras had stopped rolling, and we were dying to know why Wade reacted as he did. I overturned the box onto the desk, and out rolls a cat's head. No body, just the head. Emma, Robert, and I thought it was gross. But Bronwyn, Wade, and Austen erupted into laughter.

Wade Hanson

It was the cat's head from the pilot. Well, not the same one. It took a few minutes for Austen to fess up he had switched out the bowl for the head before the props team had wrapped the gift.

Kendra Lewis-Frost

I'll admit it. I thought it was hysterical. But we did need to return to work.

Bronwyn Davies

The property master found the bowl, and we got in place for another take. The thing is, no actor can come back after having watched someone open a similarly wrapped gift that held a severed cat's head. At some point, either while Madeline was slicing open the tape with a fingernail or while Wade was pulling back the tissue, someone on set would snicker. One of the props people would rewrap the gift, and we'd start again. They ran out of wrapping paper before we finally got a good take. If you take a close peek when you watch a rerun of the finale, you'll notice the gift is wrapped in paper emblazoned with balloons and the words *Happy Birthday*.

Bruce Leibowitz

I'm not sure I have a meditation to recite that would have rescued me from spinning out of control had they pulled a similar stunt during the live taping.

The final scene, along with one supporting scene, had also been pre-taped. Only those involved in the scene knew in advance how the show would end, and they each protected the plot secrets with their lives.

Kendra Lewis-Frost

Bruce and I had one disagreement about a storyline in the finale. I understand his point of view; I certainly recognize what it added to the finale. But I wish we had chosen a different path to our destination.

Bruce Leibowitz

Before the nonsense with Bronwyn happened a few seasons back, we had outlined a natural progression for Felicity and Peter's arc through the end of the show. We had to chuck it all out when they got divorced, but I saw an opportunity to resurrect one element from our earlier plot.

Kendra Lewis-Frost

Not only did I hate the particular plotline he suggested, but I also had the statistics to show him how unrealistic his idea was. None of what I shared mattered to him. On this one plot, he would not budge.

Bruce Leibowitz

I didn't want to give our viewers a tidy ending. I

needed to introduce the idea that multiple endings were possible. What I suggested became the hook we needed.

Kendra Lewis-Frost

To my taste, he used one of the most hackneyed plot devices on TV, one every writer trots out when they need to fabricate tension. It is all the more infuriating to me in the way it weakens the female characters. How many shows with a white, college-educated, middle-class, unmarried female lead have her experience an unplanned pregnancy? Sometimes I get the feeling it's every one of them, which statistically doesn't gel with the actual percentages of unplanned pregnancy for this demographic.

Felicity was in her late thirties at the end of *Pet Peeves*. I'm sorry, but the image of her alone in the bathroom in the scene from earlier in the final episode where she is surrounded by a pharmacy's worth of pregnancy tests, all of them positive, could not have been more illogical or unoriginal to me.

Austen Hughes

Everyone involved with the pregnancy test scene and the final scene had been sworn to secrecy. Even though both scenes were shown to the audience during the live taping, Bruce wouldn't let the cast watch the first one. Before they showed the final scene to the audience, he let us in on what had gone down in the bathroom scene.

Bronwyn Davies

I loved how the last scene came out. I shot it on location in Califon. It was my first visit to the town. Turns out, the place is really cute.

Madeline Puri

It was a three-hanky kind of evening when we shot the live episode. I teared up for the first time when Trip and Kerani said their vows. Wade did, too. But when we watched the last scene, I was bawling my eyes out. Felicity hadn't told any of her friends about the pregnancy tests. Everyone had said their goodbyes at the reception. Felicity's headed back to Florida, Trip and Kerani are headed off to Europe for their honeymoon. But then Felicity's on the walkway leading up to the front door of her former house—where Peter still lives. It's twilight. She's standing on the walkway, gazing up at the front door. You see her from the back. She appears small and unsure of herself. Slowly, the camera pulls back. Parked in front of the house is a U-Haul. The end.

Chapter 12
The Unanswered Questions

A year after the finale, I again met with the cast and crew members to reminisce about their experiences and to catch up with them about where they are today. The first question I posed to each person was, "Which was your favorite episode?"

Wade Hanson

As I told you before, "The Comfort Room" was probably my favorite. Of course, everyone thought it was stinking hilarious, but it kind of represented something else for me, too. The first season had been such a great challenge for me, for the entire cast and crew. What did I know about being funny? And since we shot only six episodes our first season, we didn't quite believe the show had a chance. "The Comfort Room," which aired in the second season, represented the moment I first felt any true ownership of my role and the series. I finally understood how we had each brought our individual talents to the table and how the show was better for it.

Madeline Puri

I know I'm not going out on a limb when I say my favorite episode was "The Gnome Home Massacre." The idea was born out of such a perfect day. And I loved how instead of using the town of Califon as a punchline, we used it for inspiration. Kendra and I have been back to hike the Columbia Trail. I'm happy to say the gnomes have rebuilt their homes and are thriving.

Emma Bates

I'm partial to "The Chew Toy." Is it selfish of me to pick one I starred in? I was pregnant with kid number one when we shot it during our ninth season. While KellyAnne would wear bits and pieces of costumes while on duty at the clinic—a headband with ears on it or maybe a tail pinned to her scrubs—she hadn't gone full-on cosplay since "The Comfort Room." The original script had me wearing big, fluffy slippers in the shape of bear paws. But since I was showing when we shot "The Chew Toy," they put me in a beaver costume to hide my belly.

The premise of the story was a Great Dane with anxiety issues would mistake me in my costume for a chew toy. Don't worry about me harming the baby or anything for the shot where the dog dragged me out of the clinic and behind a tree. They made a life-sized KellyAnne doll for the shot. But anyway, I was wrestling with an assortment of anxiety issues regarding becoming a mom. The scene near the end where the dog is lying in my lap, happily chewing on what was left of the beaver's tail, was better for me than therapy. I scratched the dog behind his ears, kind of zoned out on the rhythmic movements of his jaw against my thigh, and for the first time, believed I would have the power to soothe a creature in need.

Would you care to reveal any behind-the-scenes secrets?

Kendra Lewis-Frost

Did you know that *Pet Peeves* played matchmaker to one couple in addition to Austen and Bronwyn? Valerie Jones, our veterinary expert, met and fell in love with John Ellington, our sound editor. They married four or five years ago. Lovely wedding!

Bronwyn Davies

Do you remember the sullen-faced teenager in the waiting room with her family in the third episode of the first season? That's Erika Edmonds. Yes, *the* Erika Edmonds. She's one of the highest paid actors in Hollywood now. She had only two lines on that episode, but I remember her being really difficult to work with. Demanding, unprepared. Whatever.

Bruce Leibowitz

I don't know if you remember the story of when we hired Laird Belmont to play Archibald Edward Quinn, Duke's father and Trip's grandfather. This goes back to maybe the fourth season. We came up with the idea of having the paterfamilias retire to Califon. I thought it would be fun to trot out another member of the older generation as a recurring character. And Belmont was such a get.

Well, he comes in the second day with the remnants of the previous night's festivities still sloshing around in his gut. We had to send him home to dry out. He was fine when he came in on day three. But then he helped himself to a liquid lunch. He somehow managed to pull off his lines during the taping. We had to kill the idea of Quinn I moving to Califon. That's why we had to bring in Bostwick to play the grandfather in the finale.

Austen Hughes

How about the couch with nine lives? Did anyone else mention it? The taupe suede couch from "The Comfort Room" made its debut in the Quinns' living room on *Another Day to Live.* The set crew had found it in Moishe's dressing room. To save money, they borrowed it for a few scenes. *Pet Peeves* shows up at the same studio to shoot its first season, and there's the couch. We used it on multiple sets, including in the comfort room and, after the set designers threw a burgundy slipcover on it, in Trip and Peter's living room.

There was this one scene late in the series where Peter and Kerani were stuck sitting next to each other on the couch at the apartment. They're full of resentment for being so close together, sort of paralyzed by their mutual fear of making contact with each other. Well, there's this broken spring on the couch—that old couch didn't owe us a cent by this point—and Madeline landed on it wrong, sending her into my lap. She was slow to sit upright because she was laughing so hard. She wears this perfume. I'm no good at identifying scents, but it's floral without being cloyingly sweet. More like fresh. Really honest. Natural. A lot like her. Breathing in her scent, being warmed by her presence, all to the accompaniment of her laughter... Man, this memory has nothing to do with the show, does it?

As I was saying, Kendra decided to hunt down the couch when we moved to the studio in Brooklyn. It was still at our old studio in Queens. They sold it to her for a couple hundred bucks. When we wrapped after season 11, she brought it home with her. I hope her dry cleaner was able to fumigate the stale fart smells out of it.

Madeline Puri

You want me to reveal the secrets behind our show? Brace yourself for a dose of truth, people. Television is real. Every last thing you saw on *Pet Peeves* happened. Kerani is an actual person. Trip Quinn is a licensed veterinarian. No? Okay. How about the way you can tell when one of the actors was suppressing a laugh in a take that made it to air? Usually, if one of us was going to lose it, the take would be ruined. Someone—usually Wade or Bronwyn—would crack. Austen could keep it together better than any of us, though. In the couple of episodes where he's fighting the urge to laugh, his suppressed laughter usually made it into the final cut.

Check out "The Flea Bag," for instance. The legendary Alice Simpson plays a woman who brings her toy poodle in for a checkup. The dog scratches once. Ms. Simpson scratches once. The appointment continues. They each scratch again. She has this expression on her face conveying, "I'm a woman of means and class. I have never so much as touched fingernail to skin in public in my life." Peter finally brings up the possibility the dog has fleas. By now, she is having a scratch-fest as no one has ever scratched before, still maintaining her haughty demeanor.

Ms. Simpson elevated scratching to an art form. You can actually follow the pacing of a joke within each gesture, how it moves from set up to punchline. She'd have a subtle go at a patch of skin on her neck followed by a vigorous brush against the outside of her leg. She'd raise her hand, talons bared, toward her face. You'd anticipate another scratch. Instead, she'd swipe hair from her face. She'd wait a beat. And then she'd go to town on her scalp. Austen is watching her, plotting when to say his next line so as not to step on her shtick.

It's after the hair swipe when he starts to break. Check it out. He bites his finger. That's his tell. Any time the tip of his finger is between his teeth, where he appears to be thinking really hard, he's actually on the verge of cracking up. You can see this cute crinkling around his eyes when he does it, too.

What are you up to today? What comes next?

Bruce Leibowitz

I spent several months visiting ashrams around the world after we wrapped. My creative brain needed to experience a cleansing to remove every last trace of *Pet Peeves* from its folds. While on a two-day fast at the Desert Ashram in Shitim, Israel, an idea came to me. It remains a private thought, one not ready to be released into the world. But between you and me, it's possible you'll witness my return to network TV in the 2019-2020 season.

Kendra Lewis-Frost

What came next wasn't a daytime drama or a sitcom; it was a novel. Well, it's trying to become a novel. Writer's block isn't my plague of choice. I suffer from having an overabundance of ideas. I've written a manuscript of over two hundred thousand words. It wants to be a time travel epic, a journey into one's self, a satire. My literary agent is hacking away at it at the moment.

Blaine Carson

Things had been a little slow, work-wise, after I shot my scenes for the finale of *Pet Peeves*, but I have a new project I'm finding very exciting. It reaches my fans directly via their phones. No two days are alike, and I get to read scripts written by multiple writers. What I like best about it is how authentic my voice can be.

Robert Chang

Are you familiar with this new app, Cameo? I found our boy Blaine's profile on it. The deal is you can hire a celebrity to record a video message to send to one of your contacts. You choose from mostly B-List or B-List wannabes profiles and then you tell them what you want them to say. Lots of contestants from RuPaul's Drag Race do it and charge, like, twenty bucks per message. Blaine's going rate is $125. You should ask him how that's working for him.

Me? Nah, I'm not available for hire on the site. I found out about it when I wanted to send a funny birthday message to a friend. Acting-wise, I picked up guest spots on two of last season's shows on IBS. I'll be appearing in three or four episodes of a new show next season. Maybe it will turn into a bigger role.

Bronwyn Davies

While I'm waiting for the perfect movie script to come along, I've been focusing on my Instagram account. I'm up to nearly a quarter million followers, give or take fifty thousand. They may not be Beyoncé numbers or even up there with actors like Reese Witherspoon, but I anticipate that if I land the right project, I can build on it.

Another thing I'd totally be into doing would be filling in for daytime talk show hosts when they're on vacation. So, Hoda, Kelly, Kathy Lee, if you're reading this, you know where to find me!

Emma Bates

As you can see, I'm kind of pregnant. Well, I'm definitely pregnant. This baby debuts in August. Next fall I'll figure out if I can juggle two kids and my career.

Moishe Bronfman

I've pulled out my rabbinical robes for another run of *Fiddler*. We open on the Fourth of July at the Museum of Jewish Heritage. You'd think it would be easy to reprise a familiar role, but here's the thing: we're doing the whole *megillah* in Yiddish. My darling wife Abigail, who wouldn't have known what a knish was had one bitten her on the *tuchas* before we married, helped me to learn my lines. My mother is *kvelling*. She has her front-row ticket for opening night displayed in the center of the pictures of her grandchildren on her refrigerator. It warms my heart to see Mama so happy.

Wade Hanson

It might sound bananas to you, but I'm taking a hiatus from acting. My husband and I moved up to Hudson, New York. Justin had applied for a teaching position at their high school last spring and is now teaching ninth and tenth grade English. Over the winter, I stumbled on a local theater company in need of a new director, so I volunteered to step in. We did a run of *The Fantasticks* in the spring, and we're finalizing plans for which shows to mount in the coming season.

Austen Hughes

I'm at the tail end of a yearlong tour for my solo comedy show. It will be available for streaming on Netflix in October. When I'm back in town for good, I have a meeting with Netflix executives to discuss a new project. I have it in my mind it will be a half-hour show, a single-camera comedy but not a sitcom. Sort of a bittersweet comedy. But right now, I'm glad to be home in New York for a week before heading back out on the road. I've never been so excited to have my teeth cleaned or launder a load of shirts at my local dry cleaners.

Madeline Puri

I have a movie coming out in December, a rom-com. It's a sweet film, and I had a blast shooting it. But right now, I'm taking my time choosing my next project.

Last year, I had visited my cousin's Girl Scout troop. I went in thinking I'd tell the girls about acting on TV and in movies, discuss the importance of being on time, being prepared, getting along with everyone, you know, basic career advice. But these girls don't need to listen to some Hollywood star brag about her success. Here they are, middle schoolers, and they have already done these amazing things like creating anti-bullying campaigns in their schools and planting community gardens.

I was a Girl Scout way back when. The scouting experience has become an even more powerful tool to help these young women grow up to be badasses. I walked away from the meeting with a strong desire to become involved with the organization. To that end, I've joined the Board of Directors of the Girl Scouts of Greater New York. I'm eager to see where our ideas today will take the next generation of Girl Scouts!

While most of the interviews conducted for this oral history began with similar, pre-written questions, the answers the cast and crew members provided would themselves often lead to a new line of inquiry. Many of those questions had remained unanswered a year after the project began, thus requiring follow-up interviews. I've included the transcripts from three such interviews below.

Interviewer: May we go back to a difficult time for you, the period leading up to the contract negotiations through your return in season 11?

Bronwyn Davies: What, are you my therapist now? JK! No, you're right. I probably do owe everyone an explanation. So, when I was a freshman in high school, I had a crush on a senior, Jake Adams. But then he asked my sister Megan to the prom. And she went with him.

I: Had you told your sister that you liked him? Was she aware of how her actions affected you?

BD: No. I never told her. That's not really the point of the story, anyway. The real story is Jake was pretty drunk when he drove her home from the after party. Megan got out of the car in front of our house. I guess he didn't realize she wasn't totally out of the car, and he took off, dragging her along for about a block. She died pretty quickly, they said.

I: I'm so sorry to hear your story. Losing a sibling so young would have been a lot for anyone to deal with.

BD: I know! I spent the next three years living in the shadow of my dead sister at school. They held an all-school assembly the week after prom to pay tribute to Megan, and they made a whole display cabinet of pictures of her and her field hockey uniform and other mementos. The display may still be there. It was in a hallway right by where my locker used to be.

I: Oh.

BD: When Madeline joined the cast, it was like Megan all over again. Madeline's so pretty, Madeline's so funny. Here, Madeline, have all the awards. When Kerani and Felicity had a scene together, Kerani got all the good lines. I had to act the part of the sweet little country girl while she ran roughshod over me. And have you ever seen the way she looks at Austen?

I: I'm not sure I had ever noticed.

BD: Most people wouldn't. You won't see lust in her eyes. But it's like he's a dose of Xanax. When she looks at him, she has this sort of mellow, happy thing settling into her expression. Like I said, it's kind of subtle.

* * *

Interviewer: In addition to working on movies and for the Girl Scouts, is love on the horizon? I do remember you being adamant about not dating actors when we first started to talk. Does that rule still hold?

Madeline Puri: I'm not sure. I don't trust relationships that begin on the set. They tend to burn out quickly. I have wondered if perhaps I've been too cynical, though. For every Elizabeth Taylor or Angelina Jolie, you'd have successful couples like Tim Robbins and Susan Sarandon. But then they went and split up on me. At least Megan Mullally and Nick Offerman are still adorably loved up. I'm not ruling out actors. I'm just not going to hold my breath that I could find true love with one.

I: Returning to my original question, are love and marriage on the horizon?

MP: I'm single, big surprise. I don't mind being single; it's better than going on bad dates. But I do want to fall in love. My parents have been married for nearly forty years. I want what they have. Funny as it may sound, I think *Pet Peeves* has taught me a thing or two about what it must be like to be loved.

I: Are you referring to the impact that falling in love with Trip had on Kerani?

MP: No, that's not it, although by the point they fell in love, I had found my source of inspiration for my love scenes. It came from watching Austen, as Peter, in the early seasons when he walked into a room where he knew he'd see Felicity. He does this thing where he holds onto the doorknob behind his back with both hands, lowers his chin, scans the room, and then casts a shy yet thoroughly contented smile on Felicity when they finally make eye contact. I'd melt to be on the receiving end of such a gaze.

I: You mean you hope Austen will gaze at you with the same sentiment in his expression?

MP: No! I'm sorry. I didn't mean to deny it so emphatically.

* * *

Interviewer: I wanted to compliment you on one exquisite detail present in your first outing as a director.

The lighting on Trip and Kerani during their first kiss was absolutely transporting. I felt like angels were smiling down on the couple in that moment.

Austen Hughes: You noticed that, did you? I collaborated with Sid, one of the lighting guys, on it. It took us forever to achieve the perfect effect. I felt bad, keeping him at the studio for hours after we had wrapped for the day.

I: I definitely consider it to be worth the effort. And you chose to use it again on each of the additional episodes you directed.

AH: Are you serious? You can't be telling me you went back and studied every episode I directed just to prepare for our interview.

I: Let's just say something another person mentioned to me piqued my curiosity. You used the same lighting technique each and every time Kerani was in a scene. But I never saw any other character similarly illuminated. Would you care to, heh, heh, shed some light on my observation?

AH: No. What would be the point? She doesn't date actors.

ACT [III]

Scene [14]

OPEN ON:

EXT. STUDIO COMPLEX IN BROOKLYN - DAY

CUT TO:

INT. EMPTY SOUNDSTAGE - SAME

AUSTEN HUGHES wanders through an empty
studio, taking in his surroundings with
a sense of awakened memory. A taupe
suede couch in the center of the studio
attracts his attention. He sits on it,
running his fingers against the
upholstery. A single fixture casts a
spotlight on him. The banging of a
heavy door closing echoes within the
studio.

                    AUSTEN
        I'm in here.

[From offstage]

                    MADELINE
        Good. I thought I was late.

MADELINE PURI enters the soundstage.

295

AUSTEN

Wait a second. I wasn't
expecting you.

MADELINE

Austen?

AUSTEN

Last time I checked.

MADELINE

What are you doing here?

AUSTEN

I'm waiting to do a final
interview. Why are you here?

MADELINE

Same reason. Something's
wrong. I've always done my
interviews alone.

AUSTEN

Me, too.

MADELINE

Maybe you got your dates
mixed up.

AUSTEN

Why assume I'm the one who
mixed up the date? Maybe
you did. It's Sunday, right?

MADELINE

No, it's Thursday, you doofus.

AUSTEN

I knew that. Just checking if you did. But what's with you calling me a doofus? Don't tell me everyone's been referring to me as a doofus in their interviews.

MADELINE

It may have come up once or twice. But I swear it was always when we were talking about Peter, not you.

AUSTEN

I'm not a doofus, I'll have you know. I may be a dolt or perhaps a boob, but I'm definitely not a doofus.

MADELINE

You said boob.

AUSTEN

So did you.

AUSTEN and MADELINE cover their mouths in mock embarrassment.

AUSTEN

Hey, potty mouth. Why don't
you have a seat while we're
waiting for the interviewer?

MADELINE sits next to AUSTEN on the
couch. A second light illuminates her.
Dust motes dance in its beam.

MADELINE

Is this *the* couch?

AUSTEN

I'm pretty sure it is. Let
me check.

AUSTEN buries his nose in a throw
pillow and scoots his backside around,
evaluating each sensation.

AUSTEN

If it is, Kendra managed to
detoxify it. Ah. There it
is, the broken spring. My
butt confirms this is indeed
the same couch.

MADELINE

I remember that spring. I
believe it sent me tumbling
into your lap once.

AUSTEN

Cheeky little devil.

MADELINE

Speaking of cheeky, I never knew your butt was an expert in such matters.

AUSTEN

I assure you my butt is an expert in many matters. Geez, did I just say that? See? I told you I'm a boob.

MADELINE

Enough with the body parts.

MADELINE checks her watch, AUSTEN looks at his phone. Awkward silence.

AUSTEN

My interview should have started twenty minutes ago. We began our prior interviews on time. Did you receive a text saying anything about a time change?

MADELINE checks her phone.

MADELINE

Nothing. If you have to be somewhere, I'll stay a little while longer and let them know.

                    AUSTEN

    I don't need to be anywhere.

                    MADELINE

    Do you want to be elsewhere?

They study each other's faces for a
moment.
                    AUSTEN

    Nope.

                    MADELINE

    I'm not sure you and I have
    ever hung out, just the two
    of us.

                    AUSTEN

    It's because of that thing I
    do, right?

                    MADELINE

    What thing?

AUSTEN yodels and taps his cheeks
repeatedly with his fingertips.

                    AUSTEN

    That thing.

                    MADELINE

    I've never wanted to mention
    it, but yes.

AUSTEN repeats the gesture, this time tapping her on her face.

> AUSTEN
>
> Does this bother you?

MADELINE giggles and bats at his cheeks.

> MADELINE
>
> Now look what you made me do.

> AUSTEN
>
> I should have warned you. It's contagious.

> MADELINE
>
> Is there a cure?

> AUSTEN
>
> I find if I stay perfectly still and think serious thoughts, the episodes don't last as long.

AUSTEN and MADELINE sit woodenly in silence. MADELINE laughs first.

> AUSTEN
>
> Well, now you've done it. You laughed. There's a forty percent chance it will be incurable.

MADELINE yodels and taps her cheeks with her fingertips. AUSTEN leaps off the couch.

AUSTEN (CONT'D)

No offense, but I have my health to protect.

MADELINE grabs his wrist, pulling him back onto the couch.

MADELINE

I promise I have it under control. Please don't leave.

AUSTEN sits next to her, again studying her face. He gestures to the studio with his hands.

AUSTEN

Do you miss all of this?

MADELINE

Yes.

AUSTEN

Do you miss all of us?

MADELINE

Mostly. No. That's not true. I miss everyone.

AUSTEN

Do you miss anyone in particular?

302

After a pause:

> MADELINE

I miss Rose in the commissary. She knew to scoop out servings of pot roast for me without including any mushrooms. I hate mushrooms, or at least the kinds you'd find lurking in the commissary pot roast.

> AUSTEN

You must be leading a horrific, mushroom-infested existence without a Rose to protect you.

> MADELINE

These have been bleak days for me, yes.

> AUSTEN

I'd eat your castoff mushrooms.

> MADELINE

How was I unaware of your heroic nature?

> AUSTEN

There's plenty about me you don't know.

MADELINE

So I'm coming to realize. A
few minutes ago, I learned
your butt is a furniture
expert, for instance. Sorry,
I didn't mean to bring your
butt into this again.

AUSTEN

It's inescapable. I bring my
butt everywhere I go.

MADELINE checks the time again.

MADELINE

I'm beginning to think we've
been stood up.

AUSTEN ponders her statement. His eyes
widen, and he turns toward MADELINE.

AUSTEN

Maybe we weren't stood up.
It's possible it was always
meant to be the two of us.

MADELINE

What, like I'm supposed to
interview you?

AUSTEN

Interview may be the wrong
word. Did you two ever talk
about me?

MADELINE

Of course we did. How could we not have? We talked about everyone.

AUSTEN

No. That's not what I meant. The interviewer brought up an interesting point when we were together a couple of days ago.

MADELINE

What was it?

AUSTEN

Oh, it was nothing.

MADELINE

Clearly, it was something.

AUSTEN

Oh, all right. I had a sense the interviewer may have known a detail about me, one I didn't want to share with anyone.

MADELINE

Things just got interesting.

AUSTEN

Let's drop it, okay?

                    MADELINE

Now that you mention it, my
last   interview   became   a
little personal, a little
specific near the end, too.

                    AUSTEN

And?

                    MADELINE

You're right. It's nothing.

                    AUSTEN

Well, that was helpful.

                    MADELINE

Wasn't it, though?

Another awkward pause while AUSTEN and
MADELINE retreat into their heads.

                MADELINE (CONT'D)

Are you seeing anyone?

                    AUSTEN

What? No. Are you?

                    MADELINE

I'm rattling around alone in
my house these days. My
brother moved out. He's
engaged.

AUSTEN

Good for him! Nice work if you can get it.

MADELINE

So you're pro-marriage?

AUSTEN

Yeah. I'm a sucker for a good happily-ever-after.

MADELINE

So am I. I guess Bronwyn was never going to be that person for you, was she?

AUSTEN

I wished it had turned differently, at first. But no, she never was going to be the one.

MADELINE

You'll make someone very happy, I'm sure.

AUSTEN

You think so?

MADELINE

Yeah, I do.

AUSTEN's phone vibrates. He pulls out the phone, glances at the screen, and puts the phone in his back pocket, leaning toward MADELINE in the process. The cushions dip toward the center, forcing his shoulder to collide with MADELINE's. They move away from each other as if they had received an electrical shock.

MADELINE (CONT'D)

There's our favorite broken spring again.

AUSTEN moves ever so slightly back toward MADELINE.

AUSTEN

I'll speak to the management about it.

[A beat.]

AUSTEN (CONT'D)

Are actors still on your no-fly list?

MADELINE squirms, moving away from AUSTEN and leaning back into the cushions.

MADELINE

How'd we end up on this topic? Did it come up in one of your interviews?

AUSTEN

No, not in an interview. It just popped into my head.

MADELINE sits forward again.

> MADELINE
>
> I actually talked about my rule in my last interview. It's not set in stone, but if I were going to date an actor, I'd need him to prove he wanted the same thing out of the relationship as me. Like, right from the start and maybe in a bigger way than I'd require from a guy who isn't an actor.

> AUSTEN
>
> What exactly do you want from a relationship?

> MADELINE
>
> I want to fall in love with a man who will be my sun and my moon. I want to be both sun and moon to this proverbial man. Nothing more, nothing less. Oh, and he needs to be funny.

AUSTEN considers her answer. A slight smile tugs at the corners of his lips.

> AUSTEN
>
> The day I met you at your audition was kind of a weird day for Bronwyn and me. We had broken up a few months

earlier, but acting together again reignited the spark in me. In us.

MADELINE

I wasn't sure what the deal was with you guys. You weren't together when we first started shooting, but she made sure I knew you were off limits. That never changed, even after you guys had broken up.

AUSTEN

You think she was jealous of you? Why? It's not like you and I ever flirted with each other or anything. And you had made it very clear you don't date actors.

MADELINE

You hadn't noticed the way she behaved toward me?

AUSTEN

No, not exactly. I had figured that whatever weirdness was going on between the two of you was because you had won an Emmy.

MADELINE

Could be. I remember your breakup being mutual. She

didn't give you any reason to be mad at her, to need to end things, did she?

AUSTEN

Our second break-up was probably the least drama-filled moment between us.

MADELINE

Good. That's what I had hoped.

AUSTEN

What do you mean?

MADELINE

Um, I wouldn't have wanted her to have hurt you.

AUSTEN

That's sweet of you. Let's not talk about Bronwyn anymore if that's okay with you. So, the day we met: what did you think?

MADELINE

It was such a huge day for me. I remember thinking Wade was in over his head. I saw the two of you talking, and then when he came back, we nailed our scene. After watching how amazing you were when you read your lines, I figured out you must have been his Yoda.

AUSTEN

No! You made a *Star Wars* reference? Why did I never know you were a fan?

MADELINE

Come on! I've made *Star Wars* references loads of times.

AUSTEN

Um, no. I would have remembered if you had. You like *Star Wars* AND you think I'm amazing?

MADELINE

Had I known this would be your reaction, maybe I should have brought up my love of *Star Wars* sooner. Or not at all? I'm not sure where I'm headed with my theory.

AUSTEN

I'm glad you brought it up.

MADELINE

You are?

AUSTEN

Absolutely. Tell me about the other times you thought I was amazing.

MADELINE

You were… Wait a second. What are you trying to do?

AUSTEN

I thought you were amazing at your audition. And every day since.

MADELINE

Um…

MADELINE regards him, startled. AUSTEN reaches for her hand. She is slow to welcome it. Shyly, their fingers entwine.

AUSTEN

The cat's head was for you.

MADELINE

You sure know how to treat a gal. I thought it was meant for Wade and Bronwyn. I didn't even understand the reference at first since I hadn't been in the pilot episode.

AUSTEN

Did you ever have a cat?

313

MADELINE

No. And considering your obsession with severed cat heads, it's best you should avoid adopting any animal.

AUSTEN

I grew up with cats. I promise you not once did I behead any of my pets. Even after they had died.

MADELINE

That's oddly reassuring.

AUSTEN

I'm glad you see it that way. Most of our cats were prolific hunters. One of them, Patches, was one part fierce warrior and two parts lap warmer. She had a real soft spot for me. Anyway, every day she brought me fresh kill. You had to be careful when you opened the door for her when she was begging to come in. If she had anything in her mouth when you opened the door, she'd race inside to my room and deposit the bloody carcass onto my pillow.

MADELINE

Sounds disgusting.

AUSTEN

It was a gesture of love.

MADELINE

So you killed a cat and gave it to me as a wedding gift.

AUSTEN

I didn't kill it. You can order them online already dead and decapitated.

MADELINE

Again, I find that oddly reassuring. You know you're not a cat, right? People don't give people dead cat heads as romantic gestures.

AUSTEN

What should a person do to express such feelings toward another, then?

MADELINE

Holding hands is nice. I like it when someone brushes my hair off my face, too.

AUSTEN

Like this?

MADELINE

Mmm.

AUSTEN

How about kissing?

MADELINE

I...

AUSTEN's hand had not left her head after he had brushed aside her hair. He slides it behind her head, cradling her head and bringing her toward him. MADELINE is pliant in his hand. Their lips meet. The kiss lasts for fifteen to twenty seconds. They sit upright, contented smiles spreading broadly across their faces.

AUSTEN

You're right. Kissing is more romantic than severed cat heads.

MADELINE

Can I tell you how relieved I am that you feel that way?

AUSTEN

What? About my position on cat heads or that I have romantic feelings for you?

MADELINE

Both.

AUSTEN

And you?

MADELINE

Romantic feelings seem to be
as contagious as fits of
yodeling and face slapping.
How long have you felt this
way about me?

AUSTEN

It was a slow burn, starting
from day one, but it
definitely heated up by
season 5 or 6. Can I ask,
did you have feelings for me
before today?

MADELINE

I did, but I didn't.

AUSTEN

Well, that makes everything
perfectly clear.

MADELINE

I mean I hadn't admitted it
to myself. I knew you were
the type of guy a woman
would want in her life. But
I wouldn't allow myself to
put the two of us together
in my mind.

AUSTEN

What changed? Was it my
yodeling? Or perhaps it was
my butt's mad furniture
identification skills?

MADELINE

Definitely the latter. And maybe our interviewer had planted the idea in my head a few days ago.

AUSTEN

I found him to be awfully nosy. And I'm glad he was.

MADELINE

We should thank our interviewer for bringing us together.

AUSTEN

Thanks, Interviewer!

MADELINE

He's not here, silly!

AUSTEN

So we'll send flowers. Invite him to the wedding.

MADELINE

You think there's going to be a wedding?

AUSTEN

Maybe. We could name our first child after him.

MADELINE

Easy there, tiger. You're getting way ahead of me.

AUSTEN

I'll wait for you. But you have to admit: Moishe Puri-Hughes has a nice ring to it.

MADELINE

Hmm. I'll take it under advisement. If you believe you have any chance of me letting you knock me up, you should buy me dinner first.

AUSTEN

I thought you'd never ask.

THE END

Thank you for reading *Pet Peeves*. If you enjoyed it, please share a review on the retail site where you purchased this book. Your review may be just the inspiration another reader needs to buy *Pet Peeves*.

Cast of Characters

Dick Babcock: Senior vice president of ABS and Entertainment
Emma Bates: Actor (KellyAnne Hurley)
Rex Braithwaite: Chairman of IBS Television Network
Moishe Bronfman: Actor (Archibald Edward Quinn II a.k.a. Duke)
Stephen Burrows: Producer and writer

Bill Cantor: Agent
Blaine Carson: Actor (Dr. Harold Copeland)
Robert Chang: Actor (Thomas Huang)
D'Wayne Curtis: Writer

Bronwyn Davies: Actor (Felicity Copeland)

Bradford Ellis: ABS Entertainment chairman

Ursula Fletcher: Head of *Pet Peeves* fan club
Rob Flowers: Actor

Kym Gifford: ABS Entertainment chairman

Wade Hanson: Actor (Archibald Edward Quinn III, a.k.a. Trip)
Diego Hernandez: Theme song composer
Lucy Hernandez: Editor
Letitia Higgins: Head hairdresser, *Another Day to Live*

Ann Hughes: Mother
Austen Hughes: Actor (Peter Gluck)

Delia Johnson: Cater waiter

Bruce Leibowitz: Showrunner
Kendra Lewis-Frost: Breakdown writer, *Another Day to Live*; co-creator and executive producer
Spencer Little: Actor
Fred Long: Location scout

Floyd Martin: Assistant director

Moira O'Shea: Actor (Claudia Quinn)

Helen Price: Actor (Dr. Anita Copeland)
Madeline Puri: Actor (Kerani Flynn)
Zach Puri: Brother

Wayne Quimby: Head writer, *Another Day to Live*

Maria Rivera: Actor
Dirk Romano: Director

Sonia Santiago: Production assistant, *Another Day to Live*
Elvin Shatsky: Co-creator and executive producer
David Solomon: Director, *Another Day to Live*

Thelonious Trout: Chairman of ABS Television Network
Flip Tuttle: Comedian

Violet Vye: Casting director

Leslie "Tank" Watson: Camera operator
Julius Whelk: Assistant director, *Another Day to Live*
Al White: Stage manager, *Another Day to Live*

Acknowledgements

With gratitude, I acknowledge the many people who helped me to bring figments of my imagination into the realm of the plausible and render them into book form.

Dr. Andrea Danforth did not even blink when I peppered her with questions about animal cadavers and wet labs, supplying me instead with detailed answers about how to defrost said cadavers.

A chance meeting with Sue Clausen on a trip to Califon, NJ opened up to me the world of gnome homes dotting the Columbia Trail. Sue, along with Kimber Lee Sobeck, is the author of a lovely book, *Jerome the Gnome*.

Lindsay Galloway, my editor, trained her eagle eye on each corner of my manuscript.

Susan Traynor interpreted my collage of images and suggestions, turning them into what I'm sure is the world's most adorable book cover.

Nobody does it beta. I know, *groan*. But seriously, Phyllis and Kirsty continue to hit the sweet spot between keeping me motivated to share my books with the world and maintaining my humility as they delicately tease out the kinks and weaknesses in my manuscripts.

I appreciate the eagerness my sister and father-in-law showed for taking an early peek at what I had unleashed in my latest novel.

And finally, thanks to Kevin for laughing at all of my jokes. Making you laugh is one of life's sweetest pleasures.

About the Author

Diane Michaels is a harpist and the author of the Ellen the Harpist series (*Ellen the Harpist*, *Ellen at Sea*, and *Ellen the Bride*), *Watching the Grass Grow*, and *From Here Comes the Bride to There Go the Grooms*. When she is not spying on the world from behind her harp to collect ideas for her next book, she and her husband make up stories and songs about and for their miniature poodle, Lola. You can find our more about Ms. Michaels at DianeMichaelsBooksandHarp.com

From *Ellen the Harpist*

Chapter 1
Here She Comes

It was me and my harp versus a pair of doors. Framed by a pale gray stone archway, the twin glass and metal barriers stood like bouncers at the entrance of the church. Long silver handles invited us to try to enter. I let go of my harp cart and grasped a handle. Only by throwing my full weight into the effort could I pull one door open. Tentatively, I released my fingers from the handle, hoping the door would remain where I left it. I hopped out of the way as it slammed shut.

I peered through the doors and beyond the mosaic of stained glass-filtered light on the floor. I saw no one inside who could rescue me. And there was nothing I could use as a doorstop. My black shoulder bag lacked the heft to do the job. It held only my dress shoes, a folding music stand, the harp part to Richard Strauss' *Don Quixote* plus some light-weight bits of harp paraphernalia. I wished today's gig had been a wedding. Weighted down with overstuffed books of music, my bag would have been able to foil the door's evil plot to deny me access to the church. Out of options, I volunteered my right foot to be my doorperson. Twisting myself into the Inverted Harp Mover pose, I grabbed my harp cart and wheeled the harp backward through the open door.

The door had other plans. My foot could not prevent it from closing, and the door pushed against my harp as I shimmied through the ever-narrowing space. You would think I would be worried about harming my instrument, which is worth more than my minivan. Instead, I envisioned a scenario in which my harp vanquished our mortal enemy, reducing it to a pile of shattered glass. I'm sure my heroic slaying of the door would limit my chance of being hired for future gigs at Our Lady of the Perpetually Closing Door in Livingston, NJ.

I hoped my battle hadn't attracted an audience. Too many times, as I struggled to move my six-foot-tall, eighty-one pound harp by myself, a comedian would offer not assistance but a joke. "Don't you wish you played the flute?" they always ask.

No one responded to my klutzy entrance with a punch line, but I wasn't alone. On the right side of the sanctuary, two people engaged in a skirmish of their own. The man held a violin case and the woman held her jaw clenched.

The paperback edition of *Ellen the Harpist* and the other books in the Ellen the Harpist series are available at Amazon and Barnes & Noble. The digital editions are available exclusively through Amazon and are free in Kindle Unlimited.

www.ingramcontent.com/pod-product-compliance
Lightning Source LLC
Chambersburg PA
CBHW020247200626
46816CB00001BA/173